VIRUS 2.0

By

Norah S. Bernard

Distributed by Lulu Enterprises
860 Aviation Parkway
Morrisville, North Carolina 27560
www.Lulu.com

==

ISBN 978-0-6151-5933-1

Dedicated to the
Master of the Macabre,
Scion of Science Fiction,
Virtuoso of Virtual Reality,
Head Honcho of Horror,
Praetorian of Passion,
You Know Who You Are
My Inspiration,
Thank you.
Love,
Norah

Late last night,
I said LATE, I said...
Tommy's crackers, Tommy's crackers,
Crunching in my bed...
My Momma told me once
(Told me MORE than once)
"Eat your crackers in bed
And you'll Sleep with
crumbs."

VIRUS 2.0

TABLE OF CONTENTS

*

TABLE OF CONTENTS - continued

*

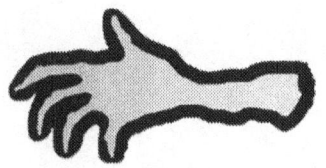

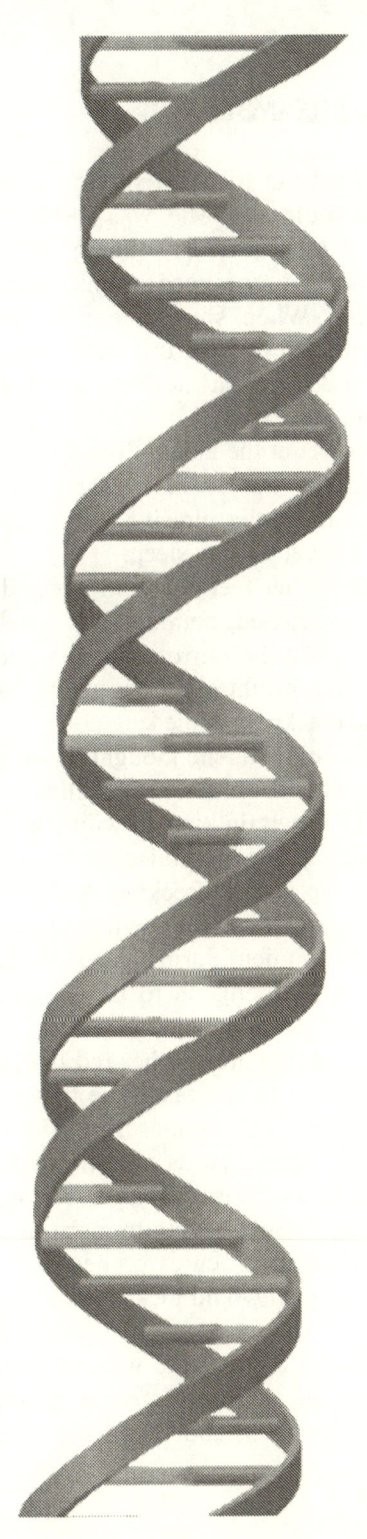

1/ NIGHTMARE, DREAMBOAT

Sydney pulled out of sleep slowly, as a fly would free itself from a puddle of molasses. She was held in the grip of a vivid nightmare while at the same time being irritated by the annoying scratching sensation of tiny jagged crumbs trapped between her skin and the bed sheets. When she came fully awake, she could not remember the dream, and thought the scratchiness must have been part of the dream, because there was nothing at all on the bed sheets. They were perfectly clean.

She looked over at the clock. Five-thirty. She did not need to be awake just yet, but she was so irritated by the nightmare which she could no longer recall, and the abrasive feeling of those particles against her skin, she could not get back to sleep.

Sydney slipped her feet out from under the covers and into her fuzzy slippers. She stretched, coming fully awake. She went into the bathroom and stared into the mirror, assessing her appearance (a daily humbling ritual). Her bright, fire engine red hair stuck out in all directions, short and crackly, untamed.

My hair is a cushball, she thought. How she had hated that hair throughout her childhood—other kids calling her "Red" or "Carrot-top." She always felt a certain kinship with Rudolph—at least with the portion of his life before he won praise for his nose-so-bright. Anyway, at least she had been spared the freckles. And there was an upside to it: Red hair seemed to draw a certain positive attention, and that could be helpful, like with the warden, during those nightmare months she still could not keep from bubbling up to the surface of her memory, no matter how she tried to weigh them down.

Her green eyes accentuated her red hair, and she had grown to accept her looks although it had taken the better part of thirty years to do so. The rest of her was nondescript, she thought—smallish in stature—perhaps best described as a well-nourished twelve-year-old. She felt she had a distinct disadvantage, starting from a position of being looked down upon, and having to make up with sparkling speech what her stature failed to procure for her, like those tall and leggy model-types on whom men would lock-on like a cruise missile from the first glance.

This was not to say that she was not attractive to men — she was, and this got her into trouble as often as not. But she had gotten pretty good at sorting it out, and found the safest path over the last couple of years was avoiding involvement and avoiding problems. So when she drove into the gas station later that morning after she awoke so early from the nightmare, she was startled by how quickly she could be catapulted into a chemical attraction on purely physical grounds once again. She really thought she had put that sort of thing firmly behind her and taken full control of her life, physically and emotionally. But apparently not.

By six a.m. she had dressed, had coffee, and hopped into her trusty old automobile, a 12-year-old Toyota which had served her well, and she assumed would continue to do so for at least another twelve years. The tank was on empty. She pulled into a Phillips 66 station, which was a little further away than her usual gas station, but they had just begun offering a free car wash with fill-up, and the old Toy was getting pretty buggy around the knees. So Sydney pulled into this new station totally unprepared for her feelings at that moment when the gas station attendant, at the self-serve pumps, leaned into her window and said,

"Can I help you?"

In spite of all of her years of experience in developing, acting out and working through relationships with men, including one marriage from the Twilight Zone, Sydney still found every one of her hard-earned defenses crumbling at the sight of the man facing her now. He might have been carved out of marble. He stood, leaning over into her window, she guessed, just over six feet tall. His thick gold-blond hair was brushed straight back to where it met his collar, and his clear tanned skin and Superman jaw were surpassed in excellence only by his peacock blue eyes, the color of which was so unusual, Sydney thought they could not be real.

She was right. He was wearing No. 2 Gulfstream Teal contact lenses. His own natural eye color was just plain blue. But the slightly aqua tint made them a whole lot easier to spot on the bathroom floor than clear lenses.

"May I help you?" he repeated. Sydney wondered if her mouth had been hanging open, and abruptly pulled herself together.

"Fill 'er up!" she managed to say, and was treated to full service at that self-service pump.

She watched as the service station attendant moved around to the rear of her car and pulled the nozzle from the pump. He had the athletic appearance of an Olympic diver—broad shoulders, slim waist, and she could not help but stare as he leaned over to put the nozzle in her tank. Above his shirt pocket a white patch with red stitching indicated that he should be called "Tommy," and at that moment, Sydney made no mental connection between this Apollo and the nightmare from which she had awakened earlier that morning.

He came around to the front of the car, and as he deftly stroked her windshield, her attraction to him gained strength. That surprised her, because it had been such a long time since she felt this way about someone she had just met. It made her feel silly and embarrassed because, after all, well, this guy was ... what? ... a grease monkey? Hardly the type who could change her mind, after she swore off men altogether, again, this last time.

As Tommy topped off her gasoline tank with the last few spurts, and replaced the nozzle back into the pump, Sydney took some cash from her wallet—then impulsively put it back and reached for a credit card instead. It worked. Tommy noticed her name.

"Sydney!" he exclaimed. "Guess your parents wanted a boy, right?" As many times as she had heard this line, she rather enjoyed it now.

"No, actually, when I was born, my mother took one look at me and felt like running away to Australia!"

Tommy hesitated for barely a second before tossing his head back and laughing, a deep, handsome laugh, showing perfect white teeth and a supple muscular neck, Adam's apple thrusting up and down with each chuckle.

"I get it!" he said. "Australia! Sydney, Australia! Pretty good!"

Well, Sydney was impressed. Really, she had not expected him to get the joke. After all, the guy probably didn't finish junior high school. Who else would be servicing cars at a self-service gas pump? He probably made about ninety dollars a week and lived with his momma. Sydney asked herself what she was doing spending even two seconds of her time on this guy? But—then again—one doesn't meet this kind of physical specimen with a brain every day, does one?

"Well, allow me to introduce myself," said Tommy, tapping the name patch on his pocket. Then he handed back her credit card and said, "Thanks, Ma'm,!" and tipped an invisible cap. "Come back again, okay?"

Sydney already knew she would. Against her better—oh, well—*what* judgment? When it came to men she only had one kind of judgment. Poor. History doesn't lie. Yes, she would be back.

2/ TRADE-OFF

Sydney drove back to her condominium apartment where she ran a computer consultation and word-processing business. She walked in and went straight to the refrigerator, inventorying the shelves, but seeing nothing but visions of Tommy in her head. It was maddening. She wasn't an adolescent anymore, and she should have better control over herself than this.

She closed the refrigerator and sat down on the stool by the U-shaped eating/cooking island in her spacious kitchen. How she loved this kitchen and this condo! It was the culmination of a life's dream when she plunked down her earnest money and for the first time in her life, became a homeowner. Who would think that a girl who had gotten off to such a bad start as she, even having done time in the Women's Federal Correctional Facility, would end up owning her own condominium in a luxurious high-rise, and running her own successful business? Life could be great in the United States of America.

For the rest of that day, Sydney forced herself to concentrate, to sit down at her computer and do the work that she had scheduled to be completed. Ordinarily she was highly disciplined about her work, and had built a reputation as a very reliable source for computer consultation needs all over the city. So many folks just wanted someone to come by and tell them how to work the darn thing.

And she noticed, too, over the next few days, that her appetite had fallen off. She hardly wanted to eat a thing, and only nibbled at her dinner (Weight Watcher's 300-calorie lasagna). Losing her appetite did not come naturally to Sydney. She kept her weight down, but only at the price of a perpetual state of war with her stomach. Now, however, her appetite for food was diminished, with Tommy's chiseled profile hovering in her head.

That night, when Sydney went to bed on her peach satin sheets under a goosedown comforter with polished cotton ticking, her comfort didn't last long. She slept fitfully again, tossing and turning, as her sleep played out nightmares which again eluded her in the morning. And again she awoke with that irritated, scratchy feeling as though she were sleeping on sand—no, something crunchier than sand—but when she pulled from sleep, there was nothing but the smooth satin underneath, and no recollection of the dream remained.

With her morning shower, Sydney rinsed off the residual feeling of having slept in a bed of cracker crumbs, and began her plans for the day. She knew she wanted to visit that Phillips 66 station again, and soon. She would need some excuse besides refueling to return, though.

Sydney took the elevator down to the parking garage and looked over her little car. She had taken such good care of it for so many years, shampooing the upholstery every six months until it started showing bald spots, and then finally quit that. The exterior as well had not been waxed in years now, and some areas of rust and primer showed through in places, like mange on an old dog.

Well, you can't stay attached to material things forever, she thought. Then she pictured Tommy again, and her resolve to get to know him better made the decision for her. She would buy a new car! After all, her business was doing great. She had plenty of savings and stocks—a retirement plan, even! Why shouldn't she have a new car? And besides—service station attendants had lots of good advice to offer about buying new cars!

"Goodbye, Toots!" she said, smacking the Toyota on the equivalent of its rump. "You've been great—And I really mean that!" she said, even as she felt a lump of guilt stick in her throat. It really WAS time to look for a new car, she argued to herself. She was NOT just looking for an excuse to act goofy over another pretty face. After all, realistically, how many more miles could she expect to get out of the little clunker, anyway? It would probably implode all at once, just as she was accelerating onto the Interstate, cutting in front of an 18-wheel semi-tractor-trailer driven by a short-tempered, sleep-deprived psychopath with a crack pipe in the ashtray and a semi-automatic assault weapon on the seat next to him. Right. Definitely need new car.

Sydney drove to the Phillips 66 station, the car moving slowly, her heart pounding fast. Fast? Tribal clans may have been called to war by slower beats—but she refused to forego her plans. As she saw the gas station sign looming closer, and finally pulled in, Tommy was nowhere to be seen.

Disappointment began to sag inside her. Perhaps this was his day off. She began to feel withdrawal symptoms at the thought of having to wait until tomorrow. Sydney looked at her gas gauge, and even though it was not even down one-quarter tank, she decided she may as well fill up, as long as she had driven there. She pulled out the nozzle and placed it in her tank, not hearing the footsteps approaching behind her. When she heard the deep, soft greeting behind her, she was so startled that she jerked the nozzle out of the tank, and gas splattered onto the pavement.

Tommy bent to pick it up and reinserted the nozzle into her tank. "Sorry I was tied up in the back," he said, and flashed his pearly whites and No. 2 Gulfstream Teals. Sydney's heart was on a trampoline. "Didn't need much gas today," he said as he hung up the nozzle and twirled the gas cap into place.

He snapped the lid closed and then began polishing his fingerprints off the car with a cloth from his back pocket. How touching! He cared enough about her rusted, dusty old clunker to polish off his fingerprints! What a sweet guy—she thought.

"Well, actually," she stammered, starting to feel the lump of guilt rising in her chest again, "I need something besides gasoline today..."

Tommy cocked his head to the side slightly and waited patiently for her to continue.

"My car's been giving me some trouble lately!" she lied, then blushed. She felt a sickening flop of guilt in her stomach—How could she say such a thing about a car that had been so dependable and faithful for twelve years??!!

After another embarrassingly long pause, Tommy decided to help out. "What kind of trouble?"

"Well, it actually—oh, it makes—you know, it makes funny noises. Yes, funny noises! You know how that is. Funny."

"Funny," he repeated, without taking his eyes from hers. "Can you, ah, be a little more specific?"

Why did I come here?

"Like this," she took a deep breath, "Oooh-ah-br-r-r-th-putt-putt-putt. Something like that."

And Tommy repeated, "Oooh -ah?" And Sydney's legs wavered underneath her and she wished she had never come back here. Then Tommy said, "Look, I'll need to drive it around to check it out. Can you leave it here for awhile? I can drive you home ..."

Drive me home! she thought, with renewed excitement. Then, *uh-oh*, her thoughts began to race in another direction. What if he drives me home and sees that I live in a luxury high-rise ... He might think himself out-classed and fearful of asking me for a date ... Or worse, he would ask me out *because* I lived there! No, better not to let him see my place just yet.

"Yes, I can leave the car with you," she said, finally. "But I'll walk back. It's only a couple of blocks. You can keep the car and see if you can figure out what's wrong with it."

"Are you sure? I can easily run you home."

"Oh, but it's such a beautiful day!" she said, waving up at the overcast sky, where heavy gray clouds had already choked off most of the sunlight. Tommy looked up and started to say something, but then just shook his head.

"Okay," he said. "Give me your phone number and I'll call to let you know what I've found. You won't be needing your car for awhile?"

"No," she said, truthfully, perhaps for the first time in this whole conversation. "I work out of my apartment."

"Oh," he said (and did his eyebrows flicker upwards for just a second?) "Well, that must be convenient."

"Yes, it is," she said, and pulled out a card from her wallet:

SYDNEY'S COMPUTER CONNECTIONS
PERSONAL CONSULTATION & TECHNICAL SUPPORT
FOR YOUR HOME OR SMALL BUSINESS NEEDS
TELE.(899) WORD-PRO

"Oh, neat!" he said, "Perhaps I might use your services some time!"

Well, thought Sydney, a line is a line. "Sure!" she said. "Let's talk about it sometime!" and she turned on her heel and walked off, as the wind picked up and some leaves and scrap paper whirled by. "Call me!"

And now the deed was done. But what was she going to do when he called and told her that her car did not go "Oooh - ah," or any other stupid thing? Well—she would cross that bridge when she came to it.

On the other hand, she thought—what if he called back and told her that she needed six hundred dollars' worth of repair work? And he turned out to be one of those crooks who trumped up a bill for any single female who was dumb enough not to get a second opinion?

Well, I'll cross that bridge right after I cross the other one, she thought, as she crossed over the Second Street bridge and saw her condo looming up ahead in the distance. It was more than a "couple of blocks" from the station. It was ten blocks, actually, but she could use the exercise, she thought. And she was sure it wouldn't rain. She just felt too exuberant for it to rain!

It began to rain about three blocks from her condo, and she wished she hadn't worn her silk dress, although she had wanted to look as alluring as possible when she drove to the gas station in hopes of seeing Tommy again. She ducked into a side store and waited about forty-five minutes until the rain subsided, and then clicked on in her high heels which had become quite painful by the time she finally wobbled home.

Sydney peeled off her wet dress. Now, she thought, now I can sit and work until I hear from Tommy about my car. But she knew that one way or the other she was going to be sorry. And just as well. She should not even be interested in this man who was seventeen rungs on the socioeconomic ladder beneath her. That is, if you didn't count things like a criminal past. But that was so long ago. She sat down at her computer and began to work.

3/ ON LOBOTOMIES

Sydney went into her office, which was the converted second bedroom of her condo, and there the decor changed from the light yellow and mint green with white rattan furnishings and pastel watercolors on the walls, to Newsbeat Central Station. There were note pads and sheaves of computer-folded paper everywhere, stacked up, stuck under paperweights, tacked to the walls, and still others in more neatly stacked alternating bundles, on every spare desk space and chair in the cluttered room.

Her computer was her life. Sydney had a real knack for using the computer and had developed the skill into a first-rate business. Knowledge of her skills was beginning to catch on in town and the outlying communities, and she had begun getting occasional requests to help develop management systems for small companies, in addition to the more common requests for word processing for printed brochures and technical support.

In her spare time, and as a respite from her daily workload, Sydney often tapped onto some of the national computer "bulletin boards" on the Internet. She even had a computer "relationship" with another computer hacker in California, for eight months last year, as they played chess games across the 'net. She never met her chess partner, but finally ended the "relationship" when she couldn't interest him in arranging a personal meeting. So much for cyberspace romance.

Sydney also picked up a lot of useful ideas for helping to design computer programs for local business clients of hers. Financially, she was doing quite well—although perhaps not as well as her family would like. They would never consider Sydney to be gainfully employed unless she were receiving a paycheck from a company listed on the Big Board.

Sydney's sister was married to a dental surgeon, so obviously, she was a SUCCESS in her parents' estimation. Sydney still hoped, in her heart of hearts, that she would attain her own success in their eyes. They just couldn't stop viewing her as a rebel and a lost soul.

Sydney sat down in the swivel chair in front of her computer, carefully stepping over the documents on the floor, and began to shift the gears of her mind into thinking about the work she had to do. Soon enough, she was pounding away at the keyboard and actually sopping up some of the information from the article which she was typing for a local professor of psychiatry.

She was shocked by the information she was typing: Lobotomies were still performed at some institutions around the country! It was still an accepted technique of medical practice! Now who would have believed such a thing could be going on in the United States of America in this day and age! She thought lobotomies were made illegal or something, decades ago—in the same class with bloodsucking slugs for "purifying" the blood!

Sydney found herself fascinated by the text she was typing. Lobotomies—or "psychosurgeries" as they were now called—had been "refined", and were performed in standard operating theatres by neurosurgeons. No longer were they performed by psychiatrists in their outpatient offices with a hand-held probe—an instrument likened to an ice pick! The old process entailed lifting the patient's eyelids and inserting the probe just above the eyeball and into the space just beneath the frontal lobes of the brain, behind the bony orbit of the eye. Then the probe was swiped in a horizontal slashing movement back and forth a few times, tearing the tissue connections between the frontal and pre-frontal lobes of the brain. That was it—a pre-frontal lobotomy!

In a nutshell, Sydney thought.

Now, the operations were done on smaller and smaller areas in the brain, areas known to be responsible for specific behaviors or emotions. Severing the connections to the cingula: Cingulotomy. Severing connections to the amygdala: Amygdalotomy. *Yer-cuttin-the-life-otomy*! Where did she hear that little saying? *I'd rather have a bottle in front of me than a frontal lobotomy!* Right.

But she was comforted to know that these operations were done only in the most drastic cases. The author gave one example of a woman with obsessive-compulsive disorder. In "milder" cases, people tend to do things over & over again, such as checking to make sure one's wallet is in one's pocket; or checking to make sure the water faucets are all turned off. Sometimes they do more bizarre things, like counting the tiles on the way to the front door—knowing full well that it makes no sense at all, yet if they try to stop doing it, they feel anxious and uncomfortable.

So depending on how severe the case is, people can get "stuck" doing these pointless things, over & over—until it interferes with their normal life activity! Fortunately, most of these patients respond to medications of one sort or another, and behavioral psychotherapy —"learning" to contradict these urges. But one woman—the most severe case this psychiatrist had ever known of—would have to "check" so many things while taking a shower, that she eventually got "stuck" in the shower and was unable to stop and get out! Her family finally came and rescued her after *thirty-three hours* in the shower. In Minnesota. In February. Long after the hot water ran out and turned to near freezing! So this woman consented to a lobotomy. Good move.

The telephone rang and startled Sydney out of her fascination with the ancient and modern techniques of lobotomies. Her heart hit the ground running as she thought it might be her golden-haired grease god, and the phone rang three or four times before she could compose herself enough to answer it. She walked into her bedroom, took a few deep breaths, and picked up the French ivory and gold telephone on her nightstand.

"Computer Connections, this is Sydney!"

"Phillips 66, this is Tommy! (chuckle) How are you?" Then without waiting for an answer, "I don't think those noises in your car are anything serious," he said, and Sydney blinked back her surprise. "I tightened up a few things, but the car is in pretty good shape for its age."

Well, dip and fry me! thought Sydney. What a nice way to deal with my made-up stupid "noises" without making me look like the idiot that I am!

"Well, that's great, Tommy!"

And now for the real test of his character: "How much do I owe you?"

"Let's see ... one hundred twenty, sixty-two fifty, thirty-one cents ... Nothing!" Then he laughed. "No charge! I didn't really do anything at all."

Sydney's blood pressure had started to rise as Tommy teased her with numbers, but she fell to giggling when she realized he was just kidding! An honest man, and cute, too! She was afraid she wouldn't be able to compose herself, she was so relieved and entertained by this guy!

"May I bring the car back to you?"

"No!" she said, abruptly ending her reverie, mid-giggle. Then, "Uh, I mean, thank you so much, but I'll come and get it, because, you see, uh ..."

"You need your exercise!" Tommy supplied, showing once again his humor and the ease with which he could help her save face. "Well, I would be happy to bring it over to you, but we'll be open 'til seven if you'd rather come by."

"I'll be by before then," Sydney answered. "And, thanks, Tommy, really. It's awfully nice of you ... Are you sure I don't owe you something?" Like dinner, she thought. Wishful thinking.

"How about dinner?" he said, and then laughed again. "No, just kidding! You don't owe me anything."

Yet, he thought.

"Oh, okay, then," she said, laughing a little, too. How sweet and funny he is!

Sydney's feet were still throbbing from the long walk in high heels this morning. She would take a cab down to the station later. She returned to lobotomies.

4/ THE JAUNT

Sydney went to her closet and began to pull out different outfits—the red shirtdress that made her waist look smaller; the lime green summer suit that made her hips look slimmer; the powder blue jumper that made her bust look larger; the canary yellow pantsuit that she bought for godknowswhat reason and that she wouldn't wear to the Micmac burial grounds.

Suddenly she realized what she was doing—obsessing over what to wear to manipulate a date with a gas station attendant! She needed a lobotomy. She would call that psychiatrist and arrange for one in the morning.

Sydney re-hung each outfit back into the closet and pulled out a pair of jeans and a sweatshirt which pictured a fat little mouse sitting in a litter-strewn living room, eyes half-closed, propped up on one shaky little paw on top of a huge crushed beer can. A caption-balloon over his head said, "B-u-r-r-r-r-r-r-p!" Her 16-year-old niece, Lila, gave it to her the last time they were together. Perfect for this occasion!

Lila was Sydney's sister Melva's oldest kid. Melva was named after one of two twin great-uncles, Sydney and Melvin. Melvin had been the oldest (by thirteen minutes, their mom had told them, whenever she talked about them. Every time she talked about them.) Melvin was a tobacco farmer and store owner in the Old Country, which in this case referred to Sirocco Bessarabia, Romania, today, but Russia back then. Great-Uncle Melvin was a very successful man by the standards of the time. He sold cigarettes and other items to the Czar's soldiers. He had candlesticks and other items of real silver in his house, which was a big house, with a separate bedroom for the boys (four) and the girls (six). People in the village were always coming to ask his advice. That's how rich he was.

The other great-uncle, Sydney, was a butcher. He was an honest man and expected the same from others, and that was a problem. When the Czar's authorities came around to weigh his meat and collect taxes, they used their own scales, which were weighted improperly, so they could collect more than they were due. Great-Uncle Sydney insisted on exposing this cheating, against his family's and all his friends' advice. For his efforts, he ended up in prison in Siberia. But he refused to give up. He wrote such eloquent and persuasive letters from prison to authorities all over Russia and even other countries, that he was eventually granted a pardon by the Czar.

In hearing these stories, Melva always preened at having been named for the rich and successful great-uncle, Melvin. But Sydney was always glad that she had been named for the poor-but-honest-and-feisty great-uncle!

The friction between Sydney and Melva seemed to worsen with the birth of Melva's first child, Lila. From the day she was born, Lila seemed somehow more bonded to Sydney than to her own mother. Even in infancy, Lila could be crying, as only babies can, red-faced, shrill, unrelenting, and Sydney had only to come into the room and reach out for her before she would stop crying and mellow out, cooing into a sweet angelic sleep. Melva could barely contain her anger and frustration about Sydney's seeming magic touch with her child.

It became less of a problem when Melva had her next two children. Their attachment to their mommy was strong, if a bit clingy, and Melva relished and encouraged it. She was fulfilled enough by her two younger darlings to ignore Lila's overt preference for her Aunt Sydney. And Lila was the only relative Sydney had who wrote to her faithfully every single day while she was in prison. The only one. Every single day. Four months, two weeks and three days.

Sydney called the doorman and asked him for a cab, then stopped in the bathroom for one last dab of perfume before heading for the elevator. The cab was already waiting for her downstairs when she got there. She directed him to drop her off around the block from the Phillips 66 station.

When Sydney arrived at the gas station this time, she saw Tommy before he saw her, which gave her time to chill down and look casual. He was making change at the cash register. The mellow glow of the late afternoon sun made his hair look like spun gold, and the muscles in his arms rippled like sand dunes on a breezy beach.

Suddenly she noticed the package of crackers in Tommy's shirt pocket, and her stomach quivered for reasons which she could not call to mind. She did not consciously recall the repeating dream she had been having recently—nightmare, really—but the close proximity of Tommy's face and the package of crackers triggered a memory that sent an unseasonably cold shiver down her spine.

Late last night, I said LATE, I said...

"Hi!" Tommy spotted Sydney and was coming over to where she stood. Her face was in the shadows of the garage bay and he did not notice how she had paled momentarily. Then the appearance of him close to her again swept away whatever uncomfortable feelings had been there a moment before. Passion can do that.

"Hi! So, ah, you're sure you didn't find anything wrong with the car?"

"I'm sure. But if you'd like me to check it again—"

"No, no, no," Sydney smiled and waved her hands in front of her. "I'm sure you've done an excellent job!"

Tommy shrugged his shoulders and blushed. What a sweet, shy guy, Sydney thought!

"It's just that I guess I'm ready for ... something new ... but it's been such a good car, and ..." she trailed off, her hand rotating in the air as though it could complete the sentence for her if it twirled long enough.

"Yeah, I know what you mean," Tommy said. "I had an old '58 Plymouth once—my very first car. It was really tough to part with the old girl..." He gazed off into the dark recesses of the repair bay behind Sydney.

Old girl? "Well, yes, that's how I feel about the, uh, the old, uh Toy, that is. My old Toyota..." Sydney fidgeted for a few seconds. "Can you help me buy a new car? I mean, can you give me some advice or recommendations?"

"Why, sure!" Tommy seemed genuinely flattered. "But cars these days are pretty expensive. And you probably couldn't get much for your Toyota now."

"Oh, that's no problem," Sydney replied, waving away his concerns with her talking hand. Then she caught herself and realized that she did not want him to know that she was so financially comfortable. "That is, I want a new car, but I realize I may need to put it on a payment plan. A lo-n-n-n-ng payment plan!"

Tommy laughed and nodded. "Do you want something sporty? Or something more for comfort?" But before she could answer, he added, almost under his breath, "I don't suppose you would want a Volvo?"

A Volvo. She had never pictured herself in one. They seemed so ... suburban. And then Sydney began to wonder why he mentioned it. Surely Tommy didn't own one? She saw him as more the genuine SUV type. Genuine, as in Jeep, canvas top, mud-spattered, no gold trim.

He went on before she could respond: "I have a Volvo you could look at, if you think it might be something you would be interested in."

"*You* have a Volvo?" Then she bit her lip, hoping she didn't come across as insulting him. Why shouldn't he have one? Stranger things had been recorded in the annals of automotive history.

"It belonged to my grandmother. She passed away recently, and I ... sort of ... inherited it." He averted his eyes, and Sydney wondered at his discomfort. There seemed to be something odd about it ...

He continued, "It's practically brand new—but I don't need it myself. I have my own rig," and he pointed to the far side of the gas station lot where there stood a mud-spattered, canvas-topped Jeep.

"Mmm-huh, I see," Sydney nodded. "Well, sure, why not? Where is it?" There was certainly no harm in taking a look at it.

"Are you sure?" Tommy asked, suddenly seeming flushed, ill at ease. "If it's not what you had in mind—"

"But it's *exactly* what I had in mind!" Sydney chirped. "I really want to see it!" *What am I talking about?*

"Okay, great," Tommy said, "I was going to go up there on Saturday. Can you come then? Around ten in the morning?"

"Sure!" she answered. "Just write down the directions, and I'll meet you there at ten sharp."

"No, you don't understand," he said. "It's fifty miles up into the mountains. I'll drive us there in my truck."

"Fifty mi—?" Sydney began to repeat, but the words stuck. She couldn't possibly go on such a jaunt with this man.

"And we should pack a lunch," Tommy continued, "because there's nobody and nothing up there for miles around the old homestead."

Oh really? Pack a lunch and go fifty miles into nowhere with this stranger? How quaint. Let's think up a quick and gracious way out of this right now.

"Oh, Tommy," she began, with a big sigh, "what kind of sandwiches would you like?" And with that she saw the last vestiges of any good judgment she ever had evaporate in the evening breeze.

5/ ODD MAN OUT

That night Sydney slept even more fitfully than before. This time there was a face in her dream. Ugly. Its skin was gray, like corroded pewter, and the eyes were tiny sparks, fiery orange sparks, like those that come off the end of a match that does not quite catch. And then the gray face crackled open in a horrible shriek that turned into a booming wicked laugh, "Mooo-o-o-o-o-o hooo-o-o-o-o-ha-ha-haaaaa!!!" and finally trailed off in a chortle like a madman.

Sydney awoke sweating and clawing her way out of the sheets and frantically sweeping, sweeping something off the bed, something crumbly, crummy, like cracker crumbs.

Late last night, I said late, I said....

Sydney sat there, shaking with fright, her heart banging in her chest like a bucking bronco at the starting gate. She headed for the kitchen. She needed something chocolate—she needed it now.

In the kitchen, with a steaming cup of fat-free cocoa in front of her, she tried to make some sense of the nightmare. She recognized that it was not the first time she had had that dream. It felt too familiar—the source of many recent restless nights.

But that face. It haunted her. Where had she seen such a horrid thing before? Yet it was familiar. Definitely familiar. She tried to recall something or someone in her past who could account for this terrifying feeling of familiarity. Nothing.

Sydney's past was, to say the least, checkered. Scotch plaid might better describe it. Her oppositional nature revealed itself from Day One, when she refused to be born. After resisting her mother's heroic efforts through thirty-eight hours of labor, she was finally pulled out with a pair of forceps, which left her with a pointed head for a week.

In school, she challenged her teachers from kindergarten on, questioning everything, talking back at every opportunity, earning frequent travelers' awards for trips to the principal's office.

It wasn't that Sydney had no respect for authority—it was just that she felt every right to question it. She seemed to have an intuitive understanding of the First Amendment before she could recite the alphabet. She loved stories of defiance, with heroes like Jack and the Beanstalk, and David and Goliath. On the other hand, she never could understand why Cinderella tolerated the abuse that she had, and didn't just pack her bags and leave with her little mice friends.

Sydney's parents did not understand this. They knew she was very bright, but it mystified them that she consistently got A's in academics and D's or F's in conduct. This was especially difficult for her father, Maury, who had been raised in an orthodox Jewish home. When he was an adolescent, barely ready for his *bar mitzvah*, he watched his own father, a tailor by trade and a lay rabbi on weekends, pour water over his hands three times, the required ritual for handwashing. Maury asked him, "Why don't you use some soap? Your hands would get cleaner than pouring water over them a dozen times," which earned him the sternest and most ferocious glare he had ever seen on his father, and one which he vowed never to provoke again. He followed the required rituals forever afterward.

Sydney's mother, Frances, was a Jewish atheist, but even so, she strained to understand her daughter's rebelliousness. She had a sense of obligation and responsibility in her marriage that was independent of her own religious beliefs. Frances kept a kosher home for her husband, including two sets of dishes, one for meat and one for dairy; two sets of silverware; and separate cupboards for dishes to be used with meat and those for dairy meals. She put her foot down at two refrigerators, though, and said that if Maury insisted on two refrigerators, she would insist on two kitchens, and two separate bedrooms, as well. Maury agreed to one refrigerator.

Likewise, Sydney's sister, Melva, never understood her. "Why do you have to question everything? You have no respect for authority. Do you like being in trouble all the time?"

Then Sydney would jump onto her soapbox and expound that if everyone were more like herself, the Holocaust of Nazi Germany would never have occurred! Melva would just shake her head and sigh. It would have been as easy to straighten up the leaning tower of Pisa, as straighten out her sister.

Melva had always walked the straight and narrow. Always diligent in school, she had never known the special joy of inspecting at close range the intricate patterns of finger markings in the corner of the classroom. She graduated college in three-and-a-half years and completed her Masters degree in Social Work; following which she became a licensed psychotherapist, and spent her days listening to people whom she considered to be far healthier than her sister.

Sydney, on the other hand, had little patience for the paper chase. She couldn't get out of school fast enough. She dropped out of high school just before the winter holidays of her junior year, having been gathering her courage to do so since she turned sixteen. She then went rapidly through two jobs, as a clerk in the Credit Bureau downtown, and a soda fountain waitress in a drugstore. She was fired from her first job on the first day, when she confided to a seemingly nice co-worker at lunch that she had not actually graduated from high school, as she stated on her job application, nor was she eighteen, as also stated. The co-worker wasted no time in reporting this to the supervisor, and within twenty minutes, Sydney was called in and handed a check for her three hours labor, and shown the door.

She did not lie about her background when applying for the job as soda jerk. She lied about her experience. After all, what was there to pouring coffee and filling out a check? She soon discovered, though, that there was an art to flipping hamburgers without grease flying everywhere, and cutting a tuna sandwich without leaving fingerprints embedded in the bread. She did not know there was a recipe for making an ice cream soda, either. And then the clean-up ritual! After the place closed at ten o'clock, she had to wash the grill and all the soda and orangeade machines! She went back to the school and pleaded with the principal to let her back in.

These experiences notwithstanding, Sydney had little idea of what she wanted to do when she graduated from high school. She wanted to make money, and she did not want to answer to any authority. So she got married.

Karl seemed to be quite a catch, really. Sydney really loved him and was happy in spite of the fact that her family loved him, too. He was, after all, a Jewish accountant, the penultimate success, second only to a Jewish doctor, whom of course her sister had married.

Sydney refused to allow her parents to throw the same kind of feeding frenzy wedding extravaganza as they had for her sister. She sincerely failed to see this as a way of tweaking her parents' noses, since they were so happy with her choice of husband that she had to punish them some other way, and depriving them of a wedding bash was effective. No, she justified this with her sincere belief that weddings were an unconscionable waste of money, and so she and Karl eloped in the middle of the night, even as her parents were up late in bed, holding hands and making plans for their youngest daughter's wedding.

But they were too happy with Karl to stay mad at their daughter for very long, so they gave them ten thousand dollars to put down on a house (Sydney refused it, but Maury got Karl alone and had no trouble convincing him to take it).

Everything went very well for three months. Sydney was able to pick up good business skills from Karl's office, and these turned out to be very helpful later on, when she needed to fend for herself. "Later on" refers to all the time after Sydney discovered, and left Karl on the same day, that he obtained his greatest erotic fulfillment not from making love to her, but in front of a full-length mirror, modeling and coddling himself in her bra and panties. Sydney had always staunchly defended anyone's right to any alternative lifestyle they chose.

But she could not accept Karl in her underwear.

The most difficult part about divorcing Karl was that she felt a strong obligation to keep his *alter ego* (read: dirty little secret) secret. Karl was a successful businessman and no one— not his family, not his closest confidante, not one other earthly soul—knew this side of him. Except his mother, and even Karl didn't know that she knew.

Sydney wanted out of the marriage, but she could not bring herself to betray Karl. Her parents, needless to say, were shocked and grief-stricken by her announcement of the divorce. They became furious with her, and even accused her of doing this deliberately to hurt them.

Sydney tried to make up an acceptable reason. She thought her mother might, just might, understand if she said that her sex life with Karl was unsatisfying (a lie). But when she told her that, her mother grabbed her by the shoulders, frantic with delight that she could solve her daughter's dilemma so easily.

"Oh, my darling little Sydney, I failed to teach you the most important thing a woman must know when she becomes a wife: Pretend!! That is all it takes to be truly happy with your husband! Pretend you enjoy it!! And before long—you will find that you *do*!!!"

Sydney sagged inside. She forced a smile and said, "Thanks, Mom. I love you." Then she left and proceeded with the divorce. Her parents did not speak to her for two years.

But Sydney put the knowledge she gained from Karl into starting her own computer business, and did very well. For awhile. Alas, she eventually ran into trouble, as all entrepeneur-anarchists are wont to do.

Tommy had been looking forward to this ever since he laid eyes on Sydney. He was taken by her hair as red as bright arterial blood, and her eyes as green as new fescue grass. She was small in stature, but had the kind of rising curves which beckoned to a man. He wanted her.

Tommy had made a note of Sydney's name as soon as she had handed him her credit card that first day in the service station. He looked up her address and was surprised to see that she lived at one of the luxury high-rise condominiums in town. Usually those people drove around in BMW's and Mercedes Benz's, not twelve-year-old Toyotas.

He drove by her condo that night just to make sure he was right about the address. He was. He decided to bide his time. Then, when Sydney returned a few days later with that story about her car "making funny noises," he knew his opportunity was at hand.

6/ THE SHOCK

Sydney got up early the next morning. It was Thursday. She did not have any more dreams about the Gray Man—or at least none that she remembered.

She got ready to go out and meet a client who had called her the previous week for some help in computerizing his business. She showered, washed her hair and plastered it back with mousse. Then she carefully applied her palest makeup, no rouge. Finally, she dressed in a high-collared cream chiffon blouse under a starkly tailored navy blue suit and matching heels. This was Business-Barbie.

Sydney had learned fast how much difference it made the way a woman dressed for business. It became apparent very quickly that if she dressed in luscious silky colors with bright makeup and a flirtaceously curly hairdo that she was more likely to be hit upon than hired.

Dates she could meet anywhere. And did, for awhile. She dated anybody and everybody. Recalling it made her cringe. All the shrinks would tell her that she was paying back the rage she bore over Karl's deceit, her sister's plodding correctness, and her parents' total lack of understanding. But knowing these insights did not stop her. Never even broke stride.

Even now she's not sure what entered into the picture to make a difference. But in all honesty, Sydney thought she just got bored to death. She felt as though a main circuit breaker was thrown and her ability to feel anything had just completely shut down.

She decided to set men aside in her life, and go full steam ahead with her business. That was what was so startling about meeting Tommy. Just seeing him had the effect of a hand reaching around in the dank and dusty darkness of the closet where she had hung up her libido, and found that old forgotten switch and suddenly threw it back on!

Let there be light!

And there was light, and love, and libido, all singing in harmony again!

Sydney finished the last touches of her dressing—no perfume, of course—and went down to the parking garage. This would be one of the last times she might be driving her old Toy.

That was the last thought she gave to her car and to her outing with Tommy scheduled for Saturday. The events of that day and the next soon overshadowed everything else.

Sydney's client was sick. She could see that as soon as she walked into his office. He rose to greet her with his hand extended, and then drew it back before she could shake it, grabbing for a big, damp, crumpled handkerchief from his pocket. He sneezed twice into it—huge thunderous wet sneezes, and then pushed the handkerchief back and forth under his tender reddened nose before stuffing it back into his pocket.

Then he extended the same hand to Sydney and she swallowed hard to keep her nausea under control as she allowed her hand to be gobbled up and shaken in his still-damp grasp.

"George Humphreys here!" he said, after Sydney introduced herself. "Sorry about the sneezing. These spring colds are the worst, y'know!"

George ran an insurance agency and had jumped for joy when he heard about Sydney's work from a business associate. He desperately needed someone who could unsnarl the computer horror story that his business had become. He had just lost his third office manager. Each of them had presented themselves as having the talent and capability to organize and computerize George's growing insurance company. Each one had convinced George that he had the improper equipment, and he needed to buy a whole different kind of computer set-up for his business; and then each, in turn, discovered that they did not have the expertise to accomplish what they had set out to do, and left.

"I'm going to go under, Sydney," he sniffled, half in desperation over his depressing situation, and half because of his cold. "I'm still running the office on my paper filing system, and it's getting completely out of control."

He stopped and blew his nose again with his now damper-than-ever hanky, and Sydney winced at how violently he rubbed over his nostrils to clean it all up. "I've worked so hard and the business has gotten so big," he said, close to whining in an even more pathetic tone for his cold, "and now I'm going to lose it all!" He rubbed his nose even harder. Sydney couldn't look. She could only imagine how hard he'd like to rub out those would-be office managers.

"Mmm-hmmm," Sydney replied, looking around at the array of equipment on different desks. There were Macs, Dells, even an old Wang, and some others.

George was waving his succulent hanky around the office. "What am I going to do with all this?!"

"Well, we could start with a garage sale, but let's get your office in shape first." Sydney asked George to show him what he had been working on. He went to one of the computers and turned it on.

"As a matter of fact, I just found a new software program that I thought might work out for me," he went on, as the blue light of the monitor swept over the screen. He tapped out some commands, and information filled the screen. A printed title stated, "ORGANIZE YOUR SMALL BUSINESS!"

"It sounded pretty good, but then once I got into it, it got confusing. Maybe I just don't know my way around computers well enough—but it seemed so simple!" Then he began to whimper again, "What am I going to do?" (Snnoorrrf!)

"Don't worry about it," Sydney said, looking at the strange program on the monitor. May I?" She pointed to George's seat, and he quickly jumped up and held the chair for her. She sat.

Sydney tapped out the commands dictated by the program, filling in necessary spaces with made-up numbers. Then there was then a bizarre string of characters and sounds produced from the computer.

Suddenly she was struck by the strangest sensation! It travelled from the top of her head, past her eyes, her chest, her belly, and ended in the balls of her feet. It was like an electrical rush, and left her with a mild tingling, which was not altogether unpleasant! It reminded her of a time when a fly had flown down the back of her dress, and the tingling sensation she continued to feel long after the fly had been liberated. Then she sneezed so violently that she had to catch herself from falling off the chair!

"G'bless ya'," George offered as he pulled out his giant juicy handkerchief again. Sydney drew back in horror at the thought of him handing it to her! But he only brought it up to his own battered nose once again. "These spring colds are terrible."

"That was weird," Sydney said, her attention back on the computer monitor again, which now stated, "End of Program." She said it almost to herself, but George picked up on it.

"What was weird?" he asked.

"Uh ... Nothing. Nothing, actually," Sydney groped for words to put him off while she tried to understand what had happened. It was too crazy to try and explain it to him. But she didn't have to. He already knew.

"Did you feel some kind of, uh, shock-thing?" he asked.

Sydney whirled around to face him, his big red nose already

sporting the beginning of another stalagtite drip. "Yes! Yes, I did!" she said. "What was that?" Then she tried to answer the question herself: "Is there some kind of an electrical short in your system?"

"No," George answered, and sat down on the edge of another desk. He rubbed his chin (which his nose must have dearly appreciated), and continued, "No, I had it all checked out electrically. There's no short anywhere. Besides," he got up and strode off toward the other side of the office, "I tried that same program in every computer, and the same thing happened in all of them."

Sydney turned back to the computer screen in front of her and stared at it. Suddenly her skin began to feel irritated, itchy ...

Late last night, I said late, I said ...

She froze with a sudden feeling of impending doom. It reminded her of the first time she had been arrested and locked up in a large holding cell with about a dozen other women, some of whom were frighteningly buff. As soon as the bars clanged shut behind her, they all turned at once and stared at her. That was similar to the feeling that she now had.

She shook it off. "There must be some perfectly logical explanation for this," she told George as she stood up from the chair and pushed it away. "You say you tried this same program in different computers?"

"Yes."

"And you felt this ... shock-thing ... from the other computers, too?"

"All of them," George corrected. "Every time I ran the program I got that same weird shock. And I must have run it a hundred times." He followed this with three more violent sneezes, leaving him crumpled over the desk. "I don't know what could possibly be causing it..."

Sydney knew enough. She knew that this was impossible. What could it be? A computer "virus" that made the User sick? Come on! The theme from the Twilight Zone echoed in her head. *Do-do, do-do, do-do, do-do...*

She looked back at George. "Where did you get this program, anyway?"

"From an email that passed my spam filter—so it must'a been okay. There was an address in western North Carolina. It was only $29.95, and sounded like just what I needed." He began looking through some stacks of papers on another desk now, his own desk. The only desk without a computer on it.

"I have the address here somewhere." He produced a charge slip receipt with a post office box number on it. It was in the mountains of North Carolina. The Smokies.

Sydney jotted the address down, for what reason she did not know, and then decided to get cracking on George's office problems. The Mystery of the Shocking Computer Virus would have to wait.

"I'll need to see your books," she said to George. "And your files. If you can review your present procedures with me today, I can begin to design a program for you."

"Really?" George was so delighted that he started going for her hand again. "Gee, thanks! That's great, just, just great!"

Sydney sneezed again, twice. George blessed her again, and then said, "Gee, I hope you're not getting my lousy spring cold."

"No, no, I don't think so," Sydney said, as she fished around in her pocketbook for a Kleenex. "Germs don't work quite that fast."

But computers do.

7/ THE CALL

Sydney got home and worked on George Humphrey's case and others, for several hours. She did not get to her Weight Watcher's meal (Fat-Free Fettucine Florentine) until close to midnight. She took a quick shower, glancing only briefly at the Jacuzzi which looked so inviting, but which she never had the time to use (the darn thing took twenty minutes just to fill up!) Then she brushed her teeth and fell into bed with her hair still damp. She fell asleep among thoughts of George and his business. So it wasn't strange that she awoke with thoughts of computer viruses.

Funny phrase, "computer virus." These were really just computer programs designed to do harm or mischief—destroy files or just flood the computer with duplicated files so that it has no more capacity to work. But some techno-doc applied the term "virus" because these programs "infect" computers the way viruses do to living organisms.

Computer "viruses" have been around for awhile—but the idea of a computer "virus" *infecting the user?* Impossible! Science fiction. Had to be.

Sydney's musings were interrupted by the telephone.

"Aunt Sydney!!" It was Melva's daughter, her niece, Lila. She sounded breathless, anxious. This was unusual, even for this teenager.

"Lila, Honey, what's the matter?" Sydney sat up and swung her legs over the side of the bed, toes scouting for her fuzzy slippers.

"Aunt Sydney!! Something has ... something has ... *happened!*" Lila sounded as though she were using all of the self-control she could muster.

"Lila, what is it? Are you all right? What's happened?" Sydney held the receiver with both hands and stood up.

"I'm okay. Well, I don't know what's happened—not exactly." Then she just stopped, and Sydney could hear her anxious breath over the telephone. It became apparent that Lila was unable to form any more words out of all that breath. It reminded Sydney of a series of obscene phone calls she had received a few years ago, which she finally terminated with the help of a two-dollar coach's whistle.

Sydney finally gave up hoping that Lila would go on, so she started asking questions: "Is it your mom, Lila? Is everyone okay?"

"Yes, yes," Lila found her voice, "Everyone's okay. Except ... well ..."

Again she fell silent, and now Sydney was beginning to feel a sense of panic. "Except what? What?? *Tell me!*"

"I can't tell you this over the phone, Aunt Sydney. I have to come and see you."

Sydney sat back down on the bed, as The Truth Began To Dawn: "Oh, Lila, are you pregnant, honey? Don't worry, I'll help y—"

Lila began to giggle and started to sound more like herself. "Puh-leeease, Auntie!" Then she pulled herself together and sounded more somber, "Can't I come out and see you?"

"But what about school?" Sydney asked. Lila was a junior in high school in the same city where Sydney and Melva's parents lived, and where they had grown up: Miami, Florida.

"We're starting spring break now. I can get on a bus and be there by tomorrow night!"

"Buy a plane ticket," Sydney said, cutting her off, "I'll give you a credit card number you can charge it to." Sydney knew how her sister and brother-in-law liked to lecture about frugality, even though they were financially well off enough to feel comfortable around Republicans. "Just tell your mom that I invited you up for spring break."

"Oh, thanks, Aunt Sydney! Oh, I can hardly wait to see you!" Lila's relief was palpable over the long-distance lines. "But are you sure I won't be interfering with your plans?"

That reminded Sydney about the trip she had planned with *Tommy de la Phillips 66* for tomorrow, Saturday—and not without some shame that she had allowed herself to get involved with this venture in the first place. Well, this would be the perfect excuse for her to cancel the plans with Tommy.

"Come in Sunday," she told Lila, marveling at how her tongue had a mind of its own. "I'll pick you up at the airport. Call me back and leave a message with your flight information, if I'm out."

"Oh, Aunt Sydney! I knew I could count on you! I love you!"

Sydney hung up the phone and hung her head in shame. Putting off her dear niece's obvious need to see her in order to carry on with a foolish trip with a poorly-credentialed hunk! ... Although ... Lila's "problem" was most likely one of those many little teenage concerns that seems like the end of the world to the kid, but is easily remedied with a few reassuring words of advice from a loving adult. And Lila seemed happy enough to come in on Sunday.

Still, Sydney felt ill-at-ease ...

8/ LILA'S DILEMMA

Lila hung up the telephone and looked around her room. She was still shaking a little, even though she felt a lot more secure since she was going to see her Aunt Sydney soon. She couldn't tell her little brother or sister, either. Maybe she was cracking up ... going insane! But she was sure, if anyone could, Aunt Sydney would know how to sort it all out.

Lila had been close to Sydney from the day she was born, it seemed. She could remember back when she was just a little bitty toddler—perhaps two or three years old. Aunt Sydney would come over and take her out. Those were the favorite memories she had from her childhood.

They would go to Peppermint Park and ride on the bumper cars and the Wild Mouse. That ride scared her more than anything! It was a high roller coaster, with each car painted like a giant mouse. The front wheels were set far back toward the middle of the car, so when it roared into a turn at high speed, the front of the car would extend way over the edge of the roller coaster, and Lila was sure the car would keep right on going and fall off the edge, crashing into the park far below! Then it would snap back as the wheels rounded the corner of the track, and the mouse's nose was once again over the track!

Lila's parents would never have taken her on such a ride at that age—but she loved the thrills and chills, and mostly, she loved her Aunt Sydney.

She wondered now, though, how she was going to tell her aunt what was happening. What if she really were losing her mind? Still, she felt a solid comfort just in thinking about confiding in her aunt, and she would ... just ... *tell* her!

Lila went into the bathroom and surveyed things again. She flushed the toilet once again—there were still charred remains floating around the edge of the water. And the smell of smoke was still in the air. It was a good thing that her room was at the far end of their long, ranch-style house. It was still early in the morning, and maybe she could air it all out before anyone got up.

But how was she going to explain the dolls? Lila had kept some favorite dolls ever since she was little. Her family had lived in this house since she was ten years old. Her father's dental practice had flourished enough by then that they could build this house in the exclusive southwestern section of Miami. And with her eight-year-old brother and two-year-old sister, they had long since outgrown the little stucco crackerbox home their parents had bought when he first graduated from dental school.

Lila had a number of dolls, stuffed animals, and little figurines that she could not bear to give away. One was a porcelain doll with beautiful features and a blue satin gown. Another was an originally white, but now gray, stuffed Snoopy dog with a graduation cap on its head which she had received from Sydney after graduating from kindergarten. (They had had a formal ceremony, with little caps and gowns, and the kindergarten teacher played a recording of "Pomp and Circumstance" while handing out diplomas.)

The last of her old favorite dolls was a somewhat sinister looking toy monkey holding two cymbals apart. The wind-up key in the back had long since departed, and Lila could not remember it ever having worked. But it held a place as one of her favorites because it had been given to her by her grandfather, who had found it in an ancient box of belongings in the attic of Lila's great-grandfather's house, after the occasion of his somewhat mysterious death.

("Mysterious" is not the most descriptive term, actually. He was found in that very attic, dismembered and strewn from corner to corner. There were no signs of forced entry into the house, and the only explanation anyone could come up with was that their previously sweet and gentle Great Dane had gone berserk and torn his master limb from limb. The fact that there was no trace of the dog in the attic—not a hair, not a paw print—was insufficient to deter the authorities from the only solution they could come up with. The case was closed, and the Great Dane was euthanized.)

Anyway, Lila kept the toy monkey. She was a loyal friend—loyal to anything with which she could form a bond. Friends, pets, even sinister-looking toy monkeys that didn't work but were handed down from generation to generation.

Lila had had a terrible dream. In it, the toy monkey had come to life. Its eyes began to turn a devilish orange-red, its gruesome grin gowing wider and wider, white teeth turning pink, then red, then livid, and stretching down into crooked fearsome fangs. Then Lila heard a noise like a key cranking a wind-up mechanism, and the monkey began to move toward her. The cymbals sewn to its paws clashed together and clashed again, making a shattering noise which pierced her ears. Lila awoke screaming with her hands over her ears.

Her heart was racing and all of her thoughts were focused on the toy monkey on her dresser and her sudden intense fear of it. Her desire for it to be destroyed became stronger and stronger ... and suddenly a small puff of smoke appeared above the monkey's head ... and in an instant it was engulfed in flames! She slapped at her own face to see if she were still dreaming, but she was really awake! The fire rapidly jumped over to the Snoopy doll and the porcelain doll. Lila ran into her bathroom, collecting enough water in a drinking cup to douse the flames ... but not before the fire had nearly consumed the three toys.

Except for the mess on her dresser and in the bathroom, and the traces of smoke in the air, Lila's room looked just the same as it always had. Her leopard-skin printed bedspread, the rock music posters on the walls, the shelves of books and souvenirs from football games, carnivals and field trips. Just like any ordinary sixteen-year-old girl's room.

Except now the porcelain doll, the Snoopy dog, and the cymbal-wielding monkey were nothing but a charred glob on top of her dresser. If they had not been sitting on a metal tray (with a picture of the Grateful Dead painted on it), the dresser probably would have been burned, too.

Lila went over and cautiously reached out with her index finger to touch the blackened remains of her dolls and see if they were cool enough to handle. They were, and when she lifted the mess she saw that only the toy monkey was still intact—*not burned at all!* Her least favorite doll—the one she wished had been destroyed—was left unscathed!

Still, she decided to dispose of it with the others. She tiptoed quietly down the long corridor which passed her bathroom, the other children's rooms, the main bathroom, and the guest room. She crossed the huge livingroom with its oaken floors and hand-cut pure woolen Chinese rugs, lamplighter chandelier, and slate-&-granite fireplace (which, in Miami, served only as a rather audacious status symbol). Finally she got to the kitchen. It was nearly as large as the living room, with a separate island cooking and eating area and gleaming hand-painted Italian floor tile.

Lila pulled open two of the lower cabinets and found some plastic garbage bags. She took them, plus a roll of paper towels, and quietly stole back to her room in the soft pinkish glow of the early spring light coming in through the glass doors. She dumped the mess from her dresser into one of the garbage bags, and began to clean up the water around it. She opened the glass doors which led out into the huge backyard, which was shaded with banana trees, avocado and mango trees, three very tall coconut trees in the very center, and bordered all around by spikey-leaved palmetto bushes.

She waved at the air to help the smoke and odor out, and then went back into the bathroom to finish cleaning that up. There was a smoke stain on the wall behind the dresser. Lila found a still-rolled-up poster of Brad Pitt, which she taped up over the smudge. There! Her camouflage attempt was complete!

She went to the telephone (Mickey Mouse, his right hand the receiver and belly button dial) to call the airlines and make reservations for Sunday's flight. She tried to think of how Aunt Sydney might react when she told her about what had happened. After all, Aunt Sydney adored her, and often said they were so close because they were both demented in just the same special way. But this was REALLY crazy!

Sydney spent most of Friday at George Humphrey's office. He was still pretty sick—if anything, he looked worse than the day before. He was pale and sweaty, and his glands looked a little puffy. Sydney would not have stayed if he hadn't told her to go ahead and work while he laid down in the back office. She wondered if she might catch something from him.

But her own sneezes from the day before seemed to have come and gone. She felt fine. She hoped she wouldn't catch whatever George had, but she did not want to lose the account, either.

Sydney would make a tidy sum for her services to George. And, when the dreaded T-Day came around, as it did every April 15th, she would declare every penny of it on her tax form. Never again would she spend her precious time behind locks and barbed wire for the ill-fated chauvinism of "free" enterprise. Because "free" enterprise was very expensive. Very.

And Sydney was glad that it had cost her no more than four months of her freedom to find out just how expensive free enterprise was. There was a certain poetic-ness there (not "justice"—she would never consider it justice). Because Sydney now had to work for five months out of every year to pay for her right to practice free enterprise. Five months of her annual income went to the federal government to pay her taxes. That was poetic.

When Sydney got home there were two messages on her voicemail. One was from Lila, giving her the time and flight number of her plane on Sunday. The other was from her sister, Melva. Lila's mother. Sydney expected that.

There was the usual pause before Melva started speaking, while Melva was allowing her hostility to flow out into the voicemail which she resented having to speak to. Afterward, her sharp, schoolmarm voice bolted off the recording:

"Sydney!" Then another long, punishing pause. Then: "I appreciate your interest in bringing Lila up for her spring break—don't think I don't appreciate it—but you might have called me first to discuss it before inviting her!"

There was something about the word "discuss" that dripped with authority—just the kind that Melva should have known by now would bore into Sydney like a dental drill. Which is probably why she said it.

"Please call me to discuss this." Another pause ... three seconds, four seconds ... click. Sydney rolled her eyes at the ceiling and snapped off the answering machine. Melva could wait until after dinner (Weight Watcher's Chicken Constantinople, 325 calories) to dis*CUSS* (accent on the 'cuss') Lila's visit!

Sydney stayed up late and worked some more on George Humphrey's account. The call to Melva went fine, as usual. Melva just wanted to give her permission, and Sydney supposed that was really quite reasonable. After all, it was her kid, and she had to maintain some semblence of authority.

She gave very little thought to the strange nature of Lila's request to come and see her. Lila was given to the same whims and excesses of normal kids her age, and Sydney thought, behind it all, that Lila may have been fishing for an invitation for spring break. That was okay—Sydney felt guilty for not thinking of it herself.

9 / TOMMY'S CRACKERS

Saturday morning. Sydney sat bolt upright in bed, stunned by the realization of what she had let herself in for today. She was going to go fifty miles from nowhere, up into the mountains with some gas station attendant she just met, to look at a Volvo (ugly) which his grandmother left him when she died (and just *how did she die*, anyway?)

She was going to get into his truck with the monster wheels and the jacklights on top of the rollbar, and after they drove maybe thirty or forty miles (to where, you might have asked?), Tommy would pull into some dense flora, slam the truck to a stop, and jerk upward menacingly on his parking brake.

Then he would turn to Sydney and give her a grotesque jack-o-lantern grin and tell her slowly and deliberately all the terrible things he was about to do.

They would not find her body for months. When she is finally found, it would be by some poor little kid and his dog. The dog would sniff a strange odor, perhaps after a heavy rain, and he would go digging in the forest floor while his young master would be tugging at his neck to come on. "Fido! Whassamatta? Dere's nuttin' dere! Come on!"

Fido would keep at his digging, though, and soon begin to back up slowly, dragging Sydney's rotted arm bone with him. When the kid sees it, he screams for his momma and runs home frantic, nearly putting out his eyes from the branches jutting into his path.

"Momma, Momma!!" he would cry, nearly delerious from the horror of his find, "Quick, call da telebijun station! You ain' t gonna belieb dis!!"

Sydney snickered at the thought and got up out of bed. She would save herself a lot of painful mental flagellation and sum it up thusly: (a) She should not go with this man; (b) She was going. End of problem. Her stomach did a quick jackknife and—just as with her better judgment—she ignored it.

Sydney made some pita sandwiches and put them into a picnic basket, along with a bottle of wine and half a cheesecake (Weight Watchers, low-fat, 175 calories per one-inch wedge). Then she forced herself to sit down and work on George's business until she could meet Tommy at ten o-clock.

She did a good job, because when she finally got up from her computer station it was five after ten! She was late! She grabbed her fringed leather shoulder bag and the ballcap with "Hotlanta!" in bold script, and didn't bother to wait for the elevator, but ran down the stairwell to the car. Locked out! She ran back upstairs, grabbed her keys, and ran back down to the car. The picnic basket! She half-ran, half-walked, half out of breath, back upstairs, got the picnic basket, and took the elevator back down to the car.

It wouldn't start. Sydney stared at the ignition in shock and disbelief. Her car NEVER didn't start. Not in twelve years did her little Toyota not start! This is a payback, she thought, pushing back a rising anxiety about whether Tommy was still waiting for her, and knowing that she probably shouldn't be doing this at all! Anxiety was shooting slingshots in her stomach.

Her dear little Toyota that had not given her a minute's trouble through twelve long and loving years, now it wouldn't start! She turned the ignition key and turned it again. Silence. It knew. It knew what she was planning. It was jealous. It was in control. It was ... It was ... It was roaring to life as the engine turned over and Sydney screeched out of the parking garage, narrowly missing a woman with a fur coat that exactly matched the little cocker spaniel she was walking.

Sydney patted the steering column as she drove on, and cooed, "But you know I'll always love you best!"

Tommy was waiting by his truck. The day was already dazzlingly bright, flowers were bursting in billows of rainbow colors, and Tommy was as comely as she remembered. More. His light gold hair was lifted a little by the slight breeze, and his supple muscular arms were folded across his chest. One leg was crossed over the ankle of the other as he leaned back against his truck. His jeans rode low on his hips and his feet sported cowboy boots.

"Hey, stranger," he said as she drove up. "You're late!" He tapped his watch crystal as he leaned into Sydney's window. His face was so close to hers that she could see how perfect his skin and even white teeth really were. His eyes reminded her of the blue-green waters of Miami's Biscayne Bay.

"The car wouldn't start!" she said, triumphantly. Now she could truly justify this ridiculous excursion which she was about to make. She *really did* need a new car!

Tommy opened the door for her and offered his hand. His grip was strong. It made her weak. She got out of the car and felt a little disappointment when he dropped her hand.

"So where are we going?" she asked.

"To grandmother's house," he answered, with a slight smile in one corner of his mouth. "It's about three hours from here," he added, lifting the checkered cloth off the picnic basket Sydney had set down.

"M-m-m-m, looks good!" He put the truck in gear and rolled slowly into the flow of traffic. Three hours, Sydney thought. She felt a small fingernail of fear scrape along her gut.

As they passed beyond the city limits and traffic disappeared on the two-lane country backroads, Sydney realized that they had said almost nothing for the nearly twenty minutes. Right after they left the Phillips 66 station, Tommy had tried to make some casual conversation. He had asked Sydney about her work, where she was from originally, and so on. But Sydney was so uptight that she killed each attempt without realizing it. Her terse, one-word answers conveyed the distinct impression that she did not want to talk. So, puzzling though it was, Tommy ceased his efforts to make conversation.

Sydney finally became aware of the lengthy silence, and decided to correct the situation. Her anxiety was remitting anyway. She cleared her throat lightly and said, "So—tell me more about this Volvo?"

Tommy looked at her and smiled. It made her dizzy. He began to talk about the car. "It's blue, less than a year old. Grandma didn't drive it much, so it's got very low mileage..."

They went on talking for the next hour. His car, her car, cars in general. It was good. Sydney felt happy and peaceful. The mountain scenery was beautiful the rhododendrons were in full bloom, as were the azaleas and dogwoods, and the countryside was filled with color and fragrance and bumblebees. As they rounded each turn in the mountain road, which took them higher and higher, Sydney looked down over the lush emerald green carpet of treetops covering the mountains.

"They're the color of your eyes," Tommy said.

"Wh-what?"

"The treetops. They're as green as your eyes. Very pretty." He said this, but continued to look straight ahead and drive.

Sydney could feel herself blushing, something she did not like to do, because it clashed with her hair. She started to say something, when suddenly Tommy let go of the steering wheel and began clawing at his eyes. He uttered something animal-like, and then grabbed the wheel with one hand while he continued to flay at his eyes with the other.

Fear pinned Sydney to her seat like a butterfly on a mounting board. She could see nothing under their wheels as the truck whipped over to the very edge of the mountain, before Tommy managed to whipsaw it back onto the road. It reminded her of the Wild Mouse ride she used to take her niece on so many years ago. Only there was no track now.

Finally Tommy brought the truck to a halt, just missing some trees on the inner edge of the road. He was still clawing at his eyes, and making garbled grunts. Now he was cupping one hand under his eye and holding it open with the other.

"Tommy ... Are you ... What's wrong?! P-Please tell me!"

"Contact lenses," he answered. Finally he sat back and relaxed, one fist curled around his lenses and the other rubbing his eyes. "Pollen gets under the lens and it's real torture!"

Finally he looked over at her, his eyes red and teary.

"Hope I didn't scare you or anything," he said. Sydney just shook her head. She wanted to scream with relief that he had not become the rampaging monster of her fantasy, flinging both of them over the mountainside.

Tommy fished his contact lens paraphernalia out of the glove compartment, brushing her knee as he did so. He went through the ritual of cleaning the lenses and putting them away. Then he took out an eyeglass case, and withdrew a pair of spectacles with the heaviest, thickest lenses Sydney had ever seen. He started to clean them with a soft cloth. They were so dense that she could see spiral after spiral within the lenses, as the images behind them were refracted over and over.

Sydney stifled the urge to tell Tommy he must be blind as a bat. Instead, she just managed to say, "Uh ... are you okay now?"

"Yeah," he answered, "I'm just blind as a bat."

"Well, uh ... can you still drive?" she asked, knowing she could not drive his manual gearshift, and wondering what they would do if he couldn't.

"Oh, yeah," he answered, still cleaning his glasses. "Just let me rest my eyes for a minute. Hey, I really hope I didn't scare you back there."

He looked at her and tears were still streaked down his face. Sydney noticed that his eyes were no longer blue-green. They were just plain blue, surrounded by throbbing red vessels. She fished in her pocketbook and handed him a crumpled Kleenex.

"Here, this is clean, I've only used it a few times ... that's a joke, really ... I've never used it!"

Tommy looked over at her and his eyes crinkled in a little chuckle. "Thanks, I'm okay now!" He put on his spectacles, which looked from the side thickness as though they could be used for the windshield on the Presidential limousine. He eased the gearshift back into drive, and released the parking brake. They pulled off the shoulder and back onto the mountain road, gaining speed slowly.

They had driven along without talking again for a little while. Both were lost in the breezy mountain ambiance. Sydney was looking out of her side window at the beautiful foliage, the sweeping mountainside carpeted with all shades of green as the clouds made little sailboats across the crystalline blue sky.

Then, without speaking, Tommy unbuckled his seatbelt and raised his hips off the seat. He reached into his left pants pocket and pulled out a package of Nabs peanut butter crackers. He turned his head so that he was looking straight through the center of his lenses at Sydney, and said, "Cracker?"

Sydney felt her heart clang like a death knell. She was nearly floating in fear at the sight of him. For, with his big eyes diminished to tiny dots behind the thick lenses of his glasses, Tommy's face now resembled that of the Gray Man. Tommy was the Gray Man of her dreams. Her nightmares.

10/ MYSTICAL BUG, MAGICAL POWER

The Center for Disease Control (CDC) in Atlanta was just beginning to get the first inkling of what was happening. Spotty reports from around the country were describing a new illness, completely unique in its character, and with no identifiable origin. It seemed utterly impossible, and the scientific and medical experts who were called in from the start were tempted to begin believing in the supernatural. Some were even going so far as to consider the possibility—in very hushed whispers, and only to the most trustworthy confidantes among their colleagues—that there might actually be a *god* at work here.

Dr. Wilhelm Nielsen tried to explain the bizarre nature of it to his wife. They were seated at the dining room table. Eva had microwaved a T.V. dinner and placed it before her husband (who never looked at what he ate). She had not known in advance that she should prepare something for his dinner because he came home at 10:00 p.m. (early for him) and realized that he had not eaten a thing all day.

"You see," he explained, as he stared up toward the ceiling while cutting into his steak-like food portion, "Diseases can develop acutely via a spontaneous genetic mutation." He waved his knife around in a slow circle in the air. Then he seemed to lapse into deep thought. His knife stopped in mid-air, as did his chewing.

"Go on, dear," Eva prodded, as she tuned in more acutely to Vanna White's voice from the living room. *Category is "Things."*

Wilhelm resumed his chewing. "Even centuries back we can often identify the time and place when a certain disease began. A virus mutates, it infects new hosts, it develops new abilities to transmit itself, it is either stopped by natural immunities in the host, or antibiotics, or—" He stopped chewing again and looked over at Eva. Her elbows were propped up on the table, chin resting on folded hands. She nodded. She could see the television if she leaned just slightly to the right. *Buy a vowel.*

"Or it wipes out the host population and thereby lays the groundwork for its own extinction." Wilhelm's eyes floated back up toward the far end of the ceiling. "But this new disease ... it's striking isolated pockets of victims around the country with no apparent means of transmission!"

He picked up his napkin and dabbed at his lips, which he pursed for the occasion, leaving a small dollop of gravy hanging off the end of his small, square-ish moustache. "And the victims," he continued, as he pushed his chair back, "they die so *quickly*."

Wilhelm looked at his beautiful wife, who was looking back at him, hands still folded under her chin. "My lovely Eva."

"Baubles and bangles!" Eva said suddenly, slapping her hands on the table and looking over toward the T.V.

"Oh ... what?" Wilhelm asked, turning in the direction of the T.V.

"Balderdash, I meant!" said Eva, walking around the table and picking up a napkin to wipe the remaining gravy from her husband's face. "Balderdash if they don't think Professor-Doctor Wilhelm Nielsen can find the answer!" That is what she always said to him.

"Why, thank you, *meine kleine blume*, my little flower," he said, as he reached up to stroke his wife's cheek (she was some four inches taller than he). "Now I must return to my work," he said, as he half-bowed to her. She heard the soft click of his heels snapping together, an old habit which he had not quite broken. He reached for her hand and kissed it with his still-greasy lips. "Good night, my *Liebling*." Then he took his still-warm hat and briefcase, and left once again for the laboratory.

Eva watched him leave. She cleared the table and threw the leftovers into the kitchen garbage pail. She scraped the plate and put it into the dishwasher. Then she removed her apron and hung it up on the hook next to the refrigerator. She turned off the lights and headed through the living room toward the bedroom, stopping only to pick up the book she had left on the coffee table, *Small World*, by Tabitha King.

When she got to the bedroom, she laid the book down on the nightstand on her side of the bed. She reached behind her shoulders and unzipped the long zipper down the back of her dress. It fell to the floor, and she stepped out of it. She surveyed her figure in the long mirror on the wall. In the mirror she saw a slight movement behind her.

"Don't move an inch," commanded a husky voice behind her. Eva stood frozen in front of the mirror, as she watched the man emerge from behind the bedroom door. He stepped slowly toward her and she could feel her heart racing in her chest. He came up behind her and slid his arms through hers. He began to caress her, as his lips brushed against her cheek.

"It's okay, darling ... He's gone for the night now ..."

When Dr. Nielsen arrived back at the lab, several of his colleagues were still there, and greeted him with a shrug, which meant "Still nothing." It was too late to go and interview any patients now, so Dr. Nielsen went to his desk to review the events of that day. Two more reports of the strange new illness had come in that day.

One victim was a computer programmer with a huge advertising company in Los Angeles. She designed programs which would allow animation of letters and figures for television commercials. This form of animation provided an exquisitely smooth movement which was not possible with animation drawn by hand. (Old-time artists grumbled that this new technique took all the "natural imperfections" of movement out of cartooning, which actually better resembled real-life movement than the computer's "too-perfect" smoothness.)

The other victim of the day was a private investigator who relied heavily on computer networking to track down the whereabouts of clients who tended to repeat their usual habits with credit cards and such, while on the lam. Both of these people, the animator and the P.I., were scheduled for arrival at the CDC tomorrow for more intensive diagnostic evaluation. They both had been evaluated by local physicians and then referred to specialists, none of whom could diagnose them.

The nature of the illness—now dubbed "CompuFlu" to differentiate it from the "computer viruses," which were not medical in nature at all, but electronic—was a complete enigma thus far. A variety of viral and allergic syndromes presented in the doctors' offices around the country. The patient may be complaining of fever, runny nose, swollen glands, sore throat, itching eyes, or aches and pains, in any or all of the above combinations. But no source of infection could be identified. No allergen, no antigen, no toxin, no infection.

At first the scientists and physicians at the CDC thought they would isolate a new strain of virus, something which would be extremely difficult to detect. But nothing was turning up. And the single environmental factor which formed a pattern among all the victims—the heavy involvement with computers in their day-to-day activities—was unnerving. You couldn't catch something from a computer!! Like, you are now entering the Twilight Zone. Or the Dead Zone.

The scientists actually discussed the computer connection very little. They merely mentioned it when describing the patient initially, and then did not refer to it again. It was so bizarre, that they could not discuss it. They were not ready to discuss such things. So they tried to ignore it. They as yet had no inkling about what else was happening to certain other computer buffs around the country, because *those* victims were not going to doctors. They were not about to, because they feared they would get carried off in jackets with extra-long sleeves which wrapped around them and tied in the back.

Mac McMulligan was a retired police officer with the Dallas Police Department in Dallas, Texas. He had been active on the force for twenty-six years—even though he had had a desk job for most of that time, so he became familiar with computers. Running license checks, prior criminal records, identification of stolen merchandise—all of that stuff was handled by computer.

Mac had run afoul of the DPD when he was just a rookie. He had been assigned to the team of officers who would be escorting a high-profile alleged murderer from the jail to the courthouse. His uniform was crisp and new, his badge and buttons gleaming, his shoes spit-shined to a mirror finish. He felt almost giddy with authority as he raced in front of the team and flailed his arms at the crowd to stay back.

Mac was one of the last ones to learn what had happened to his charge. As he arrived at the courthouse doors, he was surrounded by reporters who barraged him with questions about the murder. Assuming they were referring to the alleged murder, he answered in a knowledgable manner. But the reporters informed him that the man he was supposed to be guarding and escorting to the courthouse had just been shot—apparently by the mother of his alleged victim! That was when Mac stopped flailing and turned around to see that the man he had been assigned to protect was no longer there, but was on the ground bleeding, some distance back. Mac never lived it down.

But now—his prayers seemed to have been answered! Now, suddenly, he found himself with powers ... *real* powers! ... the kind you only read about in wonky Stephen King novels. He could ... *do* things!

At first he thought it was only a bizarre coincidence—the refrigerator door slipping open when he looked at it and thought about getting another beer; the precious stones he found on the floor after a reception by a wealthy oil tycoon for his newlywed daughter, where Mac had been hired to supply security (they were not aware of his reputation). He had stared longingly at the jewelry-bedecked women and men at the reception, wishing only that just a few diamonds or rubies would fall to the floor where he would find them. They did, and he did.

All this occurred following the new computer program he had downloaded. He saw it advertised in an email that looked pretty legitimate. It was called "SpaceWarGasm" and Mac did a double-take when he saw the name, and couldn't resist buying it.

This particular program did not seem to work right, though. Mac would set up the game, but as soon as he "fired" at the targets (furry, V-shaped blips) with his missle (an elongated mushroom-looking thing) a weird array of brightly colored symbols and dissonant sounds emanated from the computer. Then Mac felt a strange sensation float through his body. It was not unpleasant ... tingly ... kind of like someone had broken a raw egg on top of his head, and it slowly oozed through his hair and down his neck and back and chest, and finally on down his legs and feet.

At first he thought that was what was supposed to happen. Then, the more he thought about it, the more impossible it seemed ... a computer game that could cause a physical tingling sensation in his body? Then ... *things* began to happen. Like the refrigerator door, and the jewelry. He had not, though, at this point, connected either the computer game or the strange new powers with a dream he had begun to have recently ... a repeating dream:

In this dream, he was back within the halls of the court house on that fateful day. He had a handcuffed prisoner by the left elbow and was clearing people away from their path with cursory waves of his own left hand. The place was packed with reporters and crowds of other people, and flashbulbs were going off all around him like at a film festival. Suddenly, an old lady runs at them from somewhere back and to the side of them—she has a pistol out, pointed, and is shouting something at them! Mac flings the prisoner to the floor and then whirls on the old lady as he flips his pistol out of its holster and fires from hip level. He empties all six rounds into the perpetrator, who is arrested, but survives. After the crowd realizes what has happened, Mac is hoisted onto the shoulders of the citizens of "Big D" who are mighty proud of their hero!

Then comes the really strange part of the dream: Mac is carried to a door which reads "MAYOR," but instead of the Mayor, he is greeted by a shriveled old man, whom he cannot identify. The man has hair the color of steel, and wrinkles that make him look as though he's been submerged in seawater for three years. He is smiling a wide but mirthless grin, and Mac is held by his teeny, tiny eyes, which begin to light up as he comes closer. Closer and closer, Mac watches in horror as the gray man's eyes become hotter and hotter and then begin to shoot flames out at him. Mac raises his forearms to protect his face from the firey streams, and that is usually when he wakes up, sweating and choking.

But that dream is not what had been staying on Mac's mind lately. Surprisingly, he actually awakens from it with a positive feeling. It is almost as though he has finally located the *father* he never knew. Although the man in the dream and his fire-eyes are scary as hell, Mac also feels a kind of ... kinship, of sorts ... with the old man. He could almost say he loves the old gray man.

No, Mac's concerns now revolved around learning to fine-tune his newfound powers, and then devise a way to use them. The possibilities were mind boggling!

11/ WOLFGANG

Sydney could not answer Tommy's question. It was simple enough—did she want a cracker? Tommy asked her twice before he realized that something was wrong. Sydney had turned the color of wall spackle and seemed to have stopped breathing.

"Hey—are you okay?" he asked, still turning to look at her as much as he could through the center of his thick lenses (things began to get distorted as he looked through the outermost edges of them). But he had to keep looking back at the road to drive.

Sydney was in a state resembling shock, but not quite. Her blood pressure was still within acceptable limits. Otherwise, though, she was cold and clammy, and her heart pumped out a film-noir kind of discordant beat.

As Tommy looked back and forth from the road to Sydney, she kept having more and more terrifying thoughts. When Tommy looked at the road, and she could see his big beautiful blue eyes staring straight ahead, and his wide, open forehead, his athletic nose and strong, well-chiseled chin—he looked like the strong sensual guy that she wanted to be with.

But when he turned to face her and repeat, "Sydney? Are you okay?" all she could see were those beady little distorted eyeballs through his thick, coke-bottle lenses, which made his face, if you added a few thousand wrinkles, identical to the face of the Gray Man in her nightmare.

> *Late last night, I said LATE, I said,*
> *Tommy's crackers, Tommy's crackers,*
> *Crunching in my bed...*

Finally, after what seemed like an eternity, Sydney was able to pull herself together enough to answer Tommy with something resembling human speech.

"Yeah! Hey, I'm fine!" she said, looking down at her bib overalls and pressing her hand over her abdomen. "Just a little ... oh ... queasy ... these mountain roads, y'know!" Her hand once again rotated at the wrist as she groped for words to redeem her sentence.

"Do you want me to pull over for awhile?" Tommy asked, moving his foot from the accelerator to the brake.

"No!!" Sydney almost spat this out. "No! Just keep driving!"

She did not want him to stop and pull over again. But neither did she want to continue on this journey with him. Suddenly she just wished she were back home, and had never agreed to come on this foolish jaunt.

Tommy pulled over anyway, and pulled off his glasses, rubbing his eyes again. Then he turned to her and asked, "Would you like me to take you back home?"

Now, without his thick glasses on—staring into those magnetic blue eyes, that comely face—Sydney lost her fears. And her mind, she thought. "No, really, I'll be fine. Let's keep going!" Death Wish Four-Hundred-Twenty.

Tommy replaced his glasses and started back up the mountain. He drove slowly and evenly. The blue sky gradually began to darken, and about halfway to their destination it looked as though they were going to have some stormy weather. Sure enough, it began to rain in heavy sheets, and the sky was as dark as night. Thunder rolled ominously around them like the steel ball on a roulette wheel. Tommy pulled off the main road onto a side road, then stopped and parked the truck. He put on a CD —Garth Brooks.

"We'll have to wait here until the rain lets up a little," he said, as he removed his glasses. Sydney sat stiffly in her seat. She felt like a robot. Suddenly she turned around and reached for the picnic basket in the back.

"Let's eat!" she managed to say, and began rooting through the basket, pulling out sandwiches and cheescake.

"But I thought you were feeling a little queasy?" Tommy said, genuinely surprised at her enthusiastic appetite.

"Nah, I'm fine! Cheesecake?" She held the plate up to his face, and he took it.

They ate in relative silence, except for Brooks' mellow warbles, and pretty soon the rain let up and the sky brightened, and except for the crystal droplets hanging off the trees and the tiny lakes here and there, it was beautiful again, and the storm was like a bad dream. They finished eating, and then Tommy backed up the side road and started back on the mountain road.

The next hour was a less quiet one. They listened to CD's and Sydney talked and talked, the cheesecake having loosened her up a bit (sugar did that). She talked about politics, cautiously mentioning both sides of every issue, to insure that she would not insult Tommy, whatever he believed, that is, if he read the papers at all. She was careful to avoid discussing anything even remotely approaching the subject of sex, but it wasn't easy, especially when one was talking about politics. Nevertheless, they managed to pass the time, and Sydney found herself relaxing and enjoying Tommy's company in spite of her anxieties about him.

Sydney began to wonder about Tommy and the terrible repeating nightmare she had been having recently. He seemed like such a sweet guy. Could there really be some kind of a connection between him and the Gray Man? There was a distinct resemblance between the two faces, especially when Tommy had his thick glasses on.

And the cracker crumbs! Her dream always ended with that feeling as she awoke sweeping frantically at her bedsheets. But then again, what was unusual about Tommy carrying crackers around? The guy worked in a gas station—he probably lived on Nabs.

If there *were* a connection between Tommy and her repeating dream, then that would make it a clairvoyant dream, or a prescient dream—somehow knowing what was happening without being there, or knowing what was going to happen in the future! Sydney had only experienced something like that once before in her life. It was the night that her grandmother died. Sydney was sixteen. She was very, very close with her grandmother, who had been in the hospital gravely ill. Sydney had been asleep only about two or three hours that night. She thought she woke up and saw her grandmother coming toward her. Only her grandmother was walking—hovering—some distance above the ground! And she looked so beautiful! She was radiant—and youthful!

Her hair was a rich chestnut brown and flowed luxuriously down around her shoulders. She was wearing a white, diaphenous gown which flowed lightly around her, as though there were a soft breeze in the room. Then she spoke:

"Sydney, grandchild named for your great-Uncle, my brother's twin! It is so beautiful Here (she said it as though it should have a capital-H), and I have never felt so well! Please do not worry about me, child! This is a joyous and exquisite place. I am so happy! Boris is here!"

She waved to Sydney, and turned to walk back up the path she seemed to be on. Then she turned and waved once more, blew a kiss, and then disappeared.

Sydney awoke and looked at the clock. 2:07 A.M.

The next afternoon, Sydney came home from school and her parents told her that her grandmother had died the night before, just after two o'clock in the morning. Sydney did not feel a chill or sadness, as she thought she would have, but rather a warm and comfortable feeling. Then she asked, "Mom—Who is Boris?"

"Hm-m-m ... I don't know. Why?"

Before Sydney could answer, her father cut in. "Boris? That was the name they called my father when he first came to this country from Russia. His name was Baruch, but they translated it as 'Boris'."

Could it be that Sydney's grandmother had actually visited her just after she passed away the night before??

Sydney wondered now whether her recurring nightmare about the Gray Man had any significance—or any relation to Tommy? But how could it? One thing was certain, though—she would be very happy when Tommy put his Number Two Gulfstream Teal contact lenses back in and took off those horrible glasses.

Tommy pulled the truck up to a white gate which was locked with an old, rusty padlock. He got out and opened it up with a key from his shirt pocket. They drove about another half-mile down a road which was strewn with ruts and boulders, and Sydney could see that the truck's oversized wheels were necessary in a place like this.

"There's a better road up to the front of the place," Tommy explained, as they lurched and tipped over the ragged terrain, "but it's about two miles longer. I can use this entrance with this rig, and it's a lot shorter."

By the time they arrived at the homestead, a huge sprawling Victorian mansion, Sydney's stomach really was queasy. Matters were not improved when Tommy came around to her side of the truck and cupped her elbow in his hand to help her down from the truck. Twinges of excitement at his touch only churned her stomach more.

As she stepped down, her hand went to her abdomen again, and Tommy said, "Are you still feeling a little rocky? That was not an easy ride back there." He continued to hold her by the arm, and asked, "Would you like to lie down for awhile?"

"No!" Sydney answered, hoping her nervousness was not as acutely obvious to him as it felt. "I'm fine! Where's the Volvo?"

Tommy continued to look her over for a few more seconds. He noticed how she flushed when he touched her arm. He decided to hold it a little longer.

"It's in the garage at the back of the house."

Finally, he let her arm slip out of his, and he watched her subtly let out her breath, and the rose color began to fade from her neck.

They walked around the immense old house, and soon came upon the back garage. Tommy lifted the creaking door, and there sat a medium blue, non-descript, four-door Volvo sedan. Unimposing looking, as cars go, but immaculate and gleaming in the sunshine. Sydney was surprised by the personalized license plate.

"Wolfgang?"

"Uh ... yeah," Tommy said, and rubbed his chin. "That was Grandma's pet name for her car..."

"Pet name?" Sydney repeated, thinking Tommy's grandma probably needed a little tune-up more than the car did.

"Yeah ... uh, you see," Tommy continued rubbing his chin, then looked at the ground and kicked at the dirt, "She was real ... uh, attached to the car..."

"She was a little ...?" Sydney's forefinger began to rotate up around her temple.

"No, no, nothing like that," Tommy said, defensively. "She was very sharp!" Sydney felt ashamed, and started to apologize, but Tommy went on, "Although, I can see where this 'pet name' thing could seem a little ... strange."

"Well," Sydney said, "then who *is* Wolfgang?"

Tommy hesitated again, now drumming his fingers on top of the car and looking somewhat wistfully at the old house. "The car," he said, finally. "Wolfgang is the car. That's what she called him."

Him? thought Sydney. How strange. Referring to a car as "him." She looked at the car. Then she went over and lightly touched the front fender. She nearly fell backward ... *the car touched her back!*

12/ GRANDMOTHER'S HOUSE

Sydney was visibly shaken by the strange reaction she had to the car. But Tommy did not seem to notice at all. He had pulled a handkerchief from his back pocket and was buffing a smudge from the windshield. Slowly, ever so slowly, Sydney reached out to touch the car again—to see if she really felt what she thought she felt a minute ago, or if she just had some kind of tactile hallucination.

As her hand approached the Volvo's fender again, closer and closer, inch by inch—she distinctly had the sensation of a hand reaching out and meeting her own! Again she drew back as though she had just touched a hot coal. Tommy noticed. But his reaction was not what she would have expected.

"He's a nice, solid car, don't you think?" Tommy asked, and now Sydney could not restrain her curiosity, even at the risk of insulting Tommy and his dear departed Grandma.

"*He*???" Isn't that a strange way to refer to a car???"

Tommy smiled, his wide handsome smile that was so disarming. "Not if you knew Grandma!"

Sydney laughed in spite of herself. Then Tommy said, "Would you like to see the inside?" and when Sydney nodded, he reached deep into his jeans pocket and brought out a black key. He opened the door to the Volvo, and bowed with a flourish, as he took Sydney's hand and said, "Your car, Madame!"

With more than a little anxious anticipation, she slid into the driver's seat. It was soft, plush leather—the color of pale flesh—and as Sydney settled in she had the startling sensation of sitting in someone's lap. A man's lap. Even more unsettling was how completely secure and comfortable she felt, in spite of the strangeness of it all.

Tommy was pointing out some of the features to Sydney, although she barely heard him, she was so taken by the comfort of the seat.

"... solid-steel tubular passenger cage for safety, lumbar back support, digital quadraphonic sound system ..."

Tommy's voice trailed off as Sydney became more and more engulfed in the warm, almost rhythmic beating comfort that she felt sitting inside of Wolfgang. Then she heard another voice, superimposed over Tommy's ...

"Come, my little klingerschnitzel," she heard, in a deep, gutteral, masculine voice, with a record-played-backward Swedish accent. "Come and let me take you ..."

Sydney looked at the dashboard. Seven hundred miles on the odometer. "... und vee vill ro-o-o-o-o-l-l-l together." She did not remember turning on the radio, but strains of Mozart's graceful Minuet in F on harpsicord floated through the speakers.

"How do you like it?" Tommy asked her for the second time. Sydney had become totally absorbed with the cocoon she felt so comfortably encased in. As she looked out, the Smokey Mountains, colorful with flowers and green trees, looked more like the Swiss Alps—going on forever in iced beauty.

Tommy's voice finally broke through. "Sydney? Are you okay?"

"Oh, yes," she said, and tried to pull herself out of her swaddling. *But ... it ... held ... her ... It ... "He"* ... didn't want to release her. Wolfgang wanted her to stay. She began to feel as though she were sinking deeper into his hypnotic comfort, when she suddenly felt a rising panic and pushed herself out of the seat and out of the car. As she did so, the Alps disappeared and the strains of Mozart faded to nothing.

"Well, what do you think?" Tommy was asking her. Before Sydney could pull her thoughts from the frightening and yet enthralling experience she just had, Tommy answered the question for her: "You'll probably need some time to think about it. And of course you'll have to drive it before you can make a decision."

"Yes, yes, okay," Sydney answered, "I really like the way it feels, though..." She felt a little woozy at the recollection of that. "But like you say, I'll have to drive it."

Sydney already knew she would buy the car. Or ... that the car was ... *buying her?* She felt a wondrous sort of puzzlement about it, but at the same time, she felt a kind of ... *bond?* ... to it ... as though failing to take it would be a major act of infidelity, or something.

Tommy was reaching for her hand again, and started in the direction of the old mansion. "Let's go inside and look around," he said. "I haven't been back up here since Grandma died."

Sydney hesitated, but she knew as soon as he took her hand that she would follow him anywhere. They walked up the gravel driveway, stiff brown leaves from last fall crunching under their shoes. It was pretty warm in the sun now, high up in the thin mountain air, but as soon as they entered the shade under the eaves of the house, the temperature seemed to fall twenty degrees. Sydney shivered involuntarily. Then she looked up at the house and thought of Grandma dying, and shivered again.

When they stepped inside, Sydney was taken by the vast number of magnificent antique pieces in the house—the silk Victorian sofa, the Oriental rugs which looked well worn but immaculately cared for, richly hand-embroidered linen table runners, and gold-woven brocade draperies. The furniture was of carved wood, lustrous after years of hand polishing with rich oils rubbed deeply into the grain with velvety soft cloths. Ornate Rococco, Louis the Fourteenth, and Italian Provincial pieces blended together in stately fashion from their special areas under the huge, cathedral ceilings.

Tommy led Sydney up a stairwell with solid marble steps, and as they ascended she beheld the massive crystal chandelier which began at the ceiling and extended downward nearly two full floors. She almost bumped into Tommy when he stopped abruptly on the second floor balcony and opened a door in front of them. It was a bedroom.

Sydney stared at the beautiful hand-carved Colonial four-poster. It was made of darkly stained cherry wood with bronze bands around each of the posts, which were taller than Tommy. The mattress was raised high upon the bedstead, nearly to Sydney's waist, and a small set of mahogany steps sat next to the bed to climb up on. A white cotton hand-loomed jacquard bedspread with a rose pattern covered the bed, and a colorful folded wool afghan sat neatly at the foot of the bed.

Sydney felt uncomfortable. She looked away from the massive bed, and studied the wallpaper. It was pink-on-pink and had a fleur-de-lis pattern, and framed photographs hung on every wall. Most were sepia daguerrotypes of people dressed in late nineteenth- and early twentieth-century attire.

One small picture was on the nightstand next to the bed, on top of a lacy crocheted doily. It was of a man and a woman in the drab, starkly tailored style of the 1930's. The man's face was partially obscured by his bowler hat ... yet, he looked somehow vaguely ... familiar. Sydney started to walk over to it when Tommy spoke:

"This was Grandma's room."

She turned around and looked at Tommy who was standing in the doorway. His height took up most of it and his raised forearms rested against the sides of the doorframe. Without thinking, the words spilled out of Sydney's mouth, and she, like Priscilla, instantly realized that milk once spilled cannot be put back in the bottle, as she asked, "How did she die?"

Tommy's face remained coldly expressionless as he answered.

"Strangulation."

Sydney felt her throat closing up on her. She stepped backward and turned toward the door, but Tommy made no move to step aside. He continued to gaze blankly at the four-poster bed while blocking the exit.

Sydney felt a cloying terror in her chest, and all the misgivings she had had about Tommy returned like water bursting through a crumbling dam.

She turned away from Tommy and faced the bed again, which now looked less like a luxurious relic of a bygone age, and more like an ... an instrument ... of terror.

Sydney used all of her mental strength to keep from panicking. *Don't think silly things!* she thought. *This man is not going to harm you. He just wants to sell you a car. There is a car, isn't there? All that was true, right? He just wanted to revisit his grandmother's room. He's still grieving over her death, that's all. Perfectly normal. No problem here!*

She took a deep breath and strode, as casually as she could, over to the picture on the nightstand. She picked it up and pretended to study it carefully. When she was sure her voice would come out sounding somewhat normal and nonchalant, she began to ask, "Who is—"

She stopped in mid-sentence. The young man in the sepia photograph wore extremely thick spectacles. *It was Tommy!* But the picture had to be sixty years old! It was ... it was ... *The Gray Man! That was him! The man in her nightmares!!*

Sydney dropped the picture and her hands went to her mouth. She started to scream. Tommy moved in swiftly and the scream was cut short.

13/ PLANS AND POWERS

The Southside Portland (Oregon) High School "Fighting Wolfhounds" Computer Club (a.k.a. the "Hound-Bytes") was holding a secret meeting. That is, their faculty supervisor was neither present nor aware of this meeting. It was in the wee hours of Saturday morning, and the twelve club members were huddled in the basement of one of their member's homes.

Jean Bigelow's parents were out of town. Jean was seventeen, played first viola in the school orchestra, and was in the Spanish National Honor Society. She had pale blonde hair, neatly cut to encircle her face and curl up to cup her chin. She got all A's, and was President of the Hound-Bytes.

John Raymond, a thin and classically nerdy-looking fellow who actually wore a pencil-protector in his shirt pocket, horn-rimmed glasses, and pants which stopped just short of covering his ankle bones, was saying, "But how can we be so sure that this is the right thing to do?"

Jean Bigelow tried not to sound exasperated—she was a good-natured girl—but nevertheless sighed at John's question. Everyone else was in agreement except him.

"We've all been dreaming about him, haven't we?" she began, repeating the same thing they had been discussing all evening.

John nodded.

"And these strange new powers we have all developed—we know *they're* not a dream, don't we?"

John nodded.

"And he's been instructing all of us to come to him, right?"

Again the nod.

"So what choice do we have?" Jean all but raised her voice. She rarely felt so frustrated.

John raised his hands and gestured around the room, "But Jean! Guys! We don't understand any of this! If it were not happening to all of us together, we would be heading for the loony bin with wallpaper courtesy of B. F. Goodrich!" His spectacles had slid halfway down his nose, and he paused to push them up again.

"Okay," said Arthur Hurdsbeck, a pudgier version of John. "So what do you think we should do, John? Just go on about our lives like nothing's happened? Just keep meeting in secret basements and sending pencils whizzing around the room for fun and no profit?"

John pushed his glasses back up his nose again. (It took about thirty-five seconds to complete the journey back down to half-mast.)

"No, but I don't think we should go flying off on some half-baked mission to find this guy." He paused, looked around the room. Pushed his glasses up again. "I think we should notify the authorities!"

Everyone collectively groaned. John was quite alone in that idea. Jean's basement was filled at this moment with the brightest seventeen-year-old minds in Portland, Oregon. They could not figure out what, exactly, was happening, but they had some ideas ...

First, a space alien could be beaming information to them from outer space. The wrinkled old gray-haired man with the tiny flame-orange eyes that they all saw at night in their dreams could be attempting to communicate with them from a distant galaxy. Hey, it could happen! They had all pored over old copies of *Chariots of the Gods*.

And in order to get their attention, they theorized, the Gray Man transmitted his own, far-advanced telekinetic powers to them. Because that's what they had! The powers were quite real. This very evening they discovered that it was possible for them to *pool* their powers and conduct even more fantastic feats! Two of the guys stood at opposite sides of the remaining ten kids in the room. By concentrating together, they lifted the entire group up to the ceiling! (Adam White, the tallest of the group, felt his head brush the ceiling, and let out a yelp which caused the concentration of the others to waver, and the whole floating group dropped precipitously to the floor. Margaret Waldenmire twisted her ankle, but fortunately there were no other casualties.)

They had come up with a few other theories, but the space-alien theory was accepted by consensus. None of them were religious enough (or paranoid enough) to buy into any of the other possibilities—like a satanic cult, or the Second Coming, or anything like that.

"John, you *know* we can't go to the authorities!" Adam said, himself beginning to whine a little. "Remember what happened to that McGee girl?"

"Oh, yeah, *Rolling Stone Magazine*," John answered, sarcastically. "The Voice of Credibility, right!"

"Well, if it *did* happen like it said in the article," Jean went on, "then we would be committing suicide to go to the authorities. I believe it!"

The McGee girl had been the subject of a sensational article about amazing pyrokinetic and telekinetic powers. *Rolling Stone* had gotten hold of the story and contacted Jerry Springer, who was going to set up and televise a dramatic exhibition of this girl's alleged powers.

There was more tension and excitement surrounding the planned exhibition because the girl claimed that she had been virtually held prisoner by the United States government, at their C.I.A. headquarters in Virginia, because they wanted to learn how to duplicate her powers and use them for their own purposes. The girl would have been dismissed as a lunatic (she also claimed that government agents had murdered her mother and father) except for her willingness to go forward with an exhibition.

The folks at *Rolling Stone* had seen enough to be convinced that she really was the genuine article, so they brought in Jerry Springer and the television networks. This was hyped even more than Geraldo Riveras's crashing of Al Capone's treasure trove (and was hopefully going to bear more fruit than that disaster.)

The McGee girl was transported in a dazzling white stretch limousine to the site of the exhibition, Niagra Falls, where there would be plenty of water in case her pyrotechnic powers went out of control and the resulting fire would be difficult to contain. As she stepped out onto the curb, an automobile driven at high speed by an allegedly drunk driver crashed through the police cordon surrounding the girl and her entourage, killing her and four others, and wounding several others in the crowd.

The people at *Rolling Stone* maintained that the McGee girl had been absolutely genuine, and they put forth the theory that the C.I.A. was responsible for the "accident." But interest in the whole matter petered out after only a few days after the girl's death, as it had been so unbelievable in the first place.

"Okay, okay," John said, leaning back and crossing his arms over his chest to show that he was not completely won over. "So we shouldn't go to the authorities—at least not right now."

He pushed his glasses back up his nose. "But how can we be so sure that we should go out hunting for this Gray Man? He could be dangerous, you know!"

Joanne Zeidman shook her head. Everyone was relieved, because when Joanne spoke, people listened. She was the Personality Kid of the group—the star of the Southside Portland High School Drama Club, in addition to being secretary of the Hound-Bytes.

"We *have* to check him out, John," she said. "After all, *he's* the one whose *given* us these incredible powers! We have to go and see who he is!"

"And what if he wants to harm us?" John shot back. "How could we defend ourselves?"

"John," Joanne answered patiently, "if he can imbue us with these powers from across the country, or even from outer space, he can do whatever he wants, right? We wouldn't even have to go to him!"

John let out his breath slowly. He had a big crush on Joanne, everybody knew it, and everybody knew she would bring him around to their way of thinking. Actually, everybody had a crush on Joanne.

"Well," John said, weakly, "what if we're wrong about his whereabouts? What if he's *not* in the mountains—the Smokies? Are we going to travel all the way across the country on that chance?"

Joanne didn't answer. She looked from one club member to another. Then they all looked at John and nodded. John looked down at his hands and sighed.

"Okay." He looked back up at his colleagues, pushed his glasses back up his nose, and said, "But our parents are going to be *so mad* ..."

14/ EXODUS

Back at the Center for Disease Control, things were heating up rapidly. The first patient to have been stricken with the CompuFlu had died. The scientists and physicians were frantic. They could not yet isolate anything which gave them the smallest clue as the what might be causing this disease. They were hunkering down now because if news of this death leaked to the press, chaos could ensue. The country did not like diseases which eluded identification. The country did not like serial murderers who eluded identification either, but if it had to choose, it didn't like unidentified diseases even *more*. Especially fatal ones.

The victim who died was not old (which was bad—they could have blamed the death on his age), but he was in poor health (which was good—they could blame that). He was a small business owner who sold underwear by mail order. He was at least forty pounds overweight, smoked three packs of cigarettes a day, and drank beer from sunup to sundown. After sundown he drank whiskey.

Still they were stymied by the disease. They had not yet connected it to a program popping up in email boxes called "Organize Your Small Business." But every one of the victims of the CompuFlu had purchased it. And every one of them had experienced the strange total-body shiver that occurred just before "End of Program" floated up on the screen.

The victims themselves were very cooperative. They did not view themselves as prisoners—even though they had been transported to this huge building and kept isolated behind locked doors. The windows had bars. But they were pretty ill, most of them, so they really did not even notice.

And they told the doctors everything. Everything they were asked, everything they could think of. But no one thought that the computer program was somehow connected. (None of the individual victims even knew that all of the other victims were involved with computers.)

There was no way that they would connect that one strange program with what had happened to them. Most of the victims had run the program—and then ran it and ran it over again, just to see if the strange "shiver" would repeat itself (it always did). Clearly it was NOT going to help them organize their small businesses. So they just put it away for a rainy day when they might want to fool around with it again.

But as fate would have it, the news did get out. Woody Wilson, M.D., Ph.D., went home to his girlfriend's house the night after the CompuFlu took its first fatality, and sat next to his girlfriend, knocking back one neat scotch after another.

"Iss jus' crazhy," he said, the fire in the gas hearth reflecting in his half-full tumbler, and again in his large convex eyeglasses which magnified his eyes and gave him a distinctly frog-like appearance.

"What's crazy?" his girlfriend asked, refilling his glass with the bottle of J & B on the coffee table. She was barely drinking, but Woody didn't notice.

"Thiss damn diseash'!" he sputtered, waving his hand around as scotch splashed onto his tie. "We jus' can' figger it out!"

"Tell me about it, Woody, Honey," she encouraged, as she topped off his glass again.

At five o'clock the next morning, Dr. Woody Wilson was quite unconscious, and would remain so for the next eight hours; but his girlfriend, Patty Winchester, quietly dressed and left for work. She worked at WCBC News Central.

Within the next seventy-two hours the story exploded like a mushroom cloud throughout the telecommunications world, as huge banner headlines screamed it to the world: "COMPUFLU HAS DEADLY BYTE!!!"

The story was so big that it almost completely eclipsed the other countrywide phenomenon that was taking place. By the middle of the following week it was reported that twelve high school seniors had packed up and—with no evidence of foul play—disappeared from their homes in Portland, Oregon. When it came to light that they were all members of the Hound-Bytes Computer Club, the news reports went wild. On the heels of that report were added isolated reports of kids, and some adults, all over the country, who had packed their bags and mysteriously disappeared.

The connection to computers was mind-boggling. At first, entire companies, utilities, universities, courthouses, and other establishments which relied heavily on computer networks, ground rapidly to a halt, as computer operators, programmers, and everyone even remotely involved with computers began to call in sick.

They were not necessarily sick, of course—just frightened of handling their computers! No one knew why some people were getting gravely ill, and others—younger users, mostly—were disappearing! The only link was the fact that they were all heavily involved with computers.

Mac McMulligan had left, too. Just packed a bag and disappeared. But no one, not even his other retired police drinking buddies, knew that he played computer games at home. No one really knew much of anything about him, except those who knew of his disgrace during the courthouse assassination those many years ago.

Lila had not left home, but that was because she was going to see her Aunt Sydney first. Sydney would pick her up at the airport on Sunday, and then *everything would be all right*, she thought. Until then, she felt she could stave off the strong compulsion she felt to pack a bag and head for the Blue Ridge Mountains, to find the Gray Man who beckoned to her every night in her dreams. Nightmares.

But Lila did not know that the Blue Ridge Mountains were exactly where Sydney was, having driven up there with Tommy on Saturday morning. Tommy, who looked exactly like the Gray Man in the photograph.

15 / THE GRAY MAN

Sydney opened her eyes. For a moment she did not know where she was. Her feet were propped up on something. Something was covering her and restricting her movement. Something else was on her forehead.

Then the tall posts at the foot of the bed came into view and she remembered, with a sickening rumble in her belly, where she was. She looked out of the corner of her eye, afraid to make a move, and saw Tommy sitting next to her. He caught the flickering of her eyelashes, and swiftly stood up and leaned over her.

"Sydney, you're awake!" he said, as he reached over and gently touched her cheek. Sydney realized then that her feet had been propped up on a pillow. The multicolored afghan was tucked in around her, and a cool washcloth was folded across her forehead. Tommy caressed her cheek. "Are you okay? What happened? Can you talk?"

Sydney slowly started to lift her head. "Uh, yeah, I think I'm okay ... But I'm not sure what happened ..."

Tommy dropped the washcloth into the porcelain basin on the nightstand. "Don't try to stand up too fast. You might faint again."

Sydney sat up slowly, pushing off the afghan, and swung her feet down to the two stairsteps at the side of the bed. She was still a little fuzzy, and just sat there upright. "Wh-what happened?"

"I'm not sure," Tommy said, and touched her hand lightly at the inside of the wrist. He turned his other hand up and stared at his watch.

"What are you doing?" Sydney asked.

"Taking your pulse," he answered, as though it were the most natural thing in the world. After a minute he let go of her wrist and said, "Okay."

"Um ... what are you, a paramedic or something?"

"Yeah ... uh ... something like that. It's a long story. Now what happened to you just then?"

Sydney thought back. Tommy had been standing in the doorway. Something had unnerved her ... something *terrifying*. Tommy's grandmother ... *strangulation* ... *photograph* ... Sydney looked around. The photograph was gone.

Suddenly she felt ashamed. Obviously Tommy meant her no harm at all. What in the world made her think he was ... *evil?*

"Th-there was a photograph," she managed, not knowing how to proceed. But she had to ask about it.

"Oh, yeah," Tommy replied, and pulled out the drawer of the nightstand. He took out the little photograph. The glass covering it was cracked.

"Oh, no! Did I do that?" Sydney recalled that she had dropped the photograph.

"Uh, yeah, you dropped it just before you fainted. But don't worry about it. The photo and the frame are intact. It just needs a new glass, and that's easy to replace." Then Tommy looked up from the photograph, and said, "Why did this ... somehow ... *bother you*?"

Sydney sighed. How could she explain this without sounding like a dingbat? She decided to go on the offensive: "Who is that in the picture?" pointing to the man with the rimless glasses who looked like Tommy in a Prohibition-era getup.

"That's my grandfather," Tommy answered. Suddenly things began to look slightly clearer to Sydney. She wasn't sure why, but they did. Perhaps the resemblance to the Gray Man was merely coincidence, and nothing else was of any consequence.

"What happened to him?" she continued, now earnestly curious.

Tommy hesitated for several seconds. He seemed to pale slightly. Then he took a deep breath, and audibly exhaled. He seemed to be weighing his answer carefully. Finally, he answered, "Nothing. He's alive."

"Alive." *What a strange answer.* "Well, uh—does he still live around here?" Sydney said, sweeping her hand around, wondering whether this grandfather was still married to the grandmother when she died here. That photo still had a sinister look about it.

Tommy just looked away from her altogether. He took a deep breath, again, and when he finally spoke, his voice was so soft that Sydney had to watch his lips to make out every word.

"He's in a mental institution."

They both sat in silence after that. Finally, Sydney began to apologize for probing into something which was obviously painful for Tommy, and none of her business; but he held up his hand and shook his head. He smiled his wiltingly beautiful smile again, and said, "Hey, that's okay! It's just one of those things, y'know ... hard to talk about. But that's life, right?"

Now it was Tommy's turn to probe. "So what happened to you before? Something seemed to frighten you ... you dropped the picture and fainted ... Why?"

"It was just ... you said ..." Sydney stammered, combing her mind for words that would sound anything but wacky. "You said your grandmother was strangled? It just scared me ... right here on this bed!" She looked down at the rose petal bedspread.

"No, no, she wasn't *strangled*! Not *by* someone, not like that!" He sat back in his chair and took in another deep breath before going on, "She choked on a corned beef and pastrami sandwich. Choked to death. Eating in bed. Midnight snack." Tommy dropped his eyes.

Sydney looked at the photograph again. The woman in the picture next to his grandfather was a beautiful young woman, lithe and lovely. *Grandma.*The original owner of the blue Volvo. *Wolfgang.* Put seven hundred miles on him.

"Her doctor warned her about eating in bed like that," Tommy continued. "She weighed nearly three hundred pounds when she died. The housekeeper found her the next morning. Her hand was halfway down her throat, trying to dig out the corned beef and pastrami sandwich. She was blue-black. It was awful." Tommy hung his head and shook it slowly from side to side.

Then he looked back up at Sydney, and said, "Oh, I'm sorry! I shouldn't have upset you like that! I wasn't thinking."

"Oh, that's okay," Sydney said, patting him on one well-muscled shoulder.

Tommy looked at his watch. "It's nearly three o'clock! If you feel all right, we should probably be going soon. It gets dark early in the mountains."

Sydney felt a pang of disappointment, but she shelved it and hopped off the bed, feigning enthusiasm about going home. "We've got a couple of sandwiches and some cheesecake left," Sydney offered. "Are you hungry?"

"Hungry?" Tommy repeated, "Does a polar bear ..."

"... pee in the snow?" Sydney answered, and they both laughed. He took her hand and they left Grandma's bedroom.

Back downstairs in the beautiful, huge country kitchen, copper utensils hung from the rough hewn wooden walls. Cast iron skillets sat on a real woodstove oven. Tommy and Sydney sat on straightback chairs with woven reed seats, across a table covered with a red-and-white checkered cotton gingham tablecloth. Tommy had found some cans of Coors Light which still fizzed pretty good.

"Y'know," he said between mouthfuls, "A lot of people think 'light' beer means it's low in alcohol content."

"Oh, yeah," said Sydney, taking a few gulps from her own beer, which she almost never drank, because she felt the effects so quickly. Cheap drunk, she was.

"Yeah, but it doesn't," Tommy said, cracking open a second can. "It's low in calories, but it has the same alcohol content." He let out a healthy belch, and then, "Big mistake. Excuse me."

"Yer 'scused!" Sydney replied, and then let out a long, robust belch of her own. "Oh, 'scuse ME!"

Tommy seemed to get a huge kick out of that, and laughed heartily, as Sydney thought how sexy his Adam's apple was when it bounced up and down like that.

He took one more swallow from the second can, and then got up and poured the remainder down the sink.

"Driving," he said. "Don't want to have an ..." and he tightened his fist, crumpling the beer can effortlessly in his grasp, "... accident!"

"Definitely not!" Sydney chimed in. And she squeezed her own beer can, but it was half full, and beer splashed out all over her chest and arm. They both laughed. She was aglow.

"Here, let me help you," he said, and he took a dishtowel from its place below the sink and came over to her. He wiped her arm off, and then the top of her bib overalls, where the beer had splattered. When he finished, he returned the towel to its place. Sydney had an urge to pour another beer over herself.

They went back outside to the Volvo. "Can I give him a test drive now?" Sydney said, surprised at how natural it seemed to refer to Wolfgang in that manner.

"No, not now," Tommy answered, pulling up the hood. He's been sitting here for quite awhile, and I need to check him over before you drive him."

He tinkered with a few things and then shut the hood. "I brought a tow-bar. We'll tow him back to the station and I'll check him out for you tomorrow."

Sydney was disappointed and pleased at the same time. It was a strange feeling. She felt a strong desire to get back into the Volvo again, and didn't want to have to wait until tomorrow to drive it. Then again, she was happy to be able to drive back next to Tommy. Even if he did not seem to be the least bit attracted to her. She sighed to herself as she watched him back the truck up to Wolfgang and hitch him up to the tow-bar.

16/ SKELETONS

When everything was ready to go, they got into the truck. Sydney resisted the urge to slide a little closer to Tommy. This required a supreme effort, since she was feeling a little uninhibited. She really did not want to make a blithering fool of herself by coming on to a man who had no apparent interest in her except to sell her a car.

Oh, so what. She would have a nice car, anyway. And Wolfgang was so ... so ... special! That was exciting.

Tommy could tell that Sydney was mildly intoxicated. He would bide his time.

"So, tell me about yourself," he asked. They had been winding slowly down the long dirt road leading up to the front of the mansion. It was much smoother than the rocky back road they had come up on, but it was quite a bit longer.

"Well," Sydney began. Then in a moment of lucidity that could only have been born of intoxication, she decided to tell Tommy the worst about herself. After all, his grandmother may have been a wealthy woman, judging by her home—but Tommy was just a gas station attendant. Maybe that was why he didn't seem the slightest bit interested in her—maybe he felt somehow inferior to her? Yes—time to break out the skeletons!

"I'm an ex-convict, for one thing."

Tommy looked over at her with sheer incredulity, and after about two seconds, burst out laughing. "Oh, jeez," he said, wiping a tear from his cheek with the back of his hand, "You are a funny lady!"

Sydney felt herself coloring—and sobering up. Then she forced a little laugh herself, trying to join in the "joke." Then maybe she could take it back ...

But Tommy picked up on her discomfort. Her laughter was not genuine.

"Wait a minute..." he said, taking his eyes off the road and glancing at her, then back and forth from her to the road. "You were kidding ... *weren't you?*"

Sydney stopped laughing and looked down at her hands. She didn't drink often enough in her whole life to have learned how to zip up when she had a buzz on.

"No, I wasn't," she began, now straightening up and looking Tommy in the eye. "I spent four months in the Woman's Correctional Facility in California about ten years ago."

Tommy didn't say anything, but kept looking from her to the road, and back again.

"I didn't have the patience to go to college," she went on. "I did clerical work for awhile—typing, filing—but it just wasn't going to cut it for me. I don't do real well with authority figures, you see. Especially when you are hired as a secretary, and at 4:55 p.m. on your first day, you are handed a vacuum cleaner and told you can leave when you've finished cleaning up."

Here she stopped and looked at Tommy to see his reaction. Nothing. She went on. "So I decided to go into business for myself."

"Something ... illegal?" Tommy offered. Still, he showed no particular expression that Sydney could read.

"No, nothing like that. I just did contract secretarial work. Put ads in the paper to do typing, bulk mailings, stuff like that. Got a lot of calls. Actually, I did really well. In two days I could make as much as I made in a week as a secretary working for someone else."

She stopped talking then, and was looking at her hands again. Tommy tried to help. He said, "So, then ... how did you ... uh ..."

"Get in trouble?" She looked up at him again. He marvelled at her emerald green eyes and copper hair, which glinted gold in the late afternoon sun. "I read a book. That's what got me into trouble."

"A book?"

"Yeah—*DON'T PAY INCOME TAXES!,* by Merle Pinkston."

Tommy looked back at the road and already began subtly to shake his head back and forth, as in "Oh, no, don't tell me..."

"In the book," she went on, "he described in detail the laws of the Constitution—quoted them and everything—talked about the Fifth and the Fourteenth Amendments. It was very convincing. To a twenty-year-old, anyway."

"So you stopped paying taxes?"

"Worse than that." Sydney took a deep breath and sighed before going on. "If I had merely failed to report my income, I probably would have been given a fine and had to pay penalties and interest, once they discovered it. But I had to wave the flag of Libertarianism under their noses. Like a toreador, I guess," Sydney smiled here, "and boy, did I get gored!"

"What, exactly, did you do?"

"Well, I sent in blank tax forms to the I.R.S., with my signature in the proper place at the bottom. On top, I sent a cover letter explaining my 'right' to retain my earnings, and quoting the Constitutional basis for that. Just like the book said."

"So they just threw you in jail? No warning?"

"Oh, yes! They warned me, all right. They said I would be subject to prosecution. Just as Pinkston said in his book, they would try to intimidate me into giving up my 'rights'. I just stood my ground. Unfortunately, my 'ground' turned out to be quicksand."

Sydney fell silent, and Tommy didn't say anything either. The sun had dropped below the farthest mountaintop, and so it was beginning to get dusky, even though it was not yet sunset beyond the mountains. Twilight came early in the Smokies. Sydney watched the long shadow of the truck fade along with the light. After awhile, she began to talk again.

"When it came to the point where formal charges were filed against me, I hired a lawyer. There was a list of lawyers in an appendix at the end of Pinkston's book. They were supposedly 'experts' in constitutional law, and Pinkston recommended that they be retained 'in the unlikely event of any problem with the I.R.S.!'"

Sydney shifted in her seat. She reached down under the crumpled linen covering the picnic basket and fished around until she found the bottle of wine she had packed that they had not yet opened. She peeled off the tape and unscrewed the cap, lifted it to her lips and chugged down a few gulps.

"Wasn't your lawyer able to help you?" Tommy asked.

"He helped me, all right," Sydney answered, wiping a stream of wine off her chin with the back of her hand. "He helped me right into jail."

Tommy noticed that Sydney's lip quivered a little, but she kept going. "We went to court. He defended my 'right' not to pay taxes—and made a powerfully dramatic plea to the judge and jury to recognize how 'criminal' the U. S. Government is for taking its citizens' hard-earned money. And *blah, blah, blah*. Well, Pinkston and his gang just didn't think about how the average citizen would react to such a tactic. You see, everyone hates paying taxes. So these guys figured that no jury would convict someone who was doing what they all in their hearts wanted to do! They would acquit me, and then go home and tear up their own 1040's! That's what was supposed to happen." Sydney took another long swig of wine.

"They didn't ... ?"

"Well, yes, I think they agreed in principle. But on an individual basis, they would never, ever have the guts to do something like that. And I think they kind of resented me for it. They paid their taxes, and they had no sympathy for someone who avoided the same thing that they felt helpless to stop.

"So the jury did not feel any need to protect me from the government. What they really felt was, '*we've* all paid our taxes; nobody's letting *us* off the hook; and we're not letting *you* off the hook, either!' *Guilty on all counts.*"

They rode on in silence, and the shadows along the pristine mountain trails deepened, now indigo, now violet. Sydney felt the sickening sadness of that terrible chapter in her past all over again. She hadn't thought about it in such a long time, she forgot how painful it really had been. The wine seemed only to make her more melancholy, and she blinked back twinges of pain in her eyes.

Tommy spoke: "Did you ever get in touch with that Pinkston guy, by any chance? I mean, to let him know what happened to you?"

"Yeah," Sydney said, and snorted a laugh, "He's doing eight-to-fifteen in federal prison for tax evasion!"

"Well, that's a little comfort!" Tommy added.

"Very little!" They both laughed.

"Actually, prison wasn't so bad, once you got used to it," Sydney continued. "I was only there for four months, but I met a lot of interesting people. I learned a lot!"

"Like ... ?"

"Like how to conceal up to a kilo of marijuana in various bodily orifices!" Sydney broke into a goofy giggle, then abruptly became straight-faced and added, "But I'm not into that sort of thing!" Then she broke up again.

When Sydney finally pulled herself together, and wiped the tears of uncontrolled giggling from her eyes, she decided it was time to turn the tables. "Okay, now—*your turn*! Tell me about the skeletons in *your* closet!"

Tommy looked thoughtfully at the road ahead for a minute. Then he looked at her and said, "Nope—don't have any! I'm pure as the driven snow!"

"And a bigger snow job I never hoid!" Sydney said out of one side of her mouth, and tapping an invisible cigar.

"Well, okay," Tommy said, the smile fading from his face. "Actually ... I mean, since you spilled your guts so honestly and everything ..."

He hesitated briefly and then continued, "I guess you could call a malpractice suit a 'skeleton' of sorts. Even though I ... well, oh, never mind ..."

"Malpractice suit?" Sydney wasn't sure she had heard him correctly. She sat up straighter in her seat. "What do you mean?"

Tommy continued to drive in silence. Sydney recalled how she awoke in his grandmother's room and Tommy was checking her pulse.

"Were you, like, a paramedic, or something?" *Could they even be sued?* But why not? This was America, Land of Litigation.

"Not a paramedic," Tommy answered. "A physician."

Sydney was speechless. The wine was making her head hurt. Tommy was staring intently at the road, one arm stiff on the wheel, the other on the seat next to him.

"A physician," he repeated, softly, almost to himself. "A doctor. I went to medical school in Texas. The University of Texas Medical Branch at Galveston. I had always wanted to be a doctor. After I received my medical degree, I began a residency in Internal Medicine."

Sydney was trying to reconcile this new image of Tommy with the old one. It wasn't easy. She wished she had stopped with the beer, and left the stinkin' wine alone.

"During my internship I was moonlighting at an emergency room in a neighboring town about fifty miles away. Once a month I worked one straight 48-hour shift on the weekends, after I got off duty from my internship. It was good because the internship barely paid enough for an apartment and meals.

"There were a lot of gangs of petty criminal types and dopers in that neighboring town. One night about a half dozen of them came into the ER at once. There had been a 'turf war' and some of them had been shot, some badly beaten. I was on duty by myself.

"I tried to stabilize the most critically wounded, and called for backup ambulances to transport others to other hospitals. Those who had relatively minor wounds were sewn up and sent home."

Now Tommy paused again, and Sydney waited. Soon, he started to speak again, but his tone was more somber and melancholy than she had ever heard.

"There should have been at least one other doc available for backup—the staff attending physician. I was only an intern. But his wife had called in earlier and said he was sick. Everyone knew he had a drinking problem, and he frequently called in 'sick' on the weekends.

Anyway, I just tried to do the best I could by myself ... I had some super nurses helping me out—they were terrific—but we needed another doc there, too."

Tommy's face was set hard, and Sydney felt longingly to put her hand on his. But she didn't.

"Tommy, you don't have to ..."

"No, it's okay," he said. "It's been a long time since I thought about it ... a long time since I talked about it to anyone."

He took a deep breath and blew it out audibly, then went on, "One of the patients had been hit on the head, but his wound seemed minimal—he was fully conscious, vital signs stable. The x-ray equipment was all tied up with other patients, so I just asked him to sit in the waiting room for a few hours, and instructed a nurse to take his vital signs every fifteen minutes. He said he felt fine, and didn't want to stay there, and said he just wanted to go home. We were so busy, I didn't bother about locating an AMA for him to sign ..."

"AMA?"

"Against Medical Advice. A form that says the patient is leaving the hospital against medical advice, so he takes responsibility for any problems which may result. I didn't have the time to look for one, so we just let him go. He went home, went to bed, and a few hours later died of a brain hemorrhage."

Tommy paused, then drew in another long breath, and slowly let it out before going on.

"His parents—they hadn't had anything to do with him for years, since he was involved in gangs and drugs. But when they learned of his death, they filed a malpractice suit against the hospital, and named me and everyone else there that night as defendants.

"The suit dragged on for fourteen months. Finally, they settled out of court. I was exonerated—but by the time it was all over I had lost thirty pounds, plus just about all my ideals about medicine.

"I dropped out of the residency program. Before I could decide whether to re-enter or not, my father died. He owned the Phillips 66 station and left it to me. I learned that trade at his elbow, so I just took his place. I've been doing that ever since."

Sydney was still reeling from discovering this new person who sat next to her. Five minutes ago he was a grease monkey; now he's a medical doctor and business owner. *Mental whiplash.* And what a tragic story! She groped within her now-fuzzying head, as the wine was taking its ultimate toll, to find something appropriate to say.

"Do you think you'll ever go back into medicine again?"

"Well, I'm getting kind of old now," he answered. "Thirty-six. And I would still have another three years of residency to complete. Nah, I don't think ..."

He looked over at Sydney. She had fallen asleep. Her copper fire curls were resting on his shoulder. He drove on.

17/ A. W. O. L.

Dr. Esther Anna looked out the window at the rolling grass. It was so beautiful in the springtime. If she didn't have so much paperwork to do, she would go out for a walk around the grounds. She always ran into a number of her patients when she did that, and she enjoyed seeing them in a "social" encounter, rather than in her office. They were always more relaxed, and they seemed to enjoy seeing her outside as much as she did them.

She pulled her attention away from the scenic view of the window and back to the stacks of charts on her desk. There was so much paperwork to do it was depressing. It certainly did not help the patients any! It just served to provide more jobs for the state bureaucracy to pad itself. Admission assessments, treatment plans, treatment plan updates, treatment plan goals, long-term goals, short-term goals, estimated time to reach goals, reasons for not reaching goals; progress notes, and on and on, *ad nauseum.* All the paperwork was dreamed up to insure, by documentation, that the patients were getting appropriate and timely treatment. An admirable idea, but the paperwork had mushroomed to the point that it literally took more time to complete it than to treat the patient. Doctors, nurses, social workers and others would spend more time writing or dictating notes than they spent face-to-face with their patients.

Dr. Anna felt it was all a dreadful waste of time—but she was working for a publically-funded state institution, and that's what they wanted. Privately she could treat patients and make whatever notes she needed, to keep herself on top of the each patient's progress. But for the state, it was almost a trueism that medical records took priority over medical care. The patient could croak, as long as all the records were properly documented in a timely fashion! Everyone muttered about spending more time treating the charts than the patients. Maybe someday things would—

Dr. Anna's thoughts were interrupted by a knock on the door. It was Casey Quinn, the social worker who worked with Dr. Anna's patients and their families (or at least, those patients whose families still cared to know whether their mentally ill relative was dead or alive).

Casey was tall and reed thin. He wore the anachronistic shoulder-length hair and bushy beard that were the hallmarks of the flower-child era of the late '60's and '70's. Usually Casey was so laid back that you could doze off listening to him, but today he was anxious—visibly upset. Dr. Anna could not remember seeing him like this. Ever.

"Casey, what's wrong?"

"It's Ross," Casey said, swallowing hard. "He ... he's *gone!*"

This was nothing new. However, although Casey was inclined toward the dramatic, he was never this shaken up. The last time Dr. Anna saw him even close to this was just before the Joint Commission on Accreditation of Hospital Organizations made their last triennial inspection. Casey was not seen outside his office for two whole weeks before that inspection, madly racing to bring his social assessment reports up to date. Two years' worth of being mellow and laid-back was apparently worth two weeks of sleepless mania for him.

"Well, we'll have to have a grounds search," said Dr. Anna, without undue concern. Patients regularly "disappeared," usually when they felt bold enough to walk into the nearby town. Or when they found another patient interested in getting lost in the surrounding woods with them for a few hours. After all, they may have mental problems, but they had their needs and desires, just like everybody else.

"We've searched the grounds, Esther. The sheriff has been through town, too. All his usual hangouts." Casey ran his fingers through his bushy beard, something he did whenever he was nervous. "He's REALLY gone. Missing!"

Dr. Anna stared at him finger-combing his beard for a few seconds. This was unusual, even for Ross, who "disappeared" from the hospital grounds with some regularity. And another problem loomed up in her mind—this patient's wife had died fairly recently. So it might be expected that his mental state was vulnerable to decompensation. It *would* be expected.

But Ross had not decompensated when Dr. Anna told him the news of his wife's unexpected death. He responded as though he had just been told that it was going to rain tomorrow. No show of emotion. Of course that was not unusual, either, with a patient as disturbed as Ross.

Now, possibly as a delayed reaction to the news of his wife's sudden demise, he disappears. Not in the woods, not downtown. Just gone.

"Go ahead and notify the State Patrol," Dr. Anna told Casey.

"Should I tell them that he's ..."

"Yes," Dr. Anna said without needing to hear him finish, "Tell them that he is dangerous."

18/ HITHER AND YON

Tommy got Sydney home after dark Saturday night. She slept most of the way back, but was able to awaken enough to walk on her own past the doorman of her condominium and pull off a reasonable performance of sobriety. As soon as the elevator doors closed behind her and Tommy, she dissolved into giggles—the laughter of One Who Thinks She Has Put One Over On Someone Else (the doorman, who knew she was sloshed the minute she stepped out of Tommy's truck and required his assistance to walk to the door).

She giggled all the way up to her floor in the elevator, all the more for Tommy's patronizing attitude. Why couldn't he giggle just a little, too? This was pretty funny! When they got to her door, she handed him her keys and let him open the door for her. Then he took her firmly by the shoulders, turned her around, and nudged her into the darkness of her living room. He placed the picnic basket inside the door, and flicked on the entry light.

"Get some sleep, now, go on," he commanded.

Hey, what did he think she was, a german shepherd? But she was too tired and light-headed to do anything but obey, and Tommy closed the door behind her and left.

Sydney crashed fully clothed onto her bed. She slept through until Sunday morning, when she awoke with a magnificent headache. A marching band was playing John Phillip Sousa inside her throbbing temples. Why did she have to have so much wine, anyway? She knew her limit of alcohol. Nil. Nisht. Zip.

Sydney had not had any dreams or nightmares that night, at least. But she did have the strangest recollection of Wolfgang being towed along behind them all the way home. She was not even sure if it was a dream or not. In her mind's eye, she could see Wolfgang's reflection watching her in the passenger side rearview mirror. The last violet-orange halo of sunset behind the farthest mountain range glinted off of Wolfgang's chrome grill. He was smiling at her.

And she could hear in her memory the strains of "Liebestraum" by Liszt floating through the air from the quadraphonic sound system of the Volvo. It matched the tender feeling she had for Tommy when he was telling her the tragic story of his ill-fated medical career.

Sydney had no recollection or feeling about having been watched by the Gray Man.

No lights were on in the room where Grandma had died. The four-poster bed stood untouched since Sydney awoke from her faint and stepped down with Tommy's assistance. But the photograph she had dropped was now back on the nightstand where it was when Sydney first picked it up. The glass was still cracked. The lace curtains at the window were drawn to the side by a long, sinewy hand. He watched the shiny truck with the oversized wheels pull slowly out onto the dirt access road at the end of the gravel driveway, Wolfgang in tow behind it. He caught a glimpse of the cardinal hair of the girl in the passenger side of the truck, and the long flowing white hair of the passenger in the back seat of the Volvo.

As the vehicles disappeared in tandem around the bend of the mountain woods in the early twilight, he dropped the lace curtain back to its original position. He picked up the photograph from the nightstand and went back up to the attic.

It was a very busy time from coast to coast that weekend. While Sydney and Tommy got to know each other during the trip up the mountain and back down again, a lot of other activity was taking place. Plans were being made and carried out by an unprecedented number of people who knew nothing of each other at all. Still other people were sick and moribund, and the best minds in the country could not figure out why.

The twelve members of the Hound-Bytes Computer Club were emptying out savings accounts and secret hiding places that had been stuffed with birthday and babysitting and bar mitzvah money from years past. Two members sold their portable DVD players; one pawned the diamond pendant her father sent her last Christmas in lieu of a trip to see him and his new wife and baby; and another club member borrowed two hundred dollars from his older brother who was dealing again even though he was already on parole for possession of a controlled substance.

Then all the club members made their reservations for a flight from Portland, Oregon, to Asheville, North Carolina, to leave on the following Monday, just after school was to start. One-way reservations. Once they arrived in Asheville, they would take a train to Jiminy Rock, high up in the Blue Ridge Mountains. And there ... well, there ... well, they were all agreed on this, even though not one of them could explain why ... but there in Jiminy Rock, they expected that the Gray Man would meet them. And then he would explain everything, and help them understand their frightening and fascinating new powers. And then he would tell them what to do next. They all agreed on that.

Down south, in Miami, Lila was packing, too. She could barely contain her excitement and anxiety, but she just kept focused on one thing: Aunt Sydney would know what to do. Aunt Sydney would help her. She always did. So Lila packed her bag and took out her plane ticket to Atlanta for the umpteenth time, and reviewed her flight number, time of departure, and time of arrival.

In Atlanta, Patty Winchester, anchorwoman for WCBC News Central Station, who broke the original story about the CompuFlu, had triggered a swarm of reporters who descended upon anyone and everyone connected with the Center for Disease Control to dig up information. Was the CompuFlu real? Where did it come from? Was there any effective treatment? No one could answer these questions, and so the researchers and doctors imprisoned themselves, right along with the sick and dying patients, inside the institutional fortress, to avoid the news bloodhounds.

Mac McMulligan had already arrived in Asheville from Dallas. He had never felt so invigorated and alive as he did at this time. He hired a stretch limousine to drive him the twenty-some rugged miles up the mountain to Jiminy Rock. He had already discovered that he didn't need any money to do this. His newly acquired mental powers were such that he could pick up an ordinary rock from the ground, hand it to the limousine driver and say, "This is a forty-carat flawless white diamond. Take it and keep the change, my good man!"

And the driver would do just that! The limousine driver at the airport in Dallas was so overwhelmed by the illusion that this ordinary rock was a diamond, he got down on his knees and kissed Mac's hands and said, "God bless you, Sir! You must have been sent by an angel! Now my little girl can have the operation she needs! Our H.M.O. refused to pay for it because they said it is not a covered procedure—and she probably could live another six months without it—But now we can pay for it ourselves!!"

And George Humphreys, Sydney's business client, still sick with the flu, but excited that he had finally found someone who would be able to get his business into shape, sat at his computer and ran the program "Organize Your Small Business" over and over and over, feeling the same strange head-to-toe tingle each time. His secretary found him dead under his desk when she came in Monday morning. He had drowned in his own bodily fluids.

And so on, across the entire country, hundreds of citizens were packing and making arrangements to go to Jiminy Rock, North Carolina, on an unearthly hunch that a charismatic elderly man who scared the hell out of them in their dreams night after night would be there to meet them. And he would ... explain ... everything.

19 / SECRETS

Sydney was stepping out of her bib overalls that she had slept in, and began to peel off the rest of her clothes. She felt disoriented—lost in thoughts of the day before, when she drove up to Tommy's grandmother's house, and the strange feeling she had had of Wolfgang's "presence" which had followed her home, and an unrelenting hangover from the wine that made her head feel like the inside of a handball court.

Suddenly she remembered with a jolt—she was supposed to pick up Lila at the airport this morning! She looked at the clock. Ten. She had just enough time for a quick shower and a dash to the airport. She looked wistfully through the bathroom door at the beautiful Jacuzzi. Lila would probably get a big thrill out of using it. Well at least someone would get to use the darn thing!

Sydney closed the shower stall door and turned on the water. She let the cold water slice through her—punishment for her excesses of the day before. Then she gradually turned the hot water on, lathered up with this week's fruit soap (Apricot Spice In the Afternoon by L'avelle of E. Chicago, Indiana), rinsed and dried off, and pulled on a pair of clean jeans and a Falcons sweatshirt.

At the airport, Lila looked this way and that before she spotted her Aunt Sydney's bright red hair in the waiting area. She ran over and hugged her tightly.

"Oh, Aunt Sydney, I'm so glad to see you!" she nearly cried. Sydney was only mildly aware that Lila seemed more distressed than usual (which was a lot for a sixteen-year-old). Sydney's thoughts doggedly hovered around Tommy like a hummingbird over a hibiscus, and she had to force herself to pay attention to what Lila was telling her.

"How's your mom, honey?"

"She's okay," Lila answered, "but you know Mom—she was pretty ticked off that you invited me up without talking to her about it first?" (Lila tended to end her sentences as though they were a question). Her big brown eyes were wide with delight under her thick dark lashes and shiny brown hair. She took in all she could of both sides of the busy, bustling airport as they walked down to the baggage claim area. She talked about school, about her friends and all of their problems, and about her latest computer project (she knew Sydney would appreciate that. Her parents thought it was a tremendous waste of time).

Sydney's ears did perk up when Lila began telling her of her latest computer interest—a game which users all over the country could play together at the same time. The game was one that was advertised on the Internet, (*StarWarGasm*, but Lila didn't tell Aunt Sydney the actual name—didn't think she would approve. Sydney was terrifically smart and understanding, but she *was* an adult, after all). Lila couldn't get the game to work for her at home—and she just kept getting some kind of electrical short on it, because she got the strangest tingling sensation when she ran it.

Sydney's mouth nearly fell open when she heard this. She thought about George Humphreys and the program she had run at his office. She only ran it once, but she vividly recalled the strange sensation she got from it. She would have to call George in the morning, and ask about it. She had no idea that he would have already run it to the point of expiration (his).

"So what else is new?" Sydney asked her niece, not wanting to alarm her until she got more information about this computer-tingling business.

Unfortunately, Lila found it far more difficult to tell her aunt what else was actually new than she thought it would be when she called her a few days ago and asked if she could come for a visit. How in the world was she going to tell Sydney that she nearly burned down her bedroom—just by having dreamed about a madman with sparks for eyes?? Or her strange, nearly irresistible compulsion to travel to a place in her mind called Jiminy Rock, North Carolina??

Lila had been unable to bring herself to do anything else from the time she had cleaned up her room and hidden the mess on the wall from the burned dolls. She was afraid to try to do anything else—to use these terrifying powers intentionally—if that were possible. But now she found that she was even more afraid to tell Sydney what happened. What if Sydney didn't believe her? And what if she could not repeat the performance? Worse yet—what if she *could*??

No, no, it just wasn't the right time to talk about it. She would have to try to "test" this again, to see whether it was really real. She would bide her time until she had a chance to "try" something. Her aunt always took her for long rides through the bright red Georgia clay in the countryside, and she still enjoyed that as much as when she was smaller. Perhaps she would have a chance to focus her "heat power" on something along the way (Like what? A chicken house? And the farmer would eat fried chicken for the next three months?)

Lila would just try to enjoy the visit until ... until ... well, until the right time. She wouldn't think about it any more, until then.

"What was going on when you called me, Lila?" Sydney was asking now as she guided Lila through the maze of the airport gates and walkways. "You sounded kind of ... upset."

"Upset?" Lila countered.

"Yeah," Sydney said, as they approached the baggage claim area and sidled their way through clumps of people and bags and carts. "You seemed pretty upset about something. How many bags did you bring?"

"Just one. There!" Lila pointed to a bag coming along the ramp, and eased herself between the two halves of a rather substantial couple, each with three huge suitcases waiting at their feet and apparently expecting still more. Lila nabbed her bag and waved Sydney away when she tried to take it from her. They walked out toward the parking lot.

"So, what was the problem?" Sydney asked again, to Lila's dismay, who had been hoping she would forget for awhile. Lila hated the idea of lying to her Aunt Sydney, but she really wasn't ready to tell her the truth. Not yet.

"Aunt Sydney, I hope I didn't alarm you when I called? But y'know how something can look like a huge problem one minute? And then the next day it seems kind of silly? And you don't even know what the big deal was?"

"Um-huh," Sydney answered, thoughtfully. She could tell that Lila didn't want to talk about whatever it was, and she also didn't want to lie about it. "I know *exactly* what you mean! Problem over! Let's have some ice cream! Okay?"

"Super!" Lila answered. Gosh she loved her Aunt Sydney.

They had a good time that Sunday. Sydney managed to keep more than half her mind on Lila, and gave only very fleeting thoughts to Tommy. She kind of thought that he would get in touch with her some time today, though, to let her know about the Volvo, and when it would be ready to drive and everything. How much he was going to sock her for it, and stuff like that.

But when they got back to Sydney's after dropping off Lila's bag and going out for ice cream and a ride in the country, and lots of chatter about all they were both involved in, there was no call ... no messages on the answering machine ... nothing. Sydney was keenly disappointed and less and less able to keep her mind off of her wouldn't-be lover and his car. Her car. Her Wolfgang.

20/ MANIA

Tommy had been awakened early that Sunday morning by a phone call, as Sydney was sleeping in her hung over state. After hanging up he immediately jumped out of bed, took a two-second shower, put on a pair of fresh jeans, T-shirt and cotton flannel shirt, and took off in his truck toward the same mountains he and Sydney had just returned from the night before. He didn't bother with a picnic basket.

The phone call had awakened him from a discomforting dream. Sydney was in trouble. There was a man ... he was old and had a fearsome personality ... and he had Sydney in danger somehow. It was very, very dark, and Tommy could only hear Sydney's cries for help. A rumbling, revving engine was behind him. The phone jangled him into wakefulness.

"Mr. Ross?" a female voice inquired. It was a business-like voice, but there was a distinct tinge of anxiety in it.

"Yes?"

Silence for just long enough to confirm Tommy's feeling of anxiety from across the telephone lines.

"Mr. Ross, I'm Dr. Esther Anna from Broughton State Hospital."

Tommy's heart wrenched in his chest. "Is ... Is this about my grandfather?"

"Yes, it is, but," she quickly added, "we don't know if there is anything to be alarmed about just now."

"What do you mean?"

"Well, actually ... he's missing from the hospital grounds."

"Missing?"

"That's right," Dr. Anna replied. She took a breath and waited for Tommy's response. It was strange, dealing with families of mental patients. Often the family members who had the least contact with the patient over the years would become the most indignant when informed of a problem.

"Well ... uh ... Can you tell me a little more about this?" Tommy asked, "Should I come up there?"

"That could be helpful, but I'm not sure what else I can tell you. He was discovered absent for bed count the night before last. This has happened before—actually, many times over the years that he has been here—but we always knew where to look, and we always found him relatively quickly."

Tommy didn't interrupt, so she went on: "We have notified the State Patrol, and they are still searching for him. We decided we would notify his next of kin if he hadn't been found by this morning."

Next of kin. What a dreadful feeling that phrase carried with it. Tommy didn't feel like a next of kin. He hardly knew his grandfather. Most of what he knew about him was through stories that his parents had told him.

Thomson Alva Ross, Sr., was Tommy's grandfather. He lived with his wife and had only one child, Tommy's father. The elder Ross was diagnosed as manic-depressive when he was still a young man, before there was any medication known to treat it. Tommy's father told stories of how his grandfather would gradually turn into a wild man, especially in the springtime of the year. He would continue to accelerate in his speech and behavior until summer set in. Then he might break with reality completely and become a raving maniac. He had the most severe case the doctors had ever seen, his father was told.

The local police in and around the Smoky Mountain towns were all familiar with Thomson Alva Ross, Sr. When he began getting manicky, he also began drinking heavily. Many times he was picked up ranting and raving in the streets, claiming that he had super powers and was the Savior of the world. More recently he could be heard ranting about hot nuclear core rods being buried without adequate insulation which were slowly poisoning the environment of the country.

During these episodes the police or sheriff would take him to Broughton State Hospital for involuntary commitment. There he received insulin shock treatments, ice-water baths, and large amounts of sedative injections. Finally, he would wind down into a state of depression so severe as to be a catatonic stupor. He would stay in bed for days on end, finally not eating altogether. More shock treatments.

Gradually, by the fall of the year, Tommy's grandfather, would return to a state of normalcy—a slightly irascible, eccentric scientific genius. Tommy's father spoke with quiet pride of the accomplishments of his father, and his renown in the scientific community.

Tommy's grandfather had been one of the team of scientists who developed the very first computer. It was a huge, cumbersome structure which units filled entire rooms. He worked for International Computer Machines (I.C.M.), from its earliest days, when only the wildest speculators would have brought stock in it. He was with I.C.M. until it became one of the blue chip companies of the world.

In the 'fifties and 'sixties, after it was discovered that Thorazine was a miracle drug for psychosis, and lithium—a simple salt—was specific for manic-depressive psychosis, psychiatry came out of the dark ages, and the mental hospitals emptied out by two-thirds all across the country.

But Tommy's grandfather, wouldn't take his lithium once he was discharged from the hospital. No amount of begging or cajoling by his wife or doctors could convince him that he needed to take it, not even a low "maintenance" dose. He felt well, and he viewed medication as an unnecessary crutch, a sign of weakness. And until the spring came again, one or two years hence, when he would begin to accelerate again—he actually did not need the medication. Unfortunately, once he began to accelerate, and then started drinking, it was too late to stop it with medication alone. He required hospitalization.

His wife would begin to call everyone in town for help. "Thomson's gone crackers again!" she would scream into the phone. "Please, come and get him!" And the sheriff's deputies would come and he would end up committed to Broughton State Hospital for another three-month admission.

That went on for more than twenty years. Finally, one spring, about fourteen or fifteen years ago, Thomson, Sr.'s mania crossed the boundary of society's tolerance for the mentally ill.

He had been raving about nuclear reactors, and had not slept at all in days. He had begun drinking heavily, and his wife was pleading with him to go see the doctors again and start taking his medication. He stormed out of the house saying he was "going to go to work and come up with a way to rid the world of those radiation-brokers once and for all."

His wife saw him drive off in his truck, but she did not see the loaded .38 pistol under his coat.

He drove around for a long time, stopping at a few taverns to drink and rant some more. The tavern keepers didn't bother about him as long as none of the other customers complained. He did not yet sound as though he had reached his "peak", so they didn't call the police. When he left the last tavern, around three in the morning, he drove to the I.C.M. plant. He let himself in with his own key and walked through the corridors to his office. He knew there was a high security system, but he just let it happen.

When the security officer on duty heard the alarm and looked at the television screen with the blinking red light under it, he saw

Thomson Alva Ross, Sr., heading into his own office. He knew who he was—and his history—and he was worried about the erratic way he was walking—staggering? Into his office. He beeped Mr. Ross over the intercom in his office. There was no answer. He beeped again, and again no answer. He decided he had better look in on him. On his way, he passed the south wing security officer, who decided to accompany him to Ross' office.

The two security men approached Ross' office door and gingerly knocked. "Mr. Ross?" asked the first one. The door slowly creaked open. There were no lights on.

"Mr. Ross?" he asked again, entering the office tentatively and groping along the wall for a light switch.

Ross fired three times at point blank range, hitting the first man in the right lung, the right arm, and the wall next to him. The second man slid back out the door and radioed for backup. When more security officers arrived, Ross had reloaded and repeated the action. He wounded three other officers before he was subdued and apprehended.

The trial was sensational. Such a brilliant, renowned scientist, a computer genius, an alcoholic, a madman. If he had killed any of the security officers instead of only wounding them, he would surely have been convicted of murder and sentenced to death. But since they all survived, his attorneys were able to succeed in having him acquitted by reason of insanity. It did mean, though, that he was committed to Broughton State Hospital until he was determined to be no longer mentally ill and dangerous.

I.C.M. paid the entire bill for Ross' defense. And even after his virtually permanent commitment to Broughton, they kept him on the payroll. Eventually they even built a separate room for him at the hospital where he kept his own elaborate computer equipment and files. And within the confines of this arrangement, Ross still contributed incomparable ingenuity to the field of computer technology.

Now he was missing. And as next of kin—his only surviving relative—Tommy was the one who had to be notified.

"Thanks for calling me, Dr. Anna," he said. "I'm leaving now and I'll be up there in a couple of hours."

"That's good of you, Mr. Ross. I'll look forward to meeting you."

21/ HOT PURSUIT

Lila had a dream Sunday night, too. Only her Aunt Sydney was not in this dream as she was in Tommy's. Lila dreamed of fire. Fire all around her. She could feel the heat on her face, but there was no place to turn. Fire encircled her. Suddenly she heard the clashing of cymbals and a little click-click-click coming across the floor. And through the curtain of fire appeared her little toy monkey. His stiff permanent grin was wider than ever. And as he came closer and closer, he grew larger and larger. His brown suede " fur" began to smolder, rapidly turning to a charcoal gray, and then tar black. His eyes grew bigger and bigger in his head until there were huge hollow orbs where his pupils once were. Behind them were flames, licking higher and higher, getting hotter and hotter, and the monkey continued to grow and turn black. His face began to shrivel and wrinkle and then his teeth opened up to a huge cavernous snarl and Lila could either stay there and be swallowed alive or turn and take her chances racing through the fire. She turned. She ran. She crashed headlong into the Gray Man. He looked something like the shriveled, charred thing the monkey had become, only he had a strangely ... kind ... loving ... look on his face now. He spoke:

"Come, Lila. Come to Jiminy Rock. We'll all be together there. All your questions will be answered, and all of your fears will be gone. Come now."

Lila felt both intense fear, of a magnitude she had never felt before, and at the same time, a strong desire to be with this mysterious man. She sat up with a start as she abruptly awoke from her nightmare. She was definitely hot, that much was very real. Her skin felt as though she had a sunburn, and there was a light film of sweat causing her nightgown to cling to her body. Lila looked over at her Aunt Sydney in the bed next to her, fearful that her fitful nightmare might have awakened her. It had not.

Lila eased out of the bed, careful not to awaken Sydney. She went into the bathroom and quietly closed the door behind her. She peeled off her nightgown and looked in the mirror. Her cheeks were beet red! She turned on the cold water in the shower and stepped in. She could almost feel the steam rising off of her arms and body. When she got out, she toweled off and then turned off the light before opening the bathroom door again.

When her eyes adjusted to the dark, she could see that Sydney was still sleeping soundly. Lila came out of the bathroom and quietly got her suitcase and the clothes she had worn that day, and went into the living room. She got dressed, locked her suitcase, and left. It was three o'clock in the morning. The doorman's eyebrows flickered just a little when she came out of the elevator—but he made no comment other than to call for a taxicab for her. Lila stood in silence for ten minutes, writing something on a piece of paper she had fished out of her purse, until the taxi came. When it did, she reached into her purse once again, took out a five-dollar bill and handed it to the doorman, along with the note. Then she got into the cab and disappeared.

Sydney awoke with a strong jolt, as though someone had pulled the emergency brake on a train. It was five-thirty on Monday morning, and even before she turned to see that Lila was gone, she instinctively knew that something was terribly wrong. She ran frantically around the apartment, looking for Lila, looking for her suitcase, calling her name hopelessly. Finally she noticed the note that the doorman had slipped under her door two hours earlier. It read:

"Dearest Aunt Sydney—Please forgive me for running out like this, but I just had to. I don't know if you can understand this or not. I'm not crazy—at least I don't *think* I am —but some crazy things have been happening to me lately and I need some answers that I don't think you can give me.

"I've been having a terrible recurring nightmare recently. There is always a frightful old gray man in them ..."

Sydney's stomach plummeted like a bungee jumper as she vividly recalled the ominous Gray Man from her own recent repetitive nightmares. The one who she had thought was somehow related to Tommy. She continued reading the note:

"... and I feel that he can somehow provide some answers for me. You see—and this is the crazy part—strange things have been happening to me. Things I can't imagine I'll ever know how to handle. I seem to be able to ... *burn things*. I know it sounds like I'm insane, and maybe I'd welcome that, because at least it would be an answer. But for now, I just have to follow the Gray Man's instructions and go to Jiminy Rock.

"I'll call you as soon as I get there, I promise. Will you cover for me with Mom? I love you—Lila."

Cover for her with Melva? Good grief, that is the very *least* of her problems Her thoughts began racing. Where in the world is Jiminy Rock? *And why did she feel she knew where it was?* And that Tommy would know? That photograph ... Tommy's grandfather ... *he was the Gray Man*, Sydney felt so sure of that. *Tommy would know where Jiminy Rock was.*

Sydney flipped through the telephone book to the yellow pages. (She'd be darned if she'd pay a dollar to call Information). Garage Builders ... Garbage Disposal ... Garden Equipment ... Gasoline Stations: "See Service Stations, Oil and Gasoline." She flipped over to the S's, trying to keep her anxiety from turning her fingers to sludge. There! "Phillips 66—Owner, Thomson A. Ross, III." He didn't look like a "third", but that was the place, all right.

She dialed the number. It rang ten times, and then she dialed again and let it ring twenty times. Her anxiety was now just about to ring the bell at the top of the carnival hammer-slammer, so she hung up, and pulled the telephone book back onto her lap. Then she slammed it shut and dialed Information.

"Information, what city, please?" Sydney gave what information she had of Tommy, and was connected to a computerized voice which offered to automatically connect her to his number for another twenty-three cents if she pressed "1" now. Just as she was about to hang up and dial it herself, she decided to splurge, and pressed "1." Thirty rings later, she hung up, pulled on a pair of jeans and a sweatshirt, grabbed her shoulder bag and ran.

Sydney decided to drive by the Phillips 66 station before heading out of town. She didn't even know where she was going!

When Sydney approached the station, she saw that someone was there. It was nearly six a.m. Someone was turning on the lights in the station. She pulled in and he noticed her and came walking over.

"Out pretty early, Miss—can I help you?" He was a young black man with short-cropped hair, and a gorgeous smile. He wore the Phillips 66 uniform with "Kareem" stitched in red over the pocket.

"I ... uh ... actually, I'm trying to get in touch with Tommy. Do you know where I can find him now?"

Kareem stood back from her car window and looked at her pensively for a minute. This would not be the first time a pretty girl came around the station looking for Tommy. But usually not before six in the morning. And this one did look anxious in a different sort of way from the ones who were just eager to get to know Tommy a little better.

"He should be here in the next thirty minutes if you would like to wait," Kareem told her. The station didn't open officially until six-thirty, but Kareem liked to get there early and open up.

"I really can't wait thirty minutes," Sydney said, wondering whether she seemed like a total flake to this man. "Can you reach him at all?"

"Well, if it's an emergency, I could try to call him for you."

"Oh, I really would appreciate that!" Sydney answered. "Tell him it's Sydney."

Kareem nodded and went off in the direction of the office. Sydney looked around. *There he was.* At the far corner of the station lot, nearly hidden behind a display of tires for sale. *Wolfgang.* She sat and stared at him, nervously tapping her fingers and waiting for Kareem to come back out. Finally she decided to go on into the office and wait.

When she stepped in, Kareem was just hanging up. "No answer," he said. "Maybe he's already on his way over here. Is there anything I can help you with?" He flashed that dazzling smile which attracted no small number of ladies flocking to the station asking for him, too.

"No, I don't think so," Sydney said, and she smiled back at him. "But thank you." An awkward silence ensued. Sydney decided that she would wait and hope that Tommy showed up soon. She thought she may as well make some conversation to let Kareem know that she wasn't some kind of a nut, coming over and asking for Tommy at this hour. Not that she was convinced of that herself.

"I'm buying a car from Tommy," she volunteered. Then she pointed to the far corner of the lot outside the office and said, "That one, over there."

Kareem turned and leaned toward the window. "Oh, yeah. Wolfgang. That was Tommy's grandmother's car."

"Yes, and ... well, actually ... I have to go to a place called Jiminy Rock today, but I'm not sure how to get there. I thought Tommy might know. And I was wondering if the car was ready yet?"

"I see," answered Kareem. "I doubt if the car is ready. Tommy was gone all day yesterday. The station is closed on Sundays."

Sydney was stunned. Tommy had said he would check it out for her on Sunday! Perhaps he wasn't as reliable as he had seemed ...

Kareem had continued talking. "I can probably get you a map to Jiminy Rock. That's where Tommy's grandmother's house is." Sydney's mouth dropped open. She had been there in Jiminy Rock on Saturday! And *that's where Lila went??!*

Kareem pulled a map of North Carolina off of a rack next to the counter. It was marked "$2.25", and Sydney started to dig into her purse, but Kareem put up his hand. "No charge!" he said, with a wink, flashing his smile once more.

"But ..."

"No," Kareem insisted, "Tommy gave me specific instructions never to take any money for maps from gorgeous redheads who ask for him by name!"

Sydney blushed and thanked him. Then she went back out to her car. Surely Tommy would be along any minute. Then she looked over at Wolfgang again. He seemed ... somehow ... to be ... *beckoning to her*. The feeling was unmistakable ... *he wanted her to come over*. She felt an irresistible urge to walk over to the Volvo. She looked back at the station office. Kareem was busily getting ready to open for a normal business day. She walked over to Wolfgang.

She looked in the driver's side window. The front seat, back seat, floors—all immaculate. He looked brand new. The door locks were all down in the locked position, but Sydney reached for the driver's side door handle anyway. She wondered why she felt so *compelled* by this car. As her hand touched the door handle, all four locks snapped upward at once! Sydney jumped backward, but did not let go of the handle. She looked over toward the station office, but Kareem was not in view.

Once again she felt as though a hand were curling around hers, as she squeezed the door handle. The door opened and she slid inside. She looked down and touched the seat to reassure herself that she were not sitting on a gentleman's lap, just as it felt the first time. She touched the steering wheel.

Suddenly the dashboard began to light up sequentially—first the gas and oil indicators, then the gear indicator, and then the radio. The rigid trumpet of Bizet's Carmen, El Toreador, blared out at her. Now her heart began a drum roll. There was no key in the ignition. But no sooner did she look at the ignition slot than it began turning, and the engine roared to life! She heard a voice –

"Come vith me ..." he crooned, over the sharp, snapping coronets of El Toreador, "my little klingerschnitzel." Sydney sat paralyzed, her hands frozen onto the steering wheel. Then she heard a different voice.

"Listen to him, Honey," a high, sharp voice said to her from the back seat. Sydney looked up at the rear view mirror with fear and awe, and saw ... *nothing!* She thought she would pass out from fear, but she forced herself to turn around in her seat and look back.

What she saw was a huge lady with long white hair which flowed down past her shoulders almost to her waist. It looked like the "angel hair" that is sprayed onto Christmas trees. The woman wore a white diaphanous gown that flowed around her like a foamy sea, seeming to go on forever. She was smiling but very intense. Her eyes crinkled in a way that reminded Sydney of Cinderella's fairy godmother, yet still gave her a cold shiver up her spine. Her eyes were bright blue, and although she seemed to be very old, the woman had a smooth round face with shiny pink apple cheeks. For some reason, Sydney lost her fear of her.

"Let's move it, Honey! Tommy's in trouble! You didn't get your driver's license at Sears, did ya'?

"But ... who ... *who are you?*"

"Never mind that," the apparition answered. "You just put the pedal to the metal, and don't worry about speeding tickets. I've got connections you wouldn't believe!"

Sydney believed. She put the car in gear and floored it. As the Volvo squealed out of the station, fishtailing onto the road, the figure in the back seat continued talking:

"My name is Claudette, and you must be Sydney."

"Uh ... right." Sydney noticed something else about the strange old lady. There was a distinct, pungent odor drifting across from the back seat. She could not identify it at first ... but then it came to her. Corned beef.

22/ GENIUS AT WORK

Tommy hadn't worked on Wolfgang on Sunday because he had traveled back up into the mountains to Broughton State Hospital to meet with Dr. Esther Anna. The hospital was situated on several hundred beautiful acres at the foot of the Blue Ridge Mountains, about fifty miles northeast of Jiminy Rock.

"It was really good of you to come up, Mr. Ross," said Dr. Anna. She poured two cups of coffee from the Mr. Coffee on top of the file cabinet next to her desk.

"Call me Tommy, please," he answered, blowing the steam off his cup. "I take it they still have not located my grandfather?"

"Right," she said, and sat down in her wooden swivel chair. The office was sparsely decorated, except for the green plants that sat around on every spare surface. A painting of a Cherokee Indian tribal chieftain hung on one wall, and a calendar with scenes of the mountains hung on the wall next to it.

"The only place we have not yet checked out is the house in Jiminy Rock where your grandfather lived before he came here. We were glad to learn that you would be able to come up—you may want to help in that search."

"Of course," he answered. "But do you really think it's possible that my grandfather traveled fifty miles home through the mountains by himself?"

"Well—he was in excellent physical shape, even for a man thirty years younger. The mental problems he had never seemed to take their toll with him physically. But fifty miles ..." She trailed off, shaking her head.

"Would anyone have given him a ride up there?"

"I would doubt that," Dr. Anna answered. "There are signs posted on the major roadways leading to and from the hospital advising motorists not to pick up hitchhikers. It is rare for a patient to hitchhike successfully from the grounds." She took a sip of her coffee, and then added, "But it has been known to happen."

Tommy nodded. His grandfather had apparently left the hospital the day before he and Sydney drove up to the old homestead on Saturday. But his grandfather was *not* there—Tommy was certain of that, even though he had not actually searched the house. And besides, it just seemed impossible for his grandfather to have made that trip without help.

"Isn't there anywhere else that he may have gone?" Tommy asked.

"No," Dr. Anna answered, shaking her head again. "Over the years your grandfather was known to leave the hospital grounds on occasion—he wasn't supposed to—but the staff and surrounding townspeople knew him so well that it was never a real problem. If he wandered in the streets or taverns, someone eventually would put a call in to the hospital and we would send someone to pick him up. Most of the time he would raise his drink in a toast, chug down the remainder, and ask what took us so long!"

Dr. Anna drummed her fingers on her desk for a few seconds, and then went on: "Occasionally, though, when your grandfather relapsed at the hospital, and became paranoid and psychotic again, we would not take any chances. We would transfer him back to a locked ward for safety. After all, he ..." Dr. Anna trailed off and looked down.

"Shot some people," Tommy supplied. Dr. Anna had hesitated to say that which might have made Tommy uncomfortable, and she was relieved when he said it for her.

"Can you tell me more about my grandfather? I mean, I never knew him very well. He was hospitalized when I was very young. What was he like?"

"Well, that's what was so puzzling," Dr. Anna answered. "He seemed to take the news of your grandmother's death very well. We were monitoring him closely for any signs of a relapse, but he seemed to be handling it okay." Dr. Anna stopped and seemed to be deciding whether she should continue. Then, "Your grandmother visited him every weekend. She was the only visitor he had ever since your father died some years ago."

Tommy felt a heavy blanket of guilt settle over him. He tried to push the feeling away—after all, he hardly knew his grandfather—but the guilt weighed heavily on him, and he couldn't shrug it off.

I should have come anyway... I could have come up here a few times each year... I should have ...

But he had not. The last Tommy saw of his grandfather was in the photographs in the newspaper during his trial. Tommy's chest tightened and there were sharp pangs of pain in his eyes. He felt close to crying for the first time since his father died.

"... so when your grandmother died, we really expected it to effect him in an adverse way. We were prepared for a full-blown relapse. But it never happened." Then she added, "*Until now.*"

Dr. Anna stopped and looked more intently at Tommy for a minute. Then she said, "By the way, are you, by any chance, the grandson who is the doctor?"

Tommy shook his head and stammered, "Well, no, not exactly..."

"He often spoke about a grandson who was a doctor. He was so proud of him! We didn't know if it was true, or just another delusion."

Tommy looked away from Dr. Anna, at the Cherokee painting on the far wall. He could not stop his eyes from welling up. He brought the coffee cup to his lips and swallowed the hot liquid hard. He didn't look up until he felt more under control. Later he might let himself cry. For his grandfather. For the lost years. Later.

They spoke for awhile longer, and then Dr. Anna took Tommy on a tour through the hospital. She showed him the "open" wards, where his grandfather resided most of the time, and the "closed" wards, where the more psychotic patients were kept under closer watch. Then she showed him the office where his grandfather had continued to work for I.C.M.

Tommy was astonished. There must have been tens of thousands of dollars worth of computers and other sophisticated electronic equipment in the little room. There were cables running everywhere. Tommy looked at Dr. Anna.

"I.C.M. paid for all this?"

"Yes," she answered. "Apparently they felt that he continued to be worth the price. They could have put him on retirement, but they have kept him active." Then she turned to face Tommy. "Do you know what a genius your grandfather is?"

Tommy nodded his head. "Yes, my father told me ... tried to tell me ... but it's hard to believe. All this ..." he waved his hand around, "and in a mental hospital, yet!"

"It is incredible," Dr. Anna agreed. "Hopefully we'll find him before ... before ..." She trailed off without finishing. Tommy was relieved that she did.

They completed the tour of the hospital, and then Tommy set out for his grandparents' home once again. He would spend Sunday night there, and he would neither be home nor at the gas station Monday morning when Sydney would try to call him.

23/ POWERS IN THE ATTIC

As Jeanne Bigelow, John Raymond, Arthur Hurdsbeck, Adam White, Margaret Waldenmire, Joanne Zeidman, and the six other members of the Southside Portland Computer Club Hound-Bytes excitedly exited the Boeing 747 jetliner which just brought them cross country from Oregon to Asheville, North Carolina, they were being watched. They did not notice the short, stocky, granite-faced, uniformed man who stood across from the arrival area, counting heads. They did not notice that his uniform was different from the other airport security officers. His was the official dress uniform of the Dallas Police Department.

Mac McMulligan did not need a walkie-talkie, a telephone, nor any other paraphernalia to convey this information to his new boss—the Gray Man. He merely concentrated hard on a focal point just behind the center of his forehead, and his thoughts were transmitted *just like that.* He knew, too, when the Gray Man had received them. He received a telepathic *ten-four, good buddy.*

Several hours earlier in the day he had transmitted information regarding the arrival of Sydney's niece, Lila. And in between, he reported on the arrival of more than dozens of other young people, who also happened to be computer buffs, and also happened to be following a compelling dream-command transmitted by the Gray Man.

Upon arriving in Asheville, Lila took a taxicab to the Greyhound bus station. The Hound-Bytes hailed two taxicabs (the first refused to take all of them even though they insisted they could all fit) to take them to the Asheville train station, where they would board the three-forty to Jiminy Rock. And there ... there ... *that was as far as their plans went.*

Sydney would already have arrived, except for the slight detour required to evade the State Highway Patrol. She had been speeding along, as per Claudette's instructions (who by this time had disappeared again, and Sydney was not really sure whether she had hallucinated the Rubenesque apparition or not). When the trooper's blue light flashed on and the siren whooped behind her, Sydney realized that she had been doing over ninety miles per hour (one hundred fifty kilometers per hour, as the Swedish dashboard reflected). She started to take her foot off the accelerator when Claudette reappeared once again, flaxen hair flowing, chubby white cheeks glowing, and corned beef odor wafting over the back seat.

"Floor it, Honey!" she commanded, "This ain't the Easter Parade!" Sydney floored it. "Now hit the brake and turn hard left!"

When Sydney did that, the Volvo, whose anti-lock braking system had been disabled by Claudette for just such an occasion as this, fishtailed wildly, and gravel and dust flew so high that Sydney could hardly see. When the dust settled, the car was traveling in the opposite direction, and they passed the state trooper, who was quite surprised to see the redhead in the blue Volvo going past him the other way. He tried to do the same maneuver while radioing for backup, but he flipped over three times before coming to a stop. The trooper was knocked unconscious by his air bag, but was relaxed enough by the 0.12% alcohol in his system to be otherwise unharmed.

After that, Claudette instructed Sydney to stay off the Interstate, and she gave her explicit directions through back country roads, some of them in pretty bad shape. Sydney crawled across one potholed dirt road at only five miles an hour.

And all the time Wolfgang's stereo poured out the most magnificent classical music from all periods past. It did not seem to matter what station Sydney turned to—all she got was classical music. And the odometer—that was another quirky thing. It had registered exactly seven hundred miles when Sydney first sat in it at Tommy's place. The mileage seemed to roll up normally enough. But no matter how far they went, whenever they came to a stop, and Sydney checked the mileage, it registered seven-hundred-point-zero again!

Tommy, meanwhile, had arrived back at his grandfather's homestead at Jiminy Rock late Sunday afternoon, after his meeting with Dr. Anna had concluded. He walked up the steps to the mansion, and paused to look up for no particular reason, before putting the key in the front door. He only missed by seconds seeing the figure draw back out of view from the dormer window off the attic at the very top of the house.

Tommy let himself in and looked carefully around the huge foyer. An antique credenza stood along the wall and a beautiful oil painting of a nineteenth century French street scene hung above it. There was a Chinese Ming vase on the credenza. Tommy could remember from the many years past when he came to visit his grandmother that the vase was always filled with beautiful fresh-cut flowers. The house always smelled of flowers, and something baking in the oven.

His grandmother's housekeeper was a wonderful baker. Violet was a large black woman who always had a smile and something nice to say. Even when Tommy was older, in college at Appalachian State, before he went away to medical school in Texas, whenever he would come to visit, Violet had a special "stash" of cookies just for him.

After discovering the grandmother dead in her bed the morning after she choked to death on the corned beef sandwich, Violet called the sheriff and then collapsed and had to be hospitalized, from the emotional trauma and shock. Tommy had arranged for her to retire with her salary continued for life, out of his grandmother's estate.

Now there was no smell of flowers and nothing baking in the oven. Tommy walked slowly through the large rooms, stopping to look carefully at everything. To remember. When he had completed his circuit of the downstairs, he walked up the huge, winding staircase to the second floor. Room after room was filled with old familiar pieces of furniture, paintings, and antiques. The third floor was the same.

Tommy hesitated before the door to the attic stairway. He didn't believe for a minute that his grandfather was up there. Why would he be in there? Tommy could see that his grandfather was not here. Besides, it was already getting dark and Tommy wasn't sure there were any lights up there. Not to mention the dust—he might as well take his contact lenses off before even thinking about going up into the attic. He went back downstairs to the kitchen.

He found the same cache of Coors Light that he had just shared with Sydney the day before. He cracked open a can. He wouldn't be able to drive all the way home tonight—the mountain roads were treacherous enough in the daylight—and he was already exhausted. Besides, he might want to swing back by Broughton Hospital and talk to Dr. Anna again before going back home. In the back of his mind he hoped his grandfather would have returned there by the time he checked in again with Dr. Anna. He would spend the night here in the mansion.

Tommy got up and went to the telephone on the wall. It was the only contemporary thing in the whole house. There was not even a television set. He picked up the receiver and was annoyed to discover that the line was dead. He wondered why? Nothing had been turned off, and Tommy had arranged for all utilities to continue to be paid for the time being, so the house would remain livable until he could decide what to do with it.

He took his beer and walked back up to his grandmother's room on the second floor. There was another telephone in there—maybe the line was *not* dead and the kitchen telephone was just out of order. But there was no dial tone there either. He patted his jeans and noted almost absentmindedly that he probably left his cellphone in the truck—but then recalled plugging it into the recharger at home! He left so hastily, he was positive he did not take it with him. He trotted out to the truck and confirmed that.

Shoot. Kareem would open the service station as usual tomorrow morning, but Tommy would not be able to call and let him know where he was unless he drove down the mountain into town to make a call. Well, he would just have to wonder about it, because there was no way he was going to make that drive tonight.

Tommy finished his beer and opened another. He took it and two more with him as he walked back through the front foyer and into the large library. He scanned along the shelves and pulled out a beautiful gold-embossed copy of *Oliver Twist*. He settled down on the long, saddle brown leather couch and began to read. In a few minutes, he was asleep.

Tommy never woke up that night. Not even when a tall, sinewy figure came down the staircase and stood in the door of the library, watching him sleep. The figure watched for a long time. Then he walked over to Tommy and looked him over carefully, from head to toe. He bent over and took the copy of *Oliver Twist* out of his hand, which was resting on his chest. He replaced it in its slot on the library shelf from exactly where Tommy had removed it. He went back to the couch and watched the sleeping figure for a few minutes longer. Then he took the colorful woolen afghan off the back of the couch and gently placed it over Tommy. He went back upstairs.

The attic was huge, dark and dusty. The Gray Man walked through it, winding his way around old covered-up pieces of furniture, boxes, trunks, and all kinds of artifacts for which there was no room or no use in the house. Finally he reached a door at the back which opened onto a room that was almost identical to the computerized office which Dr. Anna had shown Tommy at the hospital that day.

He sat down at the main computer table and turned it on. The screen cast its blue-gray light on him. He tapped some instructions onto the screen and entered. This was met by a blank screen and a cursor. Then the screen asked, "SUBJECT?" to which he entered, "Herman Wilbur 'Mac' McMulligan." To this the screen responded with another blanking out and series of beeps. Then a wave-pattern appeared on the screen, and at the top was printed, "SUBJECT ASLEEP."

The Gray Man continued to work at his computer for the rest of the night. He wasn't sleeping at all these days. He had been thankful that Tommy had not come up into the attic earlier, when he was exploring the house. He loved Tommy dearly, in spite of not seeing him over the years—but if Tommy had come up and discovered his computer lab in the attic, he would have had to suffer the same fate as the others. The Gray Man could not jeopardize his life's work for anyone, not even his beloved grandson.

Tommy awoke around six Monday morning—just about the time that Sydney was asking Kareem to try and reach him at home. He did not notice that the afghan had been thrown over him, nor that the book had been replaced on the shelf. He picked up the empty beer can and the full ones which he hadn't opened, and went back into the kitchen. He decided that he would go ahead and drive into town and call Kareem. Then he could come back here and spend a little more time looking around. He headed out the door.

Tommy got in his truck and started the engine while the Gray Man watched him from the window at the top of the house. But Tommy never put the truck in gear. He thought, *this is ridiculous*. What am I going to come back here for? I've searched the whole house, and Grampa's not here. There's no point in going all the way down the mountain into town just to make a phone call and then coming all the way back. The only place I haven't looked is in the attic.

As soon as he thought of that, Tommy looked up at the dormer windows at the top of the house. The Gray Man stepped back from the window, but not before the morning sun glinted off his thick eyeglass lenses. Tommy wasn't sure if he saw something there or not. But he made a decision to go ahead and finish his exploration of the house before leaving.

He turned off the ignition and walked back up to the house. He went directly to the stairwell, and then realized that he was absolutely famished. He had not eaten any lunch or dinner yesterday! He turned in the direction of the kitchen and went there instead. He looked in the refrigerator. It was empty except for a bottle of grape juice. The pantry shelves were equally empty except for some cans of soup and beans. Not exactly Breakfast at Brennan's, but better than beer. He took out a couple of saucepans from under the sink and turned on the stove burners. He was relieved to find that the electricity and gas were still on, if not the telephone.

Tommy ate the beans and soup out of the pots, and finished the grape juice. Then he washed and dried everything, and put the empty cans in a garbage bag. He put the bag by the front door to take with him when he left. Then he looked up at the stairs leading to the attic, and walked toward them.

When Tommy got up to the door of the attic, he thought he heard something. A door close? Mice, more likely. He opened the door to the attic and waited a minute to allow his eyes to adjust to the darkness. He stepped in and looked around for a light switch. There was one a few feet inside, but nothing happened when he flipped it.

When his vision adjusted, he was able to make out the shape of boxes and trunks and pieces of covered furniture just from the light from the two dormers. He moved along cautiously, since the light was not reaching the floor very well, and he didn't want to trip over something. Tommy moved slowly along the whole length of the attic, winding his way carefully, and stopping to pick up and inspect an old faded photograph, an ornate table clock, and other items here and there that caught his attention. This was all his now, he kept reminding himself. It would be up to him to take possession or dispose of it all eventually.

Tommy stopped and looked back. Well, he had completed his exploration of the entire house, top to bottom, and his grandfather was not there. Maybe Dr. Anna would have some good news for him when he went back there on his way home later. Maybe they will have found his grandfather, and he would be back safe and sound in the hospital. That would be wonderful.

Tommy started to head back toward the front attic door, when something caught his eye. *A doorknob in the middle of the far wall?* He moved closer. *There was a door there—how strange!* It looked like the very outer wall of the house. There shouldn't be a door there. He walked over and reached for the doorknob.

24/ TRAVELERS

Elijah Chester Alston had been deputy sheriff of Alston County, North Carolina, for going on six years. He was related to the county by blood in more than one way. The Alstons were his great-two-or-three-grand-relatives who settled Alston County in the days before Daniel Boone moved on to Texas, and his hallelujah chorus at the Alamo. And Alston blood served to fertilize more than one patch of rich Carolina topsoil, especially in the days of the feuding Alston and Saunders clans.

Eli's maternal grandmother, Katherine, had been a Saunders, and her daddy took pity on her and chose not to pull the trigger of the double-barreled ought-thirty shotgun trained between the eyes of her erstwhile lover, Calvin Alston, who had put her in a family way. Daddy Saunders kindly shifted the double barrel from the bridge of Calvin's nose to the small of his back, and nudged him in the direction of the Alston Feed & Grain store, the large back room of which served as the town meeting place, and church, when the itinerant preacher made his way 'round to Alston County, where he was at this time; whereby Kate and Calvin were summarily joined in holy matrimony.

The new Mr. and Mrs. Alston made an ungainly looking couple, as Calvin was, at five-foot-six, the shortest of his seven brothers and three sisters; while Kate, at six-foot-one barefoot, was just middlin' tall for her family. And thus they marched, and recited their vows, and Kate had nine more children after the nearly illegitimate one. The youngest was Eli's mother, Elly Beth Alston.

Eli's paternal grandparents were distant cousins of his maternal grandparents. "Distant" because of a rather large valley which separated their mountain homes. Bloodwise, they were first cousins once removed. That was pretty routine stuff in those rather sparsely populated times and places. Slim pickin's forces one to take what's available.

Now Grandpappy Alston was not himself forced into any marriages. He was on the other end. You see, he was a preacher, so there was always at least one belly between him and any shotgun which might be gracing these holy unions. And if any anxious bridegroom began to stammer when it was time to affirm his vows, or even hesitate for one little bitty second, Grandpappy Alston would glare at him over his well-worn Bible, under his thick, wildly frizzled white eyebrows, and nod his head ever so slightly at the father of the bride, prompting him to jab the barrel of the shotgun a little more sharply into the bridegroom's withering spine. This move would invariably produce a hale and hearty "I DO!!" from the fellow.

Preacher Alston never got married himself. Even so, there was little speculation needed about the children spread far and wide across his preaching circuit, who resembled him by more than mere coincidence. Eli's own father, Jonathan, tall and lean, was one of these children. He was the only black-haired, blue-eyed child of Thomas and Heather B. Alston, both of whom were brown-eyed blondes. Neither did it help that Jonathan was, at age twelve, six-foot-two, the tallest by a head, and the youngest of the brood.

In any case, Elijah Chester Alston's own height was passed down to him from both of these sides, and at six-foot-eight and one-half inches, he was a deputy sheriff who commanded no small amount of respect.

In addition to his large frame, he had a large helping of horse sense, which tended to make him a keenly successful deputy sheriff. Sheriff Hollister Trimble, unfortunately, was more endowed with booklearning than with horse sense, and the county fathers withheld acting in such a way as to remove the sheriff and replace him with Deputy Alston only at Eli's own insistence. Besides being big and sensible, Eli was loyal and true, and he let it be known that he would never take over the sheriff's job unless Sheriff Trimble himself chose to retire. Still and all, it was Deputy Eli who was the one that got called during any real crisis or emergency, to the constant consternation of Sheriff Trimble. It was Deputy Eli who was called when the State Trooper flipped over on the Interstate and radioed for backup to help catch a fleeing redhead in a blue Volvo.

On the other hand, it was Sheriff Trimble who was called by the moonshiner up in the back woods of the mountains when he spotted a blue Volvo crossing too close to his moonshine still for comfort. The sheriff, who made a nice little side income from being discreet about this, and other stills which dotted the wooded mountainside, decided to investigate the matter himself. He did not tell Deputy Eli, who had left to investigate the accident on the Interstate, about the coincidence of another call about a blue Volvo.

By Monday afternoon, Melva was becoming hysterical, or so her husband Phil told her. They had not heard from her daughter Lila nor sister Sydney in two days, in spite of her leaving increasingly more strident telephone messages on Sydney's answering machine. Phil did not see any reason to worry. But that never stopped Melva. She was worried to begin with, because that was her modus operandi, and it came natural to her. So she shifted into high gear when she expected Lila to have returned her calls over the past two days, but didn't.

When Melva heard on the News at Noon about the bizarre epidemic of CompuFlu which was affecting computer buffs all over the country, and that the entire membership of a high school computer club in Oregon seemed to have disappeared—well, her Worry Quotient went straight through the globally warmed hole in the ozone layer. Lila was a computer buff, and it was because of the influence of her wild sister Sydney! "Sydney's Computer Connections"—What could this have led to?

Melva had a strong impulse to pack a bag and hop on the first flight to Atlanta. She would give Sydney a good tongue-lashing and shake her finger in her face, and drag Lila home by the ear! But Phil insisted that she wait until Monday evening and try to call again. After all, Sydney was not exactly Miss Regular Hours. It would not be unreasonable if she were showing Lila the town and not hovering around her answering machine.

Kareem was getting worried, too. Tommy still had not shown up by late morning on Monday. Tommy never, *never* didn't show up. The station was busy, and Kareem hardly had time to turn around, but he tried several times to call Tommy at home. No answer. Finally he called Clarence, the other attendant who worked at the station.

Clarence was a tall, pale white, lanky fellow, with rather large teeth. He was considered not too bright by conventional standards. If anyone had been concerned enough to have had his I.Q. tested while he was struggling through grade school, the results would have placed him at the borderline-retarded level. However, there would have been a remarkable disparity between the "verbal" and the "performance" scores. For Clarence was a gifted mechanic.

Tommy's father had hired him because he seemed like a decent, honest fellow, and was excited to have an opportunity to work, even though he had given up on school after failing ninth grade for the third time. He was seventeen when he went to work for Tommy's father twenty years ago. It soon became apparent that Clarence need do little more than walk over to a car, sit in it, turn on the ignition, and sometimes just drive it once around the block before he knew exactly what was wrong with it. It was Clarence's skill that gave Tommy's

Phillips 66 station the great reputation it had. And although Clarence never asked for a single raise, he now made more than the average college graduate did at his age. Tommy's dad believed in rewarding good work in the only way that counted—with money.

"What do you mean, you don't know where Tommy is?"

"Just that, Clarence," Kareem answered. "He hasn't shown up all morning. And there's no answer at his place."

Kareem hesitated to tell Clarence about the redhead who had come by this morning. She had left her Toyota in the lot and had taken the Volvo! Kareem was not sure what to do about it—after all, she was buying the car from Tommy, and she obviously had a key for it, because he knew there was no key in the ignition.

"Can you run by Tommy's apartment and see if he's there?" Kareem asked.

"Sure," Clarence answered, "but are you okay there by yourself?"

"Well, it's busy, but I'm okay. Just check on Tommy, will you?"

"I'm on my way," Clarence said, pulling his work pants off the chair by his bed and stepping into them, holding the telephone between his cheek and his shoulder.

Clarence drove by Tommy's house first. The truck was not there, and he instinctively knew that Tommy would not be there; but he stopped and went up to the door and knocked anyway. He waited, knocked again, waited. Finally, he went back to his car and drove to the station to give Kareem a hand.

The train rumbled along steadily up the rails along the mountainside. The kids from Portland didn't have much to say. First of all, they didn't know what actually was going to happen when they reached Jiminy Rock. Beside that, the springtime, flower-bedecked scenery of the mountainside was too beautiful to do anything but look at, with a certain reverence.

John Raymond broke the silence. "My folks are gonna have a cow when they find out we're gone."

The others turned to him. This very concern was on all of their minds, but they had been collectively avoiding it. Jeanne Bigelow answered him first:

"We've been over this, John. Remember, we agreed to call home the minute we get to Jiminy Rock. Okay?"

"No, it's not 'okay'," he answered, slumping in his seat and crossing his arms over his slightly concave chest. "We don't even know where this Jiminy Rock place is! And what makes you think we will be able to make a phone call from there? It's probably a cellphone black hole, for all we know!"

Joanne answered him, but without speaking. She swung her long auburn hair back from her shoulder, and focused her thoughts intensely toward John.

This, John. This is how we know we'll be able to call our folks. We don't even need a telephone. Get it?

John sat up straight again, his arms dropping down to the seat beside him. He rubbed his hand along the wear-polished wood of the train, which looked as though Abe Lincoln himself might have ridden on it in its better days.

"I get it," he said, out loud. The new telepathic power to think-talk still spooked him a little. And besides, it gave him a headache. "I'm just getting a little worried, that's all."

Soon they were all looking out the windows again at the beautiful passing scenery. The rhododendrons waved in a sea of purple-pink petals over the large green leaves. The Carolina-blue sky was cloudless. After another hour it was just beginning to get dusky, and the bright sunlit foliage began to have a gold edge to it. They all turned as the train gradually decelerated, and the conductor announced their arrival at Jiminy Rock.

The club members all craned their necks at the windows to see what was out there. But the scenery looked the same as it had all the way up the mountain.

Adam White was the first to stand up. Being so tall, he pulled his bag easily down from the overhead rack and set it in the aisle. Then he began pulling down the others' bags. Each picked up their bag from the aisle, and one by one, disembarked from the train.

Outside they saw nothing but a small waiting bench with a torn canvas hood hanging over it on four tilting posts. As the train slowly began to start up again, the whistle blew—much more shrill to the ears from outside the train than inside. They all watched as it left the way station and slowly disappeared around a bend in the mountainside. When it was completely out of sight, and they could no longer hear it chugging along the tracks, they all turned to each other. There they stood. And they waited.

Sydney felt hunger for the first time—she must have been driving for hours. She had no idea where on earth she was. She realized that she had not passed a gas station since they hit the back country, and she looked at the gas gauge. *It was full!* And even though the odometer rolled up every tenth of a mile, it still registered seven hundred miles! Pavarotti was belting out an exquisite aria on the car's stereo, and Sydney got gooseflesh listening to his magnificent and dramatic voice. She still wished she could change the channel.

Speaking of gooseflesh, Sydney had not seen or heard from Claudette since the last dirt road she had been instructed to turn down. But now that Sydney's growling stomach was competing with Pavarotti, she heard Claudette's voice from the back seat once again.

"Hungry, my dear?"

"Oh, yes," answered Sydney, knowing somehow, instinctively, that Claudette would provide for her. And provide she did.

"Have some of this," she said, and her translucently pale pudgy hand came over the back of the seat holding a fine porcelain china plate with ... with ... with a corned beef sandwich on it ... greenish-blue mold around the edges ... and *partially eaten!*

Sydney gagged and her stomach curled up like a slug under a shower of salt. She couldn't speak for fear that she would begin to retch and pass out, but she waved the plate away, and finally managed to say, "No, thanks! I'm on a diet!"

"Really? A little bitty thing like you?" Claudette clucked. "Well, have it your way, dearie," and she withdrew the plate. Sydney could hear her noisily wolfing down the sandwich in the back seat. Sydney decided that a day's fast wouldn't kill her.

25/ REUNION

The door slipped open quietly as Tommy let go of the doorknob. He drew in his breath at the sight in front of him. The room was no larger than ten-by-six feet in size, but it was crowded to every inch with computers, monitors, telephone lines and cables running every which way across the walls and floors. A blue-gray light shone from the room, and Tommy's eyes hurt for a minute until they readjusted to the stark brightness of the new light. Sitting at the main computer desk with his back to the door was a man with thinning gray hair. He was large of frame, but thin, and his shoulders were hunched over.

"G-Grampa?" Tommy began tentatively. But the man did not stop working at the computer and gave no indication that he had heard Tommy. Tommy spoke again, a little louder this time.

"Grampa?" Still the old man failed to turn around or acknowledge that he had heard anything. Tommy stood there staring for another minute, trying to take in the meaning of all this.

Suddenly the elder Ross swung around, startling Tommy, who stepped backward and tripped on one of the many cables criss-crossing the floor, catching himself on the doorpost before falling altogether.

"Hello, Tommy."

Tommy could not speak—the man he faced was so strange and yet so familiar. He had Tommy's very own face— this is what he would look like fifty years from now. And yet ... there was something about him ... something that made Tommy feel a terrible shiver of foreboding as though someone had injected ice water into his veins. He had not felt fear like this since he was a small child.

Finally he found his voice again.

"Grampa? What are you do- ... How did you ..." he trailed off, still too shaken to know exactly what to say or ask.

The senior Ross ignored his efforts at interrogation, and asked, "Don't you need to make a phone call?"

Tommy then remembered about Kareem and the service station, and his plan to call as soon as he got into town later this morning. But how did his grandfather know that?

"Well, yes, I do! But how ...?"

Ross was pointing to the wall next to the door, where a telephone hung. Tommy walked over to it and, without trying to figure things out any further, dialed the number of his gas station in Atlanta.

"Tommy! Jesus, man, where are you?" Kareem's relief at hearing Tommy's voice was apparent. Tommy explained, in a shortened version which he felt was best, that he'd been called to his grandmother's estate to handle some last-minute legal issues, and couldn't get back in time to open up this morning.

They spoke for a few more minutes about the business, and then were about to hang up. But Kareem remembered at the last minute and said, "By the way, the Volvo that you brought in?"

"Yeah, what about it?"

"Well ..." Kareem was wary about proceeding here, because he really didn't know if he should have reported this to the police or not. But he plunged on, "A lady came and got it. Was she supposed to?"

"A lady?" Tommy asked, picturing a female member of a car-theft ring who tried to sell him some stolen autos a few months ago. "Did she have blonde hair, shaved on one side, half a dozen earrings in one ear and one in her lip?"

"I ... uh, no," Kareem answered, knowing well Tommy's penchant for making jokes. But he felt a sense of urgency across the telephone wires, and decided not to carry the joke even further, such as describing other places where the lady had rings.

"She had red hair, green eyes ... real cute. Do you want me to call the police?"

"No, no, that's okay," Tommy said, recognizing that it was Sydney. He had no idea how or why she took the Volvo—Tommy had the only key to it. But somehow ... somehow, he was relieved that she had done that. He didn't know why. Not yet. But he was relieved.

Tommy hung up the phone and then turned back to his grandfather, who was sitting and watching him. He had more questions before Tommy could get back to his own.

"You've grown so tall and handsome!" he said, glowing with pride. And he didn't look so terrifying at that moment. His hunched shoulders seemed to straighten up as he looked his grandson over. "You're a physician, right?"

But he sagged again as Tommy's expression told him otherwise. Tommy pulled over a little rolling stool from under one of the tabletops and sat down. Then he told his grandfather the whole story of his ill-fated medical career.

His grandfather's face darkened, and the expression he took on was one of ... madness. "So they're after you, too," he hissed, nearly too softly for Tommy to have heard. Then he looked over at his grandson again, and said, "Well, you're with me now, Tommy! You'll have the power and the glory right along with me! We're going to have our own brave new world!"

"Grampa! What are you talking about?"

The elder Ross stared intently at his grandson for a few seconds. Tommy felt a burning sensation, almost as though he were being scanned by red-hot laser beams. But soon his grandfather seemed to relax, and smile, and he looked less threatening again.

"I'll tell you all about it, Tommy, my boy. First, though," and here he stood up and began turning off switches and lights and unhooking telephones and throwing plastic covers over computers, "I'm going to take you where the secrets of the universe will be revealed to you. Just as they were to me."

Ross gestured at the door through which Tommy had entered, and together they left the lab. He led Tommy back through the maze of the attic, and soon they were back downstairs in the natural light. When they got back to the first floor, Ross detoured to the kitchen. There he took a case of Coors Light from the large storage refrigerator off the pantry and hefted it into Tommy's arms.

"Should we take my truck, Grampa?" Tommy offered, hoping he could get him into the truck and then drive back down to Broughton Hospital. But Ross just shook his head and kept walking, out the front door and down the gravel driveway.

After reaching the main access road, he turned off onto a path leading into the surrounding woods. They walked up a slightly inclined mountain footpath, sometimes obstructed by rocks and tree roots. It would have been easy if Tommy were not carrying a full case of beer, but he managed not to stumble and fall. The woods were thick around them, and jackrabbits and wooly aphids and all manner of flora and fauna buzzed with the sounds and smells of spring in the mountains.

They must have walked for a mile before they came to an opening in the thick wall of trees. And as Tommy stepped through the opening he gasped with wonder at the sight before him.

"Welcome to Billy's Bunion," his grandfather said, sweeping his hand around. The panorama in front of him was spectacular. "Billy's Bunion" was a piece of rock about fifteen feet in diameter which jutted out from the very top of the mountain, and provided a nearly three-hundred-sixty degree view of the rolling hills and forests twelve hundred feet below.

"Sit down now," Ross said, gesturing at the ground. He took two cans of beer from the case and handed one to Tommy. "Sorry the stock is so low!" he said, chortling, and put the can to his lips and tipped it straight up in the air. His Adam's apple rocked steadily up and down for about thirty seconds, and then he took the can down from his lips, crumpled it and replaced it in the case. Tommy did the same.

Phil Maxwell, D. D. S., was a successful dentist and family man. His patients loved him, his kids loved him, and his wife put up with all his little quirks and foibles, and yes, she loved him, too, and they were very happy. Melva was a bit rigid and obsessive-compulsive, but that was good, because it complemented Phil's sometimes too laid-back style.

Phil had wanted to be an artist when he was a kid, but his mother put an early halt to that. She would not hang his little drawings on the refrigerator. They went into a file cabinet, into a folder with Phil's name on it. His little sister's pictures went on the refrigerator. Phil did not even dare tell his mother when he won, at age 15, the WTVJ South Florida Art Contest. His ribbon went straight to the bottom of his bottom-most bureau drawer, where he kept his condoms. He never did find out, thank God, which item would have created the biggest explosion had his mother discovered them.

His sister, on the other hand, was raved about for her artistic talents, her wondrous natural beauty and charming manner. Phil, in his less charitable moments, would have described these assets as primitive (the art); a fortuitous lack of acne; and a smile which obviated the need for a brain. But he loved his sister, he really did, and he knew he did, because he often went out of his way to do things for her, and he knew that she idolized him.

Phil's father was the kind, quiet type who paid all the bills and participated passively in all the activities which his mother planned and arranged for every member of her immediate and extended family. Phil did show his father the First Place ribbon he had won in the art contest. His father nodded and smiled and said, "Very nice, son!" Then he went back to reading his paper, without asking to see the drawing for which Phil was awarded the ribbon.

Phil's mother turned out to be right, of course. Phil went into dentistry, as she had recommended, and now he could afford to take care of his family in style and carry on his avocations of painting and sculpting and photography in his spare time. Had he pursued a career in art, he would be lucky to have been able to feed himself alone.

When Phil met Melva, it was love at first sight. She was tall and big-boned (like his mother), and she wore her light-brown hair pulled back severely from her temples (people would often ask if Phil's mother was of oriental background because this type of hair-do tended to cause her eyes to look a little bit slanted). Occasionally, through the years people had mentioned that Melva resembled Phil's mother, but he told them they were just wrong. He didn't understand how people could be so far off in their observations.

Presently, Phil was not really worried about Lila's apparent disappearance. He always liked Melva's sister Sydney—she sort of represented the part of him who would have enjoyed being a starving Greenwich Village artist. He never thought for a single minute that Lila was in any kind of danger if she were with her Aunt Sydney. If anything, he thought she was probably having the time of her life. But he was glad that Melva was worried, because that's what mothers were supposed to do, so he didn't have to.

Phil realized that his thoughts were drifting, and he had been staring down the mouth of his patient for the last few minutes. He had been holding the drill poised above the patient's mouth, revving it up and down, up and down. When he noticed the frozen face of fear on his patient—the large beads of sweat on his pale forehead, the stretched open orbs of his eyes—Phil realized what he was doing. He quickly removed the frown from his face, and replaced it with his most charming smile (he tried to emulate his sister in this regard).

"Now, open wide! This won't hurt a bit!" The drill bit—which may have been the "bit" he was referring to—descended and tore into the heart of the targeted molar.

26/ MYSTERIES REVEALED

Sydney looked dazedly up at the glints of light on the far mountaintop. It came out of a haze, and she could not tell if the light was flashing red and blue, or if it was just the result of her extreme tiredness and hunger. It sometimes seemed as though Wolfgang were actually doing the driving, not her. She could not have said accurately whether she closed her eyes for a few moments at a time—as Wolfgang cruised along with the enchanting orchestral strains coming from his quadraphonic speakers—or whether it was all a magnificent hallucination.

Mac McMulligan sat for a few extra minutes in the seat of his police cruiser. He did not know, nor particularly care, how the Gray Man had managed to provide such a vehicle for him. It was a fully outfitted Jeep Patrino XR6, and at the top were two lights, one red and one blue, which he could turn on with or without the whooping siren. As the group of youths visibly shrank with fear in his presence, at the same time making no effort to leave the scene, Mac had to force himself to suppress a smile. How he loved it when people showed stark fear of him! Such a rush of power could be equalled by no other feeling on earth—except for those increasingly rare instances when he was able to physically molest his arrestees. But "police brutality" charges were getting harder and harder to dodge, as the liberal pinko nannies continued to infest the highest echelons of our esteemed government more and more with every passing year.

Finally, when Mac could justify savoring their terror and holding back no longer, he spoke: "Get in." Unlike the cabbies, though, Mac allowed all twelve of the youths to pack themselves into the back seat of his cruiser. They will need to get used to that feeling anyway, he thought.

He drove, slowly at first, up the winding path toward the peak of the mountain; then faster along the horizontal road that curved around nearly at the very top, taking them around to the other side of the mountain. Below them the children—those who could see out the window—saw a sprinkling of pink and white dogwood blossoms among a canopy of treetops blending colors from Irish Kelly green to the deep sea green of the pine trees.

They enjoyed the view only briefly, though, as Mac began to speed up when the road turned downward on the other side of the mountain. Each leg of the descent was marked by a hairpin turn, as the Jeep tacked its way down the mountainside. Faster and faster they went, whiplashing into each other more and more violently at every hairpin turn. Their terror at Mac's seeming wrecklessness increased exponentially, and by the sixth or seventh turn they were screaming in concert at the top of their lungs. By the eleventh turn, judging by the speed of the vehicle and the precarious tilt as it went around the hairpin curve on two wheels, it appeared as though they would go right over the edge of the mountainside for sure. And sure enough, they did.

The Jeep went airborne straight out from the twelfth turn. The children were screaming in stark terror, their short lives flashing before them like video scrapbooks at a bar mitzvah. Mac chuckled with extreme glee. Momentarily the car thumped down onto what felt like a smooth ramp.

The kids were too paralyzed with shock to open their eyes and look at their surroundings immediately. But by the time the Jeep finally rolled to a stop, they were all staring in total disbelief. They completely forgot the death-defying ride they had just taken—for they simply could not believe what they now saw in front of them.

"Did you ever wonder about time and space, my boy?" Ross asked, waving his hand around at the sky. He didn't wait for Tommy to answer before going on. "The fact is ... they don't exist!" At this he laughed heartily. Tommy just listened. He opened another can of beer and sat back on his haunches.

"Did you ever wonder where things began ... where they end?" Ross looked intently at his grandson. "When was the beginning of time ... when will eternity end?"

Tommy wasn't sure what he was supposed to say, so he continued to look at his grandfather and listen. No answer was required.

"There are those who point out the similarities of the atoms and molecules of matter to the configuration of the solar system, the galaxies, the very universe itself. Yes?"

"I ... I guess so, Grampa. Go on."

The elder Ross plucked a blade of grass and held it in front of his wizened face. "Some say that the smallest piece of matter—even a blade of grass—is filled with vast 'solar systems' of atoms and molecules ... on which other beings, perhaps not unlike ourselves, might exist!" As he spoke, Ross had brought the blade of grass closer and closer to his face, until his tiny flint-colored eyes crossed.

"Okay," Tommy agreed. Time for another brew.

"And these metaphysical philosophers also draw the comparison of our own infinitely large universe—immeasurable billions and trillions of light years across—to an arrangement of atoms and molecules in some vastly huge blade of grass in yet another universe infinitely larger than our own!"

At this point, Ross was rotating his arm with the blade of grass high over his head, following it intently with his gaze.

"Uh-huh," Tommy said, stifling a belch, and reaching for yet another can of the rapidly diminishing supply of beer.

Ross returned his intense stare to Tommy: "It is endless, these universe-in-a-blade-of-grass theories! Endless and stupid! Don't you agree?"

"I'd like to hear your theory, Grampa," Tommy answered, half wondering what he would do if this actually began to make sense to him at some point.

"And the same mystery holds for *time*, my boy," Ross continued. "When did time begin? When will it end? How long is eternity?" He stopped and looked intently at Tommy again. Then he smiled, obviously savoring the moment as one would a delicious morsel of food.

"The answer is ... 'Time' itself is an illusion. So is 'space'. Neither exists in reality. Do you believe that?"

"I ... uh, I ... I don't know Grampa."

"I know you don't, son. So I'm going to *prove* it to you!" He chuckled merrily at the prospect. Tommy smiled. What else could he do.

"Prove ...?"

"Yes." Ross looked down for a minute and pursed his lips. Then he looked up and said, "Have you ever had a clairvoyant experience? Did you ever have a dream which predicted something that later actually happened? Ever have a sudden insight and know something that turned out to be accurate, but you didn't know where that knowledge came from? Have you ever read about anyone who did?"

"Well," Tommy answered, genuinely interested in how his grandfather intended to prove to him that time and space were illusions, "I never had such an experience ..." Tommy hesitated for a minute, as he had a sudden flashback to the morning that he had received the news that his father had died. He had awakened with such a terrible sense of foreboding that he could not eat. The moment the telephone rang, he was overwhelmed by the feeling that he would never see his father again.

He brushed the memory away, and went on, "... but I've read about such things from time to time. Some of them seem pretty convincing. Others are obviously hokey." Tommy thought for another minute, and said, "I remember reading *The Sleeping Prophet* by Edgar Cayce. He made quite a few predictions in the early 1900's that turned out to be accurate, didn't he?"

"Yes, very good!" said Ross, his head bobbing up and down, as he rubbed his palms together. He was several beers ahead of Tommy at this point, but showed no sign of slowing down at all.

"Good. So. If you accept the premise that *some* people *some*where are able to know the future—then the future is not in the future at all—*it is here, now!* The future dwells in the present! *The future and the present are one!*"

Ross stopped and stared at his grandson, to see what impression he had made. When Tommy blinked and nodded, he went on: "The future is running parallel with the present. Do you understand? It's like a narrow stream of warm water rapidly running through a larger, cooler, slower body of water." He looked at Tommy, and continued, "Like the Gulf Stream, a powerful, warm, and swift Atlantic ocean current—both traveling in the same area, in the same direction, at slightly different speeds. So," and here Ross shifted a little on the rocky ground, "if you were to start sailing on the ocean, and float along lazily, you would see the sky and the clouds and the seagulls. But if you dove down into the water, you would see a whole entirely different world. Seaweed waving, fish darting about. Things would take on a completely different look—seeming to move faster—or slower—as though you were somewhere else. But in fact, as you would see when you came back to the surface, you were in the very same place! That is why some people—people who are considered 'psychic'—are able to 'see' the future. Because it really is in the present. Do you see?"

"Hm-m-m. In a way, I do," said Tommy, resisting the urge to scratch his head. "Time as we think of it is an illusion, because the future and the present are really ... running at the same time ... in parallel?"

"Exactly!" shouted Ross. "And the past, too. It's all together!"

"And the past. All together."

"Right, right, my boy," Ross said, and clapped Tommy hard on the shoulder. That was when he realized he must be getting a buzz on, because he hardly felt the hefty clap. And because this time-and-space business was beginning to make some sense. He must be drunk.

Ross continued, "The illusion of space operates in the same way. It is an illusion that things go on to infinitely larger and larger universes, and infinitessimally smaller and smaller universes. And if Edgar Cayce is not credible enough to convince you of that, how about Albert Einstein?"

"Einstein is credible," Tommy concurred, now beginning to enjoy this little philosophical exercise with his grandfather. And that was scary. But the glow held fast.

"Good. Because Einstein proved that both space and time are illusions. You are familiar with his theory about time and the speed of light?"

"Yes," Tommy admitted. "He determined mathematically that as an object approaches the speed of light, time—the rate of decay—slows down."

"Yes, yes!" Ross was ecstatic with his grandson's accurate participation.

"So if a spaceship travelled faster than the speed of light," Tommy continued without further prompting, "then by the time it arrived back home to earth, the passengers would be younger than they should have been—they would have aged more slowly."

"Excellent. Most excellent." Ross opened yet another beer and downed it in record-breaking chug time. Still he showed no effects from the alcohol whatsoever. Tommy, on the other hand, felt his eyes crossing a little.

"Now," Ross went on, as he wiped his mouth on his shirtsleeve, "Do you know what Einstein said about the size and shape of the universe?"

Tommy knew that, too. He reached back into the recesses of his mind, fighting the thickening cobwebs of inebriation, and said, "I think he said that the universe, by his calculations, appeared to be 'round'?"

"Bowl-shaped!" corrected Ross. "Can you imagine? If the universe is 'bowl-shaped', what then lies *beyond* the bowl?"

Tommy rubbed his forehead, finally giving up trying to shake out any more information from his high school and college physics memories. "Cherries?"

His grandfather rose up on his knees, threw his head back and laughed so hard that he fell over backward. He laughed in great heaving chortles, and tears streamed down his face.

Suddenly he composed himself and went on as though he had not just dissolved in a puddle of laughter: "Now I ask you, my dear boy—if Einstein calculated that the universe is bowl-shaped; and time 'slows down' if you travel fast enough—is that not evidence that our whole concept of time and space as we think of them is an illusion?"

He stared at Tommy, who was now so caught up in this excursion that he decided to challenge his grandfather.

"Okay, Grampa. You've proven it to me. Time and space are only illusions. They are not real. They don't exist at all. I accept that. But can you explain how the illusion is pulled off? If time and space are illusions, then what is the *real reality of it all? What is behind the illusions?* Tommy sat back and crossed his arms over his chest, but his deteriorating sense of balance caused his backward motion to continue, and he had to uncross his arms to catch himself before falling over completely.

Tommy's grandfather was so enthusiastic at this grandson's challenge that he actually rubbed his hands together. "I'm so glad you asked that question!" He leaned forward so that his face was only inches from Tommy's. He spoke in a whisper.

"The answer is: It's all done with *mirrors*! MIRRORS! It's so simple, it's exquisite! Like Occam's Razor!" He looked at Tommy.

"I know, I know," said Tommy. "Occam's Razor was the theory that the simplest explanation is probably the correct explanation, right?"

"My boy! You make my heart swell with pride! Right you are!" Ross then picked up the last full can of beer, tapped it, and set it on the ground between them. Then he went on. "Now tell me—if you took two mirrors and placed one on each side of this can—what would you see?"

Tommy started to answer, when the reality of the truth of it began to sink in. You would see an infinite number of beer cans seeming to go off in an unending parade in both directions! A complete illusion! All done with mirrors! *Time and space ... all illusions with mirrors!*

Ross seemed to have read Tommy's mind, as he said, "It is right, eh, my boy?" An Illusion of Infinity! Time and space! Ah-ha-ha-ha," and he lifted the beer and cracked it open and took a sip, then held it up to Tommy. Tommy chugged it down in four swallows, a new Personal Best.

Then he stared at his grandfather. He was a true genius. And a raving manic psychotic. It was mind boggling. He could not stop from delving further into this mind of extremes.

"So," Tommy said, "Just—is there any purpose to this? WHY do these illusions exist? Answer me that!"

"Glad to," answered Ross, and he cleared his throat, "Stage props!"

"Stage ...?"

"STAGE PROPS!" Ross repeated. "These illusions are the stage props for the greatest play ever performed!"

Tommy was bereft of a response. Ross went on, louder now than before, "Actually, it's not so much a stage play as it is a GAMESHOW! Time and Space are the illusions which form the backdrop for a *grand eternal gameshow*!!"

Tommy felt a sudden sobering plop of fear in his gut. His grandfather was getting louder and louder, and Tommy wondered if he were falling off the edge of what sanity he had. And he didn't know how to stop him.

"You see, GOD was bored!" Ross stood up now, raising his arms over his head. "*Bored*! And *lonesome*! Who wouldn't be, with all of eternity out there and no one to share it with?!!"

"Uh-huh," Tommy said, nodding.

"And what stimulates the libido and gets the blood racing?" He didn't wait for Tommy to answer, he was unstoppable now—"Good old COMPETITION! Right?"

"Yeah, right," Tommy agreed.

"So God decided to beam off some of His own energy force, and make another One. A *Companion*! A *Competitor*! Do you see?"

Tommy nodded.

"And the Competitor was none other than Lucifer! Beelzebub! The Devil himself! And They agreed to *challenge* each other to see *who could win the most number of souls!* So They created *Man*, and They designed all of these illusions to fool us into thinking They weren't really there, and They gave us Free Will to do whatever we wanted, and—"

Tommy drew back at this point. He remembered from his short-lived medical career that when patients begin ranting about God and the Devil, it was Dial-A-Shrink time.

"*Grampa!*" he cut in. Ross stopped talking in mid-sentence and stared at his grandson. His face began to darken.

"Grampa, please! Let me take you back to the hospital. Please! Dr. Anna is worried about you, and ..."

Ross cut him off with a rising fury that changed the color of his skin to livid. He spat on the ground. "YOU! *You're one of them*! I should have known! Dr. Anna—that devil's handmaiden—you're in league with her! You're part of the CONSPIRACY!!"

Tommy tried to get up, but he was a little unsteady and totally unprepared for his grandfather who lunged at him. His grandfather was no physical match for Tommy under normal circumstances—but now he had the energy of mania coursing through his veins. Tommy could hardly resist as his grandfather pushed him little by little, farther and farther toward the edge of Billy's Bunion, and Tommy could see the twelve-hundred-foot drop down to the carpet of trees below. He fought with all the strength he could muster, but the beer had denervated him.

Closer and closer to the edge they fought, around and around, pushing and tugging, inching toward the very lip of the cliff, until his grandfather was able to give one final mammoth *shove*.

27/ DANCE MACABRE

Sydney recognized the final turn that led up the mountain road which covered the last twenty miles of the journey back to Tommy's grandparents' estate. Claudette had once again disappeared, and now Sydney shifted into low gear, as Wolfgang brought her steadily closer and closer to ... to ... to what she was not sure. She had no idea why she was going back up to Tommy's grandparents' place.

But finally, as the car ascended and moved around the last bend in the road, she could see the huge Victorian mansion looming up ahead. She started to drive toward the gravel driveway, but Claudette's voice rang out from behind her once more:

"Keep going straight! Up there!" and a pudgy white finger pointed over the seat back to a small footpath going off into the woods from the road.

Sydney pulled to a stop and got out. "Go!" shrieked the ample apparition, "Hurry! Tommy needs you!"

Sydney took off at a run into the footpath and the thick woods around it. She tripped on a high overgrown tree root and landed on both her forearms, scraping them on the dirt and rocks. After she got up, she limped on as quickly as she could, having badly stubbed her toe on the tree root. She continued through the woods, nearly running again when the path smoothed out; then slowing down cautiously when the path became obstructed. Soon she was panting hard from the steep, difficult climb, and she became acutely aware of not having eaten or drank anything all day. Her vision blurred momentarily, and she began to feel dizzy.

When Sydney saw a little brook down a few feet from the footpath, she wondered if it were a mirage. She detoured over to it and got down on her knees, scooping handfuls of the crystal clear water from where it washed over the smooth, water-polished rocks, and drank deeply. Evian never tasted so good.

Just as she began to feel her strength coming back, Claudette's shrill voice rang out and stabbed at her like a cattle prod, "Go, damn it! This isn't Starbucks! Now move that little ass of yours before we run out of time!"

Sydney scurried to her feet, her heart pounding from fright—she half expected to see Claudette's billowing shape floating above her like a huge cumulonimbus cloud—but Claudette was nowhere to be seen. Sydney began running again, refreshed from the water and spurred on by Claudette's admonishments.

After what seemed like an endless trudge up the mountain path, just when Sydney really and truly did not know whether she could go another step, she heard the scuffling and shouting. She could see the end of the path about twenty feet ahead, and ran up to the clearing.

There she was stunned by the sight of Tommy grappling with an old man—who seemed very strong indeed. Each had their hands on the other's shoulders, and they were struggling this way and that, in a bizarre polka that was leading them toward the very edge of the mountaintop. She ran toward them and yelled Tommy's name, but neither of them seemed to hear. Now the older man had Tommy backed right up to the edge of the cliff. Sydney was within ten feet of them when she saw the older man give one final horrendous push, and Tommy went over the edge of the cliff.

The older man got down on his knees—to look over the edge and watch Tommy fall the distance—and his features were distorted into a horrible grin. Sydney's hands went up to her ears as she tried to block out the torturous wailing shreiks. She did not realize that they were coming from herself as she pealed off one scream after another.

Finally she recognized, even in her shock and grief, that she, too, was in danger. She turned around and headed back for the footpath as fast as she could, and ran so hard into the man standing there that she knocked herself unconscious. He bent down and lifted her up. He wore the uniform of the Dallas Police Department, and when Sydney came to, he was standing in front of her. She was handcuffed to a pine tree.

28/ HOMING IN

Melva's concern was finally matched by her husband. They still had heard not one word from Lila or Sydney. It was Monday night, and the news reports on television were taking on the importance of a national emergency. Phil called the police. They told him to come down and fill out a missing person's report—but they cautioned him that the disappearance of their daughter Lila may well be linked to the disappearance of the hundreds of other young computer buffs from all over the country. And, no, there still was no confirmation of the tie-in between those disappearances and the burgeoning epidemic of CompuFlu.

By one o'clock the following morning—Melva had been up watching the news and crying, while Phil was down at the police station doing the paperwork—there were reports that the disappearing youngsters might have been headed toward Asheville, North Carolina. A second report about a half-hour later confirmed that the investigation definitely seemed to be centering around the Asheville area.

When Phil returned from the police department, he found Melva packing a suitcase. She informed him that she was taking the next Piedmont Airlines flight to Asheville. He protested at first—then realized it was useless. Nothing he said would deter her. They agreed that Phil would stay back and await any word that might come from the local police; and Melva would call him as soon as she arrived and learned anything at all.

Phil drove her to the Miami International Airport, and Melva waited seven hours until she finally got a flight to Asheville. After several stops, they finally set down in Asheville around noon on Tuesday. Melva had no idea where to go from there.

She called Phil. She told his receptionist that she didn't care if he *were* in the middle of a root canal, she should get him on the phone. Phil came to the phone and they talked the situation over for awhile. News reports were now suggesting that the activity in the investigation was centering around a place high up in the mountains called Jiminy Rock. Phil begged her not to go, while at the same time planning his patient's next injection placement. Eighteen years of marriage to Melva taught him, if nothing else, that she would do what she wanted. He would save his energy for the dental drilling.

On the television screen in the airport terminal, tuned to the local news station, WASH, videocameras scanned the little way station where the train engineer had discharged the twelve Hound-Bytes from Portland, Oregon; where the Greyhound bus had discharged Lila; and where numerous other missing youths had been deposited—the last time any of them had been seen. Teams of searchers were combing the woods around Jiminy Rock, and helicopters were overflying the surrounding mountainsides. They even filmed the Ross mansion, the only home within twenty miles of the way station. The news mentioned that no one was living in the mansion since the mistress of the estate had died about a month earlier.

Melva watched the news reports, and felt utterly helpless. She had no idea what to do now. Phil told her to go to the Asheville Police Station and wait there until further developments arose. She said she would. Then she hailed a taxicab, gave the driver two fifty-dollar bills, and said, "Take me to Jiminy Rock." She would tell Phil of this change in plans later.

Lila pressed her hands and her face against the little glass-enclosed cell and looked out. The glass in front of her was hexagonal in shape, and the glass sides of the cell conformed to fit the hexagonal shapes of the six cells which surrounded hers. It was very tiny—she could not have stood up in it, and she could reach both sides of the cell with her arms still bent at the elbows. She was seated on a round, cushioned, high-backed chair, as were the others she could see. Her knees just fit under a tiny desk, and a personal computer sat on top of it.

Lila didn't look at the computer, nor at the others all around her. She just sat with her face and hands pressed against the glass, tears steadily rolling down her face, and onto the glass, and down to the glass floor beneath her feet. Below that was another person in an identical cell.

29/ FORE!

Sheriff Hollister Trimble rubbed his hand along the side of his pockmarked face, as he listened to Caleb Peck's tale of the blue Volvo which had passed along an all-but-abandoned gravel road within spitting distance from his moonshine still. Peck was drawling on about how the Feds were gettin' too bold for anybody's good anymore, and whatever happened to the good-as-gold guarantee he had gotten, from Sheriff Trimble himself, after handing over five hundred bucks cash AND six jugs of his best Smoky Mountain White Lightnin', anyway? Peck went on to say that if he had had his shotgun handy right then, why, he woulda'...

"Now, don't you go doin' nothin' foolish, Peck," Sheriff Trimble cut him off. "I know fer a fact that the Feds are gonna leave you plum alone. 'Til the next installment's due, anyway, you know that."

"Then what was that thar blue furrin car doin' comin' up old Baker Road, eh?" Peck shot back.

The Sheriff straightened himself up. He was nearly six feet tall, but weighed only one hundred forty-seven pounds, and he tended to slump down badly, as too-thin folks are wont to do. He hiked up his jeans and then held his hands up in a gesture to calm Peck down.

"Now hold on there, Pecker," (only the sheriff and Peck's very closest drinking buddies were allowed to call him that to his face), "For one thing, the Feds don't drive around in no blue furrin cars. Yew ever see one in anything besides a brown Plymouth?"

Peck stared intently at the sheriff, and puckered his lips. "Yer right, boy," he said, after a minute. Then he ran his hand through his oiled down hair and began to get more agitated again. "Well, then who in tarnation was that who drove through yonder?"

"Dunno," Trimble answered, rubbing over his gullied face again, and slumping back into his normal stance. "But we gonna find out, that's for sure." He did not wish to share the little bit of information which he did have about the Volvo. He had heard the police radio transmission—to his deputy, Elijah Chester Alston, the sonovabitch—about the blue Volvo with the red-haired driver who had Failed To Stop For A Flashing Light and also Evaded Arrest, causing a State Trooper to be involved in a one-vehicle accident.

Well, Deputy Eli Alston was not going to win this little feather in his cap. Trimble was going after that Volvo himself. He tossed a black, greasy forelock back from his face and hiked up his jeans once more with vehemence, before getting back into his own brown Plymouth. He backed away from Peck and his still, and rolled north onto Baker Road.

Mac stepped aside as the Gray Man came over and stared intently into Sydney's face. She knew immediately who he was. His hair was thin and the color of wet cement. His rimless spectacles were similar to those in the photograph next to Tommy's grandmother's bed. And except for the deep criss-crossing lines and wrinkles and sallow complexion, the shape and planes of his face were identical to Tommy's. This was Thomson A. Ross, Sr. Tommy's grandfather. Claudette's widower. The man of her nightmares.

Sydney struggled momentarily with the handcuffs binding her to the tree, but of course it was useless. The policeman standing off to the side snickered at her helpless squirming, but the Gray Man looked sharply over at him and the snicker fell from his face. Mac McMulligan stood at attention smartly.

"Who are you?" Ross asked Sydney in a quiet—but not gentle—voice.

The horror of having watched Tommy pushed over the edge of the cliff came barreling back on her in a rush of grief, and Sydney began to gasp and draw in breaths in ragged hitches, trying not to start crying and screaming all over again.

"S-s-sydney," she finally managed, as the Gray Man continued to stare closely into her face, almost as though he expected to see into her brain with x-ray vision.

"What are you doing here, Sydney?" he asked, certain that he knew who sent her and what her mission was. *One of Dr. Anna's disciples, no doubt! Even if she does look rather wholesome. The key was lipstick! And, even though this woman was not wearing any lipstick, she was in cahoots with Dr. Anna. Had to be.*

"I don't suppose you know anything about computers?" he asked suddenly, not even waiting for her answer to his first question. He knew that answer.

Sydney was taken so off guard by the question that she stopped hitching and gasping, and stared back at him. Was this a trick question?

"Well, yes, as a matter of fact—I do!" she said, after a moment's hesitation. Then with more assurance, "I run a computer consultation business in Atlanta."

"Well! Is that right?" answered Ross, backing away from her face just a little. Then he asked her to describe the configuration and technological operation of a computer motherboard.

Sydney launched right into the description, and soon began to notice that the rings of light refraction within the Gray Man's thick spectacle lenses seemed to be ... moving! They were beginning to spin ... and ... take on different colors ... and ... Sydney snapped her eyes away from the Gray Man's face, realizing that he was somehow *hypnotizing* her! She finished her recitation on computer design while staring at the ground.

"Hm-m-m-m," Ross said, rubbing at his chin as she finished. Then he looked over at the policeman and said, "Let's take her to the ship."

Ship? Did he say ship?

The Gray Man quickly disappeared down a path into the woods, and Mac McMulligan came over and pulled a tiny key from a chain looped to his belt, and unlocked the handcuffs. Sydney rubbed her wrists and flexed her arms. As soon as Mac had replaced the key, he took her left upper arm in a crushing grip and started to walk briskly with her in the same direction the Gray Man had gone.

"C'mon, Red," he said, the snicker back on his face.

He shouldn't have said that. Sydney bared her teeth and said, "Don't you call me 'Red', Buster!" Then she made a fist with her free right hand and drew it back.

Mac nearly laughed out loud at such a pathetic attempt to throw a punch at him. As he raised up his left hand to clamp around her little fist, the arrogant snicker remained on his face.

Sydney never threw the punch. As Mac went to grab her raised fist, she kicked him in the knee hard enough to dislocate his kneecap. The surprise and pain were so acute that Mac let go of Sydney altogether and she fled in the opposite direction. Mac was on the ground wailing and writhing in pain.

Sydney flew down the footpath which had brought her up to Billy's Bunion. She ran, heedless of the branches groping for her eyes and the rocks and tree roots laying in wait for her toes. She ran, and she looked back only once, after she had run down the footpath at least fifty yards. She saw no one.

When she turned to look forward again, the Gray Man stood directly in her path.

Sydney stopped so short she fell to her knees. Then she started to cry. The Gray Man walked right up to her, passed her, and continued up the path she had just raced down. As he passed her, he quietly said, "Come."

Maybe he was a wraith like Claudette—or maybe he had magical powers that she didn't understand. But whatever he was, Sydney knew clearly that she could not escape from him. And her sorrow over Tommy was draining her resolve to try. Part of her longed to do a swan dive off that same cliff and join her would-be lover below. She got back up on her feet and followed the Gray Man, as instructed.

They made their way back to the clearing overlooking Billy's Bunion and continued on to another footpath leading in the other direction down the mountain. About a half-mile down, they came to a slightly wider path—just barely big enough to accommodate the jeep which had been parked and left there. They met Mac there, his face still contorted with pain from his dislocated kneecap. He had a rag wrapped around two tree branches, splinting the leg. He glared at Sydney with a ferocity that she refusd to acknowledge, and kept her own sight on the Gray Man's back. They got into the Jeep, and Mac whipped out his handcuffs again, this time snapping one cuff on Sydney's left wrist and the other on his own right one. The Gray Man drove.

It was hard to judge distances, but Sydney felt that they had travelled at least twenty miles—probably down to at or near the bottom of the mountain. They were now driving through another small rutted road through a forest in the valley between the mountains. When they stopped, Sydney became filled with terror. There was nothing but forest all around them. What could they be planning to do here except to kill her and leave her body in this isolated wooded valley? She could feel the tears beginning to well up in her eyes again, and then she thought of Tommy. Somehow that made it a little easier.

I won't cry, she thought. *I'll die like a woman.* Then she started to cry.

The Gray Man picked up a remote control device of some kind and aimed it at the dense woods in front of them. To Sydney's incredible surprise, the woods on each side seemed to slant away—and she realized that she had been staring at two gigantic mirrors, each reflecting the woods from the other side, and hiding what was really there.

A golf ball. A thirty- or forty-story tall building in the shape of a golf ball. It was perfectly round, probably a football field or more in diameter, and yellow-green in color. It had indentations, just the like the "dimples" on a golf ball, all over it, each indentation perhaps ten feet across. Then Sydney heard a heavy whirring noise, and a large square piece of the front of the golf ball—or whatever this thing was—began to open up. A ramp was coming down. It was wide enough for at least two or three vehicles abreast to drive through.

When the ramp came to rest on the ground, the Gray Man put the Jeep into gear again, and slowly drove inside the gargantuan golf ball.

30/ DEARLY DEPARTED

When Melva's taxi approached Jiminy Rock, she could already see a large crowd of people, police cars, and television news vans up ahead. She told the taxi driver to let her out right there—away from the crowd. She walked up slowly, keeping to the trees along the way, so that no one could see her. Why she did that, she could not say. She had no earthly idea what she was doing.

As she came up through the trees closer to the milling people, she could see the back of the Ross mansion. There was still no information of any connection between Ross and the arrival of the missing youngsters here in Jiminy Rock—but Melva felt intuitively that she should go into that house. A small gathering of law enforcement and other official-looking persons were talking near the back entrance as she stood under the cover of what were once used as stables. The group seemed to be preoccupied with their conversation and less so with watching the back door. Melva fished around in her pocketbook and found the I.D. badge she had been issued when she went for a parent-teacher conference at the high school (it was issued to all visitors right after they passed through the metal detector and the drug-sniffing dog). With badge clipped in place on her collar, she walked right up to the back door. She tried the doorknob. It clicked open.

No one was in the house, so Melva began to roam freely and quickly around. She went through the kitchen, the foyer, the living room and the library. Then she went to the second floor, already feeling foolish—what did she expect to find? Lila hiding under a bed? With little heart, she continued upward to the third floor, but half of her motivation was the fear of being caught snooping around once she finally came down again. How embarrassing that would be! The other half of her motivation was one of the strongest forces known to the human race—woman's intuition.

When Melva got up to the attic, the afternoon sun was shining directly into the two dormer windows on the western side of the roof, and so there was quite a bit of light in there. She threaded her way through all the long-forgotten belongings, exactly where Tommy had himself tread so recently. She looked at everything and wondered about the people who had lived there. She had no knowledge of the Ross family at all.

As she reached the far end of the attic, she turned around to go back the way she had come. Just then a mouse skittered across her shoe, and Melva screamed and flung herself backward—and fell through the door to Ross' computer lab. She got to her feet slowly, gaping at a room which looked to her like a scaled-down version of Command Central at Cape Kennedy's NASA Space Center.

Melva had only the most superficial knowledge of computers. She had refused to join the New Wave and learn what she could, even though her daughter, Lila, had developed a considerable expertise and had offered to teach her.

The main computer appeared to have been turned off, but she saw the red on/off switch on the side, and, without even knowing why, she threw it on. Immediately a list of names, in alphabetical order, blinked onto the screen. Melva sat down and read them. Some of them were familiar—she knew it! These were some of the missing kids who had been mentioned on all the television reports recently! She saw the little indicator arrow key on the keyboard, and pushed the "down" arrow. The list of names immediately began to move upward, new names rolling up from the bottom of the screen as the names at the top disappeared.

Her heart quickened as she reached the "J's" and then the "K's." Finally the "M's" rolled into view. Mabry, Shiela Karen; MacLaughlin, Garvin Robert; Maxwell, Lila Elaine ... LILA!!! *Oh, my God!* thought Melva, biting her lip and feeling tears stinging her eyes, *I've found her!* If only she knew what to do now!

Melva went on pure instinct and a little prayer. She moved the "up" indicator arrow until it rested directly over Lila's name. Then she pushed the "Enter" key. The screen went blank while Melva heard it beeping steadily. Then some words appeared on the screen:

```
Lila Elaine Maxwell, Age 16
Coral Gables Senior High School
Miami, Florida
Major: Mathematics
OGPA 3.9
```

Below that came some additional words:

```
EEG pattern
Thought Search
Transport
```

Transport? That sounded intriguing. Melva moved the indicator arrow directly on top of the word "Transport" and depressed the "Enter" key again. Again the screen went blank, more beeping signals were emitted, and then the screen lit up with two new headings:

Laboratory | Home Base

Melva moved the indicator over "Home Base" and depressed the enter key once more. The room went dark. A scintilla of lights spun around Melva and she became dizzy and light-headed. A mild, pleasant sucking sensation surrounded her. Was that a slight wind she felt at her back?

Momentarily she lost consciousness. When she came to, she was sitting squashed in, without an inch left over, on the round cushioned chair practically in Lila's lap in the little hexagonal glass cell.

Lila looked at her with shock and utter disbelief. *"Mom??!!!"*

"Lila!!!" Melva responded, and they hugged each other and cried.

Deputy Elijah Chester Alston just sat in his cruiser staring at the Volvo which had been so hastily abandoned by the side of the road that the driver's side door was left wide open and the car still buzzed the signal that the keys remained in the ignition. Even more bizarre was the fact that there were no keys in the ignition! No redhead in sight. And the Two Big Mysteries were: (1) There was nothing out here besides the Ross mansion, which the car had passed at least 100 yards back down the road; and (2) The Volvo was owned by Mrs. Claudette Ross who died recently, and it had been bequeathed to her grandson, Thomson the Third, who owned a gas station in Atlanta. If some (redheaded) person or persons stole the automobile from the Ross mansion, why would they drive it all the way back up here just to abandon it like this?

Just at that moment, something caught the massive deputy's scanning vision—the footpath. It was all but hidden by overgrown trees and branches. And there was at least one clear, heavy footprint as though from someone running. Fresh.

Eli ducked his head and stepped out of his cruiser, placing his mountie-style hat on his head as he rose to his full height of six feet eight and one-quarter inches. He passed the Volvo and walked over to the edge of the footpath and dropped down to one knee. Yep. He or she definitely headed up this path after his or her rapid exit from the Volvo.

But judging by the size of the print, it was a *she*. The dirt was freshly kicked aside and small plants recently trampled. Bent and broken stems, but still fresh. And, it seemed as though *several different-sized footprints* led off into the woods.

Why? What was up there, anyway? This footpath led to ... Billy's Bunion, maybe? Some people stole a car, went for a joyride, and then went on a sightseeing hike? Eli pushed the brim of his hat back and scratched his head. He should call for reinforcements to help search the area ... But it was still pretty light. He headed up the footpath.

The Jeep came to a stop just inside the golf ball structure, at the top of the ramp. The Gray Man turned around and pressed the remote control device once more. The ramp began to lift from the ground and close up the huge doorway behind them. Then he eased the Jeep into one of several slanted parking slots just to the left of the door.

Ross turned around and swung his arm over the back of the seat. He looked at Sydney and said, "Welcome to the *Ship of the New Millenium!*"

If the structure itself were not so vast and intimidating, Sydney would surely feel that this man was a madman. Instead, she just said, "You must be quite a golfer."

Ross threw his head back and laughed whole-heartedly. He was finding himself enjoying this little spitfire of a woman, and *wanting* to believe that she was *not* in the enemy's camp.

"Oh, no, my dear—I'm not that big on golf! Allow me to show you around. The 'golf ball' shape is merely the most aerodynamically economical structure that can be devised. That's why golf balls are designed that way! But in actuality, this is a ship. A *transport* ship."

A ship, thought Sydney. *A ship goes places.* She did not want to go anyplace in this ship. But she followed Mac as he slid out of the Jeep, half jerking her along by their mutual handcuff. They all stood in front of two massive doors, which seemed to partition off a small slice of the outermost edge of the ball-shaped structure which the ramp, now pulled completely up, closed in. Ross pushed a green button on a small control panel just to the side of the massive doors. They opened.

Sydney drew in her breath at the awesome sight before her. Hundreds and hundreds of glass honeycomb-like cells protruded up and down the inner walls of the huge structure. And each seemed to contain ... a person?!! Each person seemed to be seated at a little desk or table, and there barely seemed room for anything else beside the person and desk in each little glass cell. There were hundreds—perhaps a thousand or more—of these cells!

"This is the main control center," Ross was telling her, directing her attention to a circular control station at the center of the vast expanse of floor. The control center was filled with computers, lights, dials, switches, and video monitors on every spare surface. There were several chairs in the open space within the circle of controls, but no one was in there. Outside, however, stood at least ten sentries, all in various law enforcement and other types of uniforms. One wore green Army fatigues; another wore the uniform of the California Highway Patrol; another was a Brinks security guard; and another—Sydney wasn't sure, but it looked like—the uniform of a Salvation Army officer.

But Sydney looked past this motley crew and blinked several times before she could believe what she saw at the other end of the huge room. In what looked like a 17th-Century anachronism in the midst of this futuristic assembly, sitting on a bare wooden bench attached by the ankle to a heavy chain, elbows resting on his knees and staring at the floor ... was *Tommy! But I saw him fall off a twelve-hundred foot cliff!!* Sydney wondered if he were a hallucination, like Claudette. *Another ghost?*

Softly, almost too softly for the Gray Man to have heard, she said his name. *Tommy!* But he *did* hear her.

Ross stopped in mid-sentence, annoyed that Sydney was not paying attention to his Grand Tour spiel, when he recalled that Sydney had witnessed him flinging Tommy over the edge of the cliff back up on top of the mountain. She probably thought he had been killed!

"Yes, that's Tommy over there," he said, with a dismissive flip of his hand in Tommy's direction, "He's fine. I'll explain about him later. Now, over here we have ..."

But Sydney broke and started to run. However, as she was still handcuffed to Mac, she jerked him off his good leg and he fell onto his dislocated knee, and bellowed in pain, falling over on his face, and dragging Sydney down to her knees.

"Tommy!!" she yelled, and her voice echoed through the huge structure.

Tommy raised his head up from his hands. He stood up and stared at the little redhead on her knees across the whole expanse of the ship, attached to the bellowing beached whale in the Dallas Police uniform on the floor next to her.

"*Sydney!*"

31 / THE TEST

Ross looked down at Mac McMulligan, wailing and groping on the floor, over his destroyed knee. He was struggling pitifully to get back up, but Sydney was struggling equally hard to move farther in the direction toward Tommy, keeping Mac from regaining his balance. Ross felt annoyed, but he wasn't sure why. He did not know for certain if this young woman was or was not in league with Tommy—and Dr. Anna, and the others involved in The Conspiracy. Obviously she had been involved with Tommy in some way. Perhaps Tommy had pulled the wool over her eyes and she was really a *victim* of The Conspiracy, like himself. Ross had not even realized that his grandson was part of The Conspiracy until he started talking about Dr. Anna "worrying" about him, and wanting to take him back to the hospital, and all that.

As Ross watched Sydney's fervent efforts to move closer to Tommy, he found himself feeling ... a little ... jealous. But even *he* knew that was preposterous. Right now he could not be certain whether this feisty little redhead was friend or foe. She certainly knew her way around computers, having proven that with her in-depth expose of computer design back up on Billy's Bunion. Ross decided that he would bide his time. He would know soon enough if he must dispose of her ... or if he would be able to have her ... in some ... more *useful* capacity.

Finally, Ross could take no more of Mac's ear-shattering wails. The acoustics inside the ship made them deafening. He walked over to Mac and put both hands on his shoulders to get his attention. Mac sniveled down and became quiet. Sydney stopped trying to pull him toward the opposite side of the ship where Tommy was. Ross gestured toward Mac's pocket of keys, and Mac retrieved the handcuff key. He unlocked the handcuff from his own wrist and started to put the key away. Ross pointed to Sydney's wrist, and Mac, realizing that the old man intended to set her free, began to curse in protest.

"That little bitch broke my goddam knee!" he shouted, and he started to lunge for Sydney, still with the handcuffs dangling from her one wrist.

But Ross did not let go of Mac's shoulders. He locked his gaze onto Mac's own—and Sydney recalled with a shiver the hypnotizing quality of that stare. But soon Mac was being more than just hypnotized. He began to sweat freely, and his skin became pink, then rose-colored, then beet red. He said, "Stop ... STOP! PLEASE, Mr. Ross, ST-O-O—"

Mac's entreaties were cut off mid-sentence. Steam began to rise up out of his collar and spray from his ears, just like an angry cartoon character. His eyes widened and enlarged, and then steam began to come from around his eye sockets, and in a few seconds they burst open, clear bubbling fluid spilling out onto his cheeks and down his police jacket. Then his swollen red tongue burst out of his mouth, little steaming pink pieces flying in all directions. Finally, as the life went completely out of him, his bladder emptied itself and urine spread about his crotch. It, too, began to steam, and the pungent aroma of boiling ammonia filled the air. Mac's corpse fell forward onto its face, with hissing fluid spreading in a puddle on the floor all around him.

Ross picked up the handcuff key from the floor, testing it first to see how hot it was, and then unlocked Sydney's other cuff himself. Sydney was horrified by what she had just witnessed. She wanted to scream herself into oblivion, but decided it was wiser not to direct Mr. Ross' attention to herself. So she just stared at the grotesque boiled carcass and uttered not a sound.

Ross motioned to two of the sentries standing around the central control desk to come and dispose of Mac's remains. They went into one of a bank of doors which opened onto several cubicle-like offices at the far side of the ship, nearby to where Tommy was standing shackled to the bench. The sentries came out with a canvas stretcher, and lifted Mac's soggy body onto it. Then they carried him to the large doors through which Sydney, Ross and Mac had entered. Ross leaned over the control panel and pressed a green button. The doors opened and the pallbearers exited. He closed the doors behind them. On one of the monitor screens, the outer ramp of the sphereship could be seen lowering slowly to the ground outside. Then a view of the forest was broached by the two sentries carrying Mac's boiled remains. They continued through the woods and were soon out of view of the screen.

Ross stood back up from leaning over the console and looked at Sydney. "Are you all right, my dear?" he asked. Sydney was both gratified and appalled that he would address her like that ... this madman ... this sorcerer ... this ... whatever the heck he was.

"I've been better," she answered. Then she added, without sensing Ross' feelings of irritation at the question, "I want to talk to Tommy. May I?"

Ross hesitated for just a second before nodding his head once. He thought, *This will be the telling moment about this woman, one way or the other.*

Sydney walked slowly across the vast tiled expanse. She walked around the control center and the sentries, without taking her eyes off of Tommy. When she got to him she just stood there, staring up into his tired but still perfect face, his gold hair disheveled and dusty, and she wondered if this really was all a terrible dream and she would wake up and he would really be dead after all? Or a nightmare within a nightmare, and she would again awaken and they would be sitting together back in Atlanta, in a little sidewalk cafe drinking frapuccino?

When she was finally able to find her voice, she said, "Hi, Tommy. I thought you fell off a cliff."

"Actually, I did," he replied, nonchalantly. It was so wonderful to see her again ... But Tommy sensed danger in displaying any emotion or affection. He wasn't sure why, but he held back.

"And?" Sydney prodded, curious that Tommy was not volunteering more information, while at the same time overjoyed at being near him again, believing now that he was really here, alive ... how could it be? But she was thrilled that it seemed to be.

"And I don't know," he said simply. "I'm not sure what happened." Then he lowered his voice to a near-whisper and said, *"My grandfather seems taken with you."*

The elder Ross' feelings for Sydney were obvious. If it were not so obvious by the way Ross had responded when Mac McMulligan had cursed Sydney, then it was obvious by the way he stared after her—at her hair, her eyes, her figure. It was obvious by the shackle on Tommy's ankle and the absent one on Sydney's. It was obvious.

"That's crazy, Tommy," Sydney said, even as she became more aware of Ross staring at her from across the room. "Besides, I don't care ... I'm not going to ..."

Tommy cut in, "Please, Sydney!" Then more softly, *"Please ...* just be careful ... will you?" Tommy glanced at her lovely green eyes and China red hair. He wanted so much to touch it. *"He's dangerous."*

"Tell me about it," Sydney responded. She, too, held back, wanting to reach up and smooth Tommy's hair back, and pick the leaves off his shirt.

Ross stood and watched them. He was glad that they had not embraced. That was good. The woman would be his. Just one final test. He walked toward them, past the sentries and the control center, and stopped a few feet from them. Tommy and Sydney both looked at him, expressionless. Ross held out his hand to Sydney in a gesture for her to come to him. She took a deep breath, and then took a step in his direction. Ross reached out and took her hand and led her across the tiles to the bank of doors to the cubicles just to the side of where Tommy was sitting.

He pulled out a key ring of his own and opened the first door. It was a bedroom, sparingly outfitted with a double bed and a small chest of drawers. The bed looked somehow out of place there. One would have expected to see spartan bunks, tightly packed with perfectly squared-off sheets and thin, army-style woolen blankets tucked in so tautly that a quarter dropped on it would bounce back up into your hand. Instead, the little bed was covered with a powder blue, cotton-embroidered bedspread. It was familiar, too ... yes! It was exactly the same style as the bedspread in the second-floor bedroom of Tommy's grandmother's mansion! One would think she might have picked it out herself...

Ross didn't say anything, but he turned to face Sydney squarely and stared at her. She did not feel that he was trying to hypnotize her now. He wanted something else. Sydney turned and looked over the bedroom, slowly, and then back at Ross.

She held his gaze for a few seconds, and then said, "I'll sleep in here, Mr. Ross—*alone*." He nodded and closed the door. She had passed the test.

32 / THE DEMONSTRATION

Ross took Sydney by the arm out of the little bedroom and together they went to the control center. He lifted a slice of the desk top and they walked into the inner circle. Then he dropped it back into place behind them. Sydney stared at all the electronic equipment surrounding her. Ross sat down in one of the swivel chairs with rollers, and pulled up another for Sydney to sit in. She sat, and only then realized for the second time this day that she had not eaten one thing all day. She was achingly tired, and wondered how long Ross would keep her there. She wondered how long she could stay up.

"I know that you have a lot of questions," Ross began. "You may ask me now."

Sydney resisted the urge to ask when dinner would be served, and instead asked, "How did Tommy survive the fall from the cliff?"

Ross again shook off his irritation at her interest in Tommy, and focused on the pride he felt in his not-insignificant accomplishment. "Levitation, my dear! Simple levitation!" He rubbed his hands together.

Levitation? Sydney had just read something about that ... British and Dutch scientists had succeeded in creating a magnetic field a million times stronger than that of the earth. They were able to levitate a frog inside of a magnetized cylinder until it floated in the air! But a full-grown man ...?

"Franklin!" Ross beckoned to one of the sentries, and the man in the green army staff sargent's uniform turned around to face him and snapped to attention. "Be still now, I'm going to give a demonstration for my lady."

Franklin started to tremble in spite of his lengthy training to the contrary—after seeing the "demonstration" Ross had performed on Mac McMulligan, he was not exactly enthusiastic about being the star of one himself.

"Just relax, now, Franklin. You're a good soldier, man, and I need your cooperation now," Ross told him in a firm but soothing voice, and Franklin was visibly relieved in spite of remaining at rigid attention. Ross continued to stare at him and told him that he was *going to feel a floating sensation.*

Franklin did indeed feel something strange—the sudden weightlessness that one feels the minute one steps off of a high diving board. Franklin looked down and saw that his feet were no longer touching the floor, and his arms involuntarily went out to the sides to try and stabilize himself. He was nearly choking with the effort to restrain a scream.

Slowly, agonizingly (to Franklin), he continued upward and upward. The glass-encased honeycomb of cells lining all the walls of the ship stopped just below a curved window cap at the very top of the structure, and Franklin rose, still flailing his arms while trying to remain at "attention" to the very top. He reached up and touched the window over him, easily three hundred feet above the ground.

"Excellent, Franklin!" the Gray Man called to him, his voice reverberating throughout the entire sphereship, which was acoustically perfect. Franklin seemed to be smiling, but still holding onto the window cap sill as though that were somehow keeping him safe.

Then Ross leaned toward Sydney and spoke softly, just to her, "Now watch, my dear," and as he turned back to look up at his experimental subject, Franklin dropped abruptly and began plummeting towards the floor at accelerating speed. Everyone—all of the hundreds of people in the glass honeycomb cells, too—drew back in horror. The other sentries guarding the control center forgot their parade-rest stances, and gasped and backed away, watching in horror as Franklin dropped, screaming, toward a certain death.

After only a few seconds—when Franklin was perhaps forty or fifty feet above the floor—Ross began to stare more intently at him, knitting his brows together and gritting his teeth. And ... Franklin ... began ... slowing ... down. His deceleration was astounding! Slower and slower he fell, until he came to a complete stop, his feet dangling about four feet above the floor.

Ross turned to Sydney and said, "You see how easy that was? *I can transfer to you the very same capability!*" He looked back at Franklin, almost as an afterthought, still dangling in mid-air, and set his brow in one more intense stare. Franklin crashed the last few feet to the floor, as though a rope holding him had been shot through. He grunted and scrambled to his feet, looking all around himself as though he were not sure he were really whole. Then he noticed Ross still staring at him, and snapped to attention again.

"At ease, my good man! Well done!"

Franklin smiled a grateful and relieved smile, and shifted into parade rest stance.

Ross looked back at Sydney. He began to review how he had similarly "reverse-levitated" Tommy safely to the foot of the mountain after pushing him off. Relieved and satisfied, as well as reeling somewhat from the shock of the demonstration, Sydney was now overwhelmed with tiredness and hunger, and she felt faint.

"That was quite fascinating, Mr. Ross," she managed. "But I haven't eaten, and ... well, it's been such a long day ..."

Ross actually felt a stab of guilt that he had not thought to ask Sydney if she had eaten, nor tended to any of her needs. He took her gently by the arm—and Sydney was surprised at suddenly feeling the same sort of magnetic sensuality in his touch that she did when Tommy had first taken her arm and helped her out of the Volvo at his grandmother's mansion. She thought that seventy must not be as old and crotchety as she had previously believed. Ross led her back to the same little sleeping area she had seen before, pointed out a small bathroom and shower room, and a cabinet which he said contained food. Then he left. Sydney laid down on the bed and was instantly asleep.

Sydney did not know how long she had dozed, but she awoke to the sound of her stomach growling, and she decided to check out the food cabinet. It was a long pantry-like storage closet next to the door to the tiny bathroom and shower stall. Sydney opened it up.

It was stacked from top to bottom with silver foil packets about the size of a vending machine snack pack. Only there was nothing as appetizing as that inside! When she ripped open a packet, a few different-sized tubes fell out. One was labeled "beef", one "carrots", one "apples", and so forth. She saw nothing to drink, but there was a stack of small paper cups from which she could drink water from the faucet.

Sydney uncapped the "beef" tube and squeezed some out into her palm. (She did not know that they were intended to be squeezed directly into the mouth for minimum waste and maximum sanitary conditions!) It tasted very strong, and Sydney supposed it was concentrated, but she didn't know how much. She washed it down with a cup of water and felt an immediate full pressure in her stomach! The little tube actually contained a full three helpings of roast beef, when expanded with water! It was fortunate that she had eaten only a small amount before drinking the water!

Sydney put the remainder of the tube back in the packet, and went into the little bathroom to wash. No mirror—just as well! She was sure she must look like a space alien by now. She went back to the bed, first hesitating by the door to the room. Was it locked? Probably. But was it?

Tentatively she reached over to it. After all she had seen in the past two days, she didn't know what to expect. She touched the doorknob. She wrapped her fingers around it and gave the slightest turning pressure. It was locked. She was locked in. She was sorry she checked. She went back to bed and flopped face down onto it. Within seconds she was deeply asleep once more.

Tommy sat and watched as the elder Ross came out of the room where he had deposited Sydney and went back to his control center. Tommy was fascinated by, as well as fearful of, his grandfather. He knew that he was a paranoid madman, and yet somehow he had managed to develop some kind of supernormal or paranormal capabilities. He built this entire structure ... this "transport ship"... somehow. And Tommy had had no idea how he had survived the twelve-hundred-foot fall from the mountaintop until the demonstration his grandfather had just performed. Tommy thought he had probably passed out along the way, and perhaps had landed on some soft brush. Now he knew. But he needed to know more.

Obviously it had been a terrible mistake to have mentioned Dr. Anna to his grandfather, and to have suggested that he go back to the hospital. Now the elder Ross was convinced that Tommy was part of his delusional "conspiracy." And although it was obvious that his grandfather was taken with Sydney, he felt that one wrong move—one mistaken word from her—and she would be in terrible danger. Tommy was certain that he was alive now only because he was the grandson that Ross had loved in absentia for all these years. But—he felt that it would not take very much to convince his grandfather that he, too, should be disposed of. Look how quickly the old man had turned on McMulligan, whom he had trusted and put in charge of all the others!

Tommy looked at the shackle around his ankle. He wondered if he could loosen it, little by little. He wondered how much time he would have to try. He watched his grandfather at the control panel. The man never slept! Tommy laid down on the bench and, uncomfortable though it was, soon fell asleep from total exhaustion, as had Sydney, in the room not twenty feet away from him.

33/ THE VISITOR

Sydney did not know what time it was when she was awakened by the soft, almost imperceptible click of the doorknob turning. In fact, it was about one o'clock on Tuesday morning—just about the time when Melva had still been at home in Miami, frantically watching news reports about the missing children, and making plans to get a flight to Asheville.

Sydney did not get up but lifted her head and stared just to the side of the doorknob. In the darkness it was slightly easier to see an object when not focusing directly on it. Yes, it was definitely turning. She closed her eyes and dropped her head back down on the pillow—not sure she wanted to confront whoever or whatever was rattling her cage. Too late, she thought of dashing into the little bathroom—perhaps she could have locked or barricaded herself in there somehow.

The tall slender man came into the bedroom slowly and stared in Sydney's direction for a minute before turning and gently, quietly, closing the door behind him. He locked it with a key which he dropped into his pocket. When he got to the side of the bed, he just stood there. Sydney's heart was pounding so hard and so fast that she was sure he could hear it himself. She felt that it was the Gray Man standing there, but would not risk opening her eyes to find out. Perhaps if she continued feigning sleep, he would leave. Perhaps ...

"Sssssssydney," he said, in a hissing whisper, still standing next to the bed. She opened her eyes. It was Ross. He sat down next to her and took her hands in his. His hands were hot, hot and dry, as though he had been holding hot stones. "Sssssssydney, I want you to be my Queen, my glorious, red-haired Queen ... Would you like that?"

She didn't answer. She couldn't. She swallowed and could feel her heart in the way. As she squirmed, his grip on her hands became tighter, and she felt the bones in her hands crowding against each other.

"Will you be my Queen, will you, Ssssydney?" he asked again, and his face came down to hers and she could feel the heat radiating from him, and his skin was so hot she thought he would burn her. And he kissed her and it was scalding, and his face felt like scales, and Sydney tried to scream, but his kiss was smothering and burning.

Sydney twisted her face away from him and the Gray Man sat back and glared his intense, frightening glare, the same one she had seen in her nightmares, and then flames licked up behind the pupils of his eyes and began to shoot forward toward her. And suddenly she heard crackling sounds, and smelled a dense, acrid smokey odor, and her own hair was on fire, and she screamed, but still the Gray Man held her, glaring, watching as the fire caught on her clothing. One scream rang louder than the next, and the next was louder still until her ears hurt from the reverberation of her own screaming.

The screams faded as Sydney sat up with a jolt, fully awakened, shaking and sweating, and no one was there, and there was no fire. She broke into heaving sobs, and fell back down on the bed. She lay there for an hour before her heartbeat was back to normal, and her mind had stopped replaying the terrible nightmare. The she got up and went into the tiny bathroom and curled up on the little floor space, barricading the door tightly closed with her own body. And she slept.

When Sydney awoke again, there was light coming in from somewhere, and she realized that there was a tiny window at the very top of the bathroom wall above the shower stall, which was at the very back of the entire structure. The window was less than one foot square, and Sydney wished she had something to stand on and look out.

She got up and tried to stretch the kinks out from the ungainly position in which she had slept. She wondered if anyone *had* tried to enter her room last night? She ignored the thought, however, and decided to step into the shower. It was heavenly to feel the cool water rinsing the dust and dirt and nightmares away from her, but it cut off after only one minute!

Sydney pulled her grungy jeans and sweatshirt back on—but when she walked out of the bathroom, she saw a dress laid out on the bed. It was made of a filmy material, light blue, with a gold string belt. That madman did come in! But now she just felt angry more than fearful. Sydney resisted the impulse to ball it up and throw it into the commode! She headed for the pantry.

Now she noticed that the foil packages were all labeled on the back with their contents. She found one that said, "Eggs, Cereal/Milk, Oranges, Bananas," and ripped it open. She remembered to eat just a little of the paste and drink some water after it. Again she found herself full after just a mouthful of each paste.

There was a knock at the door. It startled Sydney into dropping the packet, and she was busily picking up the different tubes, and trying to decide how to answer the knock. Obviously, Ross had come into her room and left the dress for her while she was sleeping. And the chilling memory of that awful nightmare she had had still gagged her.

The door opened and Tommy stuck his head in. "Sydney?"

She nearly lost it. Was this another dream? She started to run to him, but he lifted his hand in a gesture which was meant to hold her off. Tommy looked over at the dress on the bed. He did not come further into the room.

"Tommy!" Sydney half-whispered, half-cried. "Are you okay? Are you free now? What's ..."

"It's okay, Sydney. I spent a long time talking with my grandfather last night. I think he trusts me now. I'm not sure, though. But he unlocked that ankle bracelet." Then, moving a little further into the room, he asked, "Are you all right?"

Sydney did not think she would ever forget the horrendous dream she had the night before, and how she slept curled up on the floor of the bathroom with her back against the door.

"Never better!" she said, with a huge smile. Tommy smiled back, and Sydney could feel the tears pushing to get out. But she wouldn't let them. Who knows how long she would be with him, and why spoil it with blubbering?

Tommy nodded toward the dress on the bed. "Are you going to put it on?"

"No," she answered, now feeling the anger rising again.

"Are you sure?" Tommy raised his eyebrows, "It might make him ... feel ... more sure about you, Sydney... less paranoid ...?"

"That's his problem," Sydney answered. "Besides, blue is not my color. Now, move, please. I'm going out to talk to your grandfather."

Ross had been watching them from the work station where he had been sitting and working all night. He had not so much as dozed for more than a few minutes. He had spent several hours talking with his grandson. He had tried to wheedle more information about Dr. Anna, and whatever "plans" she had to re-hospitalize him. And maybe because he loved his grandson so very much—even in his highly paranoid, and manic state—he wanted very much to believe that Tommy was not really in league with Dr. Anna.

After all, it was Tommy's baby photograph back in his room at Broughton Hospital which kept him going all these past terrible years at the institution. When the racing thoughts and sleepless nights brought him to the brink of total exhaustion—then plunged him into the depths of hellish despair—it was Tommy's picture that he clasped in his hands and slept with beneath his pillow that kept the thoughts of suicide from winning his soul for all eternity.

So it was not all that difficult for him to change his mind and decide that Dr. Anna had duped his grandson. He released Tommy from the ankle iron and let him sleep in one of the sentries' empty quarters.

When Sydney walked out of her bedroom, Ross was visibly annoyed to see her wearing her own clothes. But she walked right up to the control center and motioned for one of the sentries to open the entranceway for her. Tommy walked with her, concerned, but hoping she knew what she was doing and wouldn't act too impulsively. When she got inside the inner circle, she stood there, not going any farther, not making any move to sit down.

"You did not like the dress?" Ross asked, an accusatory edge to his voice.

Sydney ignored the question, but countered in the most authoritative voice she could muster, "What right did you have to enter my bedroom while I was sleeping?"

Tommy's stomach crushed in on itself as he wondered why Sydney would provoke a madman like this. *Was she crazy?*

But Ross became suddenly contrite—he almost stammered in his haste to apologize to Sydney, and said he would never do that again! Tommy was flabbergasted!

"I accept your apology," Sydney replied, her chin jutting up in stately defiance. Then she pulled up a chair to within a few feet of Ross and sat down. Ross waved for Tommy to do the same.

"Now you may explain all of this to us," Sydney said, matter-of-factly, waving her hand around in a sweeping motion.

"Yes, of course," Ross answered, still maintaining his more contrite posture. "I certainly shall."

Sheriff Hollister Trimble ducked his head as he sprinted under the whirling rotors of The Bird. The helicopter was the crowning glory of his reign over Alston County. After years of painstaking political connection-weaving, he succeeded in appropriating the funds he needed from the county commissioners for the chopper, and he felt not a pang of guilt that the money was lopped off the public school budget.

The Bird swooped upward at an angle and the ground fell away beneath it, the distance soon making his Plymouth look like a Micro Machine. Soon the trees and shrubs lost their outlines and melded into a lush green carpet below The Bird. They hovered for a minute and then

Sheriff Trimble pointed due north. The pilot tilted the steering wheel and The Bird followed obediently.

They whirred through the air for nearly half an hour before reaching the road where the blue Volvo was originally sighted. They followed a path up the mountain range, and past Peck's moonshine still. From this vantage point, it soon became apparent to Trimble that the Volvo had been headed toward Jiminy Rock. The Bird turned and gracefully headed in that direction. At the very topmost point of Jiminy Rock was the Ross mansion. Even from miles away, Trimble could see the masses of police cars and yellow cordons that had been put up, as the investigation of the missing children centered there. Just beyond the ridge of the road leading up to the mansion, Trimble spotted the blue Volvo itself. Behind it was the patrol car of Deputy Eli. But the massive deputy was nowhere to be seen.

The Bird hovered in the area for a few seconds. Fuel was getting low—he should have gone back, but was too eager to take a look. Now Trimble needed to go on because he would be dipped and fried if he would allow Eli to solve the mystery of the blue Volvo before he did. The Bird glided over the trees and swooped around on an arc which took them directly to the other side of the mountain.

34/ NEW WORLD MILLENNIUM

Ross began his lecture directed at Tommy: "The human body is quite remarkable, you know." He turned to Sydney, "And you are familiar with the exciting capabilities of manufactured computers." She nodded.

"Well, the human brain is infinitely more complex than any computer imaginable," Ross went on, and seemed to relax as he talked about that which he knew possibly better than any other human on earth. "You may have heard it said that throughout our lifetime we do not use more than one-tenth of our brain's capacity?" He looked back and forth at Sydney and Tommy. They nodded in unison.

"Well, that's not true! We use perhaps one-hundredth of our brain! Perhaps only one-thousandth of our true brain capacity!" He smiled and then looked around.

"This entire structure was built on brainwaves!"

Now Sydney spoke up, "This structure? How could it possibly...?"

"But it's here, isn't it?" he answered, bushy gray eyebrows raised into arcs. "It's here, and I did it, didn't I?!"

"But ... how ...?"

"You have heard of telekinesis?" he asked.

"Yeah," Tommy answered, still not as comfortable with his grandfather as Sydney seemed to be, "Like that guy who can bend spoons with his mind?"

"Right! But that really is mere child's play, y'know. Do you think"—and here Ross paused for emphasis, staring first at his grandson and then Sydney—"that if people had the power to *move objects* with their minds, they should spend their time bending spoons?" He laughed with a short snort.

"No ... THIS," he went on, waving his hand in a large circle overhead, "THIS is what you can do when you have honed *telekinesis* to its most extreme capability!"

"And ..." Sydney began, tentatively, then plunged ahead, "what about that policeman? What did you do to him?"

"Oh, McMulligan," Ross answered, "*Pyrokinesis*! Another useful skill which man has failed to train his brain to do, but sits there with so much unused potential!" He rubbed his chin, and went on, "The mind can move matter. Heat matter! Bend it! Lift it! The mind is nearly limitless in what it is capable of! It can be trained to do so much!"

Sydney & Tommy were silent. They were both recalling the horrifying sight of Mac McMulligan sizzling on the floor yesterday; and the demonstration of levitation with Franklin flying through the air with the greatest of unease.

Sydney then asked the questions whose answer she wanted and dreaded the most, for reasons she did not quite understand: "Who ... are ... all these people?"

Ross' gaze followed Sydney's open hand upward. He looked around at the hundreds of glass cells, the honeycomb covering nearly all the inner wall space of the entire structure. Row upon row of transparent hexagonal cocoons up to the window cap at the very top of the structure.

"These people will make up the population of the New World in this New Millennium," Ross answered. "I gave these young people special powers. And now they will help me start a new world."

"*New world?*" repeated Sydney. And she felt sick with fear.

"Yes!" Ross answered, and then his face darkened and began to contort ... he looked more manic ... more paranoid ... "The world is self-destructing, you know." He seemed almost to be talking to himself now.

"The world will not survive in its present state. War, AIDS, drugs, promiscuity, godlessness, godlessness, everywhere ..." he trailed off, and neither Tommy nor Sydney could say a word, they were so frozen with fear of this man.

"WE MUST START OVER!" he said, banging his fist down on the desk, pencils and paper clips jumping, "Just like Sodom and Gomorrah, and the great flood after it rained for forty days and forty nights! THIS IS NOAH'S NEW ARK!!"

Ross relaxed as suddenly as he had accelerated. His face calmed to a more natural appearance, and he sat back in his chair.

"I wanted young people, of course—young, BRIGHT people. So I directed my efforts at designing a computer program—a 'virus' really—which would provide a link between myself and such people. I invented *'StarWarGasm'*," and he stopped to chuckle at his own cleverness.

"The name, of course, would appeal to the very prurient interest which is destroying these same young people today. But these youngsters in particular are all still young enough and untainted enough to be salvaged.

"The program was so simple, so exquisitely simple," he went on—and now Sydney thought Ross would laugh out loud, but his face straightened up again, and he continued. "It is not a *game* at all, but a series of electronic emissions which, when entered into another computer, will DIRECTLY AFFECT THE USER!"

"Affect ... the *user*?" Sydney ventured, fearful yet fascinated by this madman's diatribe. Could he possibly be accurate about all of this? The implications were staggering...

"That's right, my dear," he answered, "It is no more complicated than a cellular telephone! You can call someone halfway around the world, just by pressing a few buttons! No wires, no visible connection! By the same technique—well, almost—I used a series of electronic emissions, and programmed them into the StarWarGasm game. And just as the correct code punched into a phone miles away will stimulate your cell phone to ring, so the electronic emissions from the game will stimulate the pineal gland of the user!"

Now it was Tommy's turn to be curious. "The pineal gland?" He knew that this was a vestigial organ—a useless item in the body, like the appendix on the intestines. It may have served some function in primeval man, but no longer.

"That's right, my boy!" Ross answered. "Scientists consider it merely myth or legend that the pineal gland is not a vestigial organ at all, which you were probably taught in medical school. But—it is also known as the 'pineal *eye*'! And others call it the '*third eye*' and believe that it is the *seat of psychic ability* in the human brain! And guess what? *They're right*!!"

A shiver went simultaneously through Sydney and Tommy. Ross went on: "By designing the program properly, anyone who went through the instructions of the 'StarWarGasm' game would have had their pineal eye electronically stimulated, and would discover, sooner or later, that they could move objects by telekinesis—or burn them by pyrokinesis—just by thinking about it!!"

Ross was waving his hand around as he spoke—gesturing again at the crystalline prisons and the myriad of inmates that inhabited them.

"All of these people??" Sydney looked up and around, really trying to see the faces of the people within the glass honeycomb. But they were too far away.

"That's right! They all experienced the ability to perform telekinesis or pyrokinesis, as well as reading each other's thoughts without speaking—mental telepathy—and many more phenomena which are mistakenly referred to as 'paranormal' by people whom I consider to be 'para-scientists'! Hah!! *What do they know?*" And here

Ross threw back his head and laughed—the same terrifying laugh that Sydney heard so many times in her nightmares. Ross trained his gaze back on Tommy and Sydney, and continued his explanation about the people in the glass honeycombs.

"Once they tapped into my game, and their pineal 'eye' came to life, they became both transmitters and receivers. Then I was able to reach them through mental domination ..."

"'Mental domination'?" Sydney broke in. She had heard nothing so sinister as that in all her life.

"That's right! It is a highly-evolved power on the order of telekinesis. One can make *objects move* at will ... and one can make *people conform to their will!*"

Sydney felt as though an iceberg were sliding down her spine. Her stomach tightened, and she closed her eyes. She felt that Tommy felt the same thing. The same iceberg, in the same forbidding sea.

Ross seemed oblivious to their sense of fear and despair. He continued lecturing and gesturing as though they were in a college classroom on a sunny spring day, and his students were enthusiastically hanging on his every word, and then they would all go to Einstein Brothers after class and sit outside at the plastic tables and continue listening to their fascinating professor and muching humus bagels.

"...unlike ordinary hypnotism—wherein one can only *suggest* things to one's subject, and the subject may not comply if the suggestion is contrary to his moral values—*mental domination is unfettered by the subject's will or mores*! He *will* carry out your commands regardless of his personal values!"

Ross stopped and looked back and forth at his "students"—and, satisfied that they were enthralled, he continued. "And so I commanded all of these youngsters to come here and join me!"

"C-commanded?" Sydney managed to ask, in a near whisper. "You mean they are all here against ... their ... will??"

Ross hesitated for only a second before answering. "Yes and no. They *will want* to be here. Eventually. In time." Ross seemed to want to say more, but he stopped. *Sydney and Tommy would see—that he was a true Savior—that he had saved these children by bringing them here—and he would save his grandson and this lovely young woman, too. They would see. He, Thomas A. Ross, Sr., is the Messiah.*

"And do they still possess these telekinetic and pyrokinetic powers even now?" Tommy asked—hoping that would alleviate some of their fears about the helplessness of these imprisoned youngsters. If they had those powers, they could, perhaps, come and go, if they so chose ...

"Oh, no, not within the hexcells," Ross answered. He thought of the cells as in biology, "individual organism units," but failed to see the other definition of cells as "prison units." Nor did he notice the suggestion of "black magic" which the word "hex" conjured up.

"No, they are blocked by a strong electronic force-field which runs through and around each hexcell, and interferes with any mental transmission they might try to emit."

"How ... how do they get out? How do they get to exercise? What do they eat?" Sydney asked, one question stumbling over the next.

"Well, actually ..." Ross responded somewhat hesitantly—he knew the answers would be upsetting—"they don't! *They don't need to eat!* Energy is transmitted to their bodies' cells electronically! Glucose is merely a storable form of energy. In these youngsters, energy is stored in its pure form! And they do not need exercise, either! *They are exercising their brains!* They have their computers in front of them, and when I give the instructions, we shall all make mental and electronic communications with each other. They will help me to bring us all into the New World Millennium!!"

Ross smiled brightly, but Tommy and Sydney were in shock. They could not answer.

"We shall use our combined telekinetic powers, and ..."

"*But when will they ever get out of there??!!*" Sydney interrupted, now verging on panic.

Ross stared darkly at her, then said, slowly and deliberately, "When the time comes for them to come down, there is a spiral ramp which winds down around the entire sphereship, just inside the outer shell. It runs behind every hexcell. When the force field is turned off, they can leave the cell by the rear, and simply walk down the ramp. *When the time comes.*"

Then Ross brightened and finished his lecture: "As I was saying, with our combined mental and electronic ability, we shall be able to transport ourselves, within the sphereship, to a new time. This will be a time beyond the Great Destruction, and we shall call it the New World Millennium, and I shall be ..."

Sydney could not help herself. Again she interrupted. "*'The Great Destruction'?* What is ..."

"Yes, that's right." Ross was trying not to be irritated. After all, she was ignorant of this and needed to be instructed. At least his grandson knew how to be quiet and listen. Men were superior in that regard.

"You see, after we are all safely transported away from the earth, then I shall enable the subjects to reinstate their pyrokinetic powers. My subjects—through my mental domination, if they are not ready to listen to reason voluntarily—and myself, shall then emit enough mental 'firepower' to annihilate all of the remaining populations of the earth. Then we shall return to the earth to start a fresh new civilization. But of course, not until the earth has had time to re-stabilize its eco-systems."

Ross looked at Sydney and quickly held up his forefinger, showing her that he anticipated her next question before she could ask. "How long will that take, right?"

Sydney nodded, and Ross went on, "The earth will restabilize relatively quickly—less than a hundred years, to be sure—and new growth, new trees, clear rivers and streams, new flora and fauna, all pure and new, will return. Then we shall return to begin the New Millennium!"

"A hundred ... years?"

"Well, probably less—not to worry!" Ross chuckled here. He so enjoyed his own sense of humor. "We shall take the sphereship out by spinning at Pho-ten," he said, raising his forefinger toward Sydney again. "That's ten times the speed of light. That's just under two million miles per second. Okay?"

Sydney nodded, even though she could not imagine what could possibly be okay about it.

"When we return to earth, after travelling at that speed," he continued, "one hundred years will have passed down there—but we in the sphereship will have *aged only a few years!* Perhaps less than ten years!" Ross sat back and clasped his hands behind his head. "Not bad, eh?"

Sydney's thoughts had drifted back to Lila. Her young niece was up here! She was imprisoned somewhere in one of the hexcells. That's what led Sydney here in the first place. Her heart was aching. She would gladly give herself to this madman's plan if only he would let Lila go home. But would such a suggestion enrage him? She had to think.

"...And there will be no disease in the New Millenium World, either!" Ross went on. He gestured grandly with both hands as he espoused his vision. "I have taken care of that, too!"

"No disease?" Tommy asked.

"That's right, my dear and glorious physician grandson! No work for you! Ah, ha, ha, ha!" He wiped a tear from his eye, and then became intense again: "No disease! I have tapped into the electronic 'secrets' of the thymus gland, as well as the pineal gland!"

Tommy knew about the thymus gland, too. The human body's immune system, which forms white blood cells and the capability of fighting disease, develops in embryonic stages from the thymus gland. Later, the thymus gland shrivels into a relatively useless organ.

"So," Ross continued, "I devised a second program—'Virus 2.0'—to test the possibility of manipulating the immune system in another generally healthy subject population. *Small business owners*."

Sydney did not think she could get sicker than she already felt at the realization that Lila was being held prisoner in a little glass cage not big enough to stand up in, until she heard Ross mention *small business owners*. And *disease*. George Humphreys! The *CompuFlu!*

"Under the title 'Organize Your Small Business' I designed a program which would electronically trigger the thymus gland of the user to be re-stimulated. The body would then behave as though a foreign body—or a disease organism—had entered the bloodstream, and had to be fought off. Only there was no foreign body! So the body's immune system would just start fighting itself! Eventually it could overwhelm the organism completely..."

"You mean ... k-kill ... *anyone who used the program?*"

"Wel-l-l, not necessarily," Ross answered, entirely detached from the emotional aspects of killing someone for merely using a computer. "It would make them sick. But the more times they ran the program, the sicker they would get. If they ran it enough times—yes, it would probably kill them." Then he brightened up and added, "Of course, in the New Millennium, this process would be used to *rid people of all disease!* That's the beauty of it!"

Sydney was fighting faintness now. Her stomach was trying to give the paste breakfast back up, and she began breathing slowly, deeply, trying to keep the rising nausea from taking over. She wondered how George Humphreys was? Was he still alive? She was grateful that she had only run the program once herself—and yet even that was not comforting, as she felt a certain "survivor guilt" about it.

Then she thought of Lila again, and this time she didn't think she could stop from gagging. She saw spots before her eyes, and her field of vision darkened, then lightened, then darkened again. She fell sideways off the chair, into Tommy's arms, as he came off his chair just in time to break her fall.

He lifted her and stood there, knowing that his grandfather would be jealous, insane and jealous. But he held Sydney tightly and walked over to the control station entryway. A sentry looked at Ross, who squinted his eyes and frowned—but then nodded, and the sentry opened the desk entryway for Tommy to pass. Tommy headed for the rooms at the back of the sphereship; and his grandfather glared at his retreating back.

35/ FAMILY HISTORY

When Sydney opened her eyes again, she thought she knew how Sleeping Beauty must have felt. Tommy was sitting at the foot of the bed watching her.

"Doctor, oh, Doctor," she said, propping herself up on one arm, "I seem to have a problem. Can you help me?"

"Well, I don't know," Tommy said, moving around to the side of the bed next to her. "What seems to be the matter?"

"I keep losing consciousness. Is that normal?"

"Uh, perhaps," Tommy answered, stroking an invisible beard. "Have you, by any chance, been under any ... unusual ... stress lately? Hmmm?"

"Stress?" she repeated, rolling her eyes upward and pursing her lips. "Why, no, I don't think so. Nothing unusual, I would say." They both managed half-hearted smiles, but no real mirth. The situation was too dire, and they both knew it.

Tommy reached over toward Sydney and pushed back a curly red lock of her hair which had fallen onto her forehead. Sydney knew—they both knew—of the danger surrounding them, but she could not help herself. She sat up and pressed against Tommy and hugged him tightly. Then she tilted her chin up and moved to kiss him—but he leaned back, and then he took her arms and gently pushed them from him. "Sydney, we can't ... this is not the time ..."

"Why not?" Sydney looked up at him with her beautiful green eyes, and he wanted her so much. "When, Tommy? Who knows how much longer we'll be here? Or if we'll even survive and get back home again?"

She started to slip her arms back around him, but again he stopped her. "Sydney, I hope—I plan—that we'll survive this. *Together.* Right now, though—this is all so bizarre—and I don't want to do anything—with you—that you might regret later on, understand? I don't want to take advantage of you ..."

"Tommy! Please! I'm not exactly a child, you know—don't you think I have a brain?" She slipped her arms free of his grip and held his hands in hers. "I should have a choice in this, too, right?"

Tommy smiled, but shook his head from side to side. "No, Sydney. We'll wait. Then, when this is all over, if you still feel the same way, nothing will stop us!"

Sydney pulled back and dropped her head. "Okay, then—if that's the way it has to be."

Then she looked up at him once more.

"Tommy?"

"What?"

"Would it be all right ... Would it be asking too much ..." Sydney dropped her eyes down once more, not really wanting to lay her ego on the chopping block again, but unable to stop herself. "Would you just kiss me? Just one kiss?" And she tilted her head up. Tommy leaned down and lightly brushed her lips with his. And then he pressed against her more intently. And they kissed again. And so it went.

Ross watched it all on a video monitor in the control center. He was enraged ... and yet sorrowful at the same time. Enraged because these two betrayed him after all, and that meant that they would have to die. Sorrowful because, as he watched them feverishly, desperately making love, he knew that this kind of youthful, volcanic passion was something that he would never again know. And in the short time that he watched them yielding to that passion, the small, nearly extinguished, but still winking spark of the last ember of sanity within his mind cried out to him, *"This is the way it should be! This is right and true! There is your beloved grandson and the woman he loves, and they belong together! Stop this madness!"*

He switched off the monitor. And with it he doused that last ember. He thought for a few minutes and then called two of his sentries into the inner area of the control center with him.

Tommy and Sydney sat together on the edge of the bed, arms around each other. They were both quiet. Both knew that it may be a matter of minutes or hours, but they would soon have to face Ross and his madness.

Suddenly, Sydney sat up straight and drew in her breath. She turned to look at Tommy and grabbed both of his hands.

"Tommy!" she cried, in a sharp whisper. She could hardly contain her excitement. "Oh, Tommy! I almost forgot! We're saved, we're saved!"

Tommy took her hands and looked at her. "What are you talking about?"

"How could I forget? Claudette! And Wolfgang! They'll save us!!"

Tommy stared at her in disbelief. "Claudette? My grandmother? She's dead! What are you talking about?"

"No, no, she's not dead!" Sydney replied, nearly giddy with delight. "Well, she IS ... but she's HERE! She's here to help us! And Wolfgang ..."

"Sydney! Stop!! What's the matter with you?!"

Tommy was holding her by the upper arms now and had to resist the urge to shake her. "*My grandmother's dead!* And her car ... Is that what you meant when you said 'Wolfgang'? Her *car??!*"

"Yes!! The Volvo! Wolfgang! Claudette is in there! In the car! She drove up here with me, and she wants to help us!!"

Tommy half stood over Sydney now and gripped her arms even more tightly. "Stop it!! Stop it!! You're talking crazy, Sydney! *Please, stop it!*" He pulled her to her feet and dropped his voice to a desperate pleading whisper, "*Don't do this, Sydney! Don't flip out on me! I need you ...*"

Sydney pushed hard on Tommy's chest and he let go of her. Then she stood her ground and shouted in a hoarse whisper, "*Listen to me!!* Take my word for it!! I know it sounds crazy, but it's true!! *How do you think I got up here??* Claudette was waiting for me in Wolfgang, and I ..."

Tommy cut her short with a slap in the face hard enough to send her reeling back onto the bed. She was stunned by the pain, and tears instantly began to stream down her face, as she held her hand up to her cheek, which stung with pain.

Tommy stared at his hand as though it were a separate being. *He had never hit anyone in his life!* The closest he had ever come was in grade school, when a class bully began to taunt a girl walking home—He grabbed the bully by the collar and held up his fist in front of his nose. The bully—who was really a big coward who only threatened people smaller and weaker than he was—started to cry. Tommy let him go and he ran away.

Now he could not believe his own terrible action. He and Sydney just stared at each other for just seconds ... then he began to move toward her.

"Sydney—*I'm so sorry!!* I ..."

But Sydney did not wait to hear the rest of his apology. She scrambled over the bed to the other side and laid her head down on the edge. She clasped her hands in front of her head and began moving her mouth ... praying ... without making any sound except an occasional hitching sob when she drew a breath.

Tommy just stared at her. He was stricken by the recollection of his mother's own fanatical praying and religious rituals when he had been a little boy.

Jennifer Cooke Kensington Ross was a woman of extraordinary beauty. She had the face of a fine porcelain doll, and her hair was thick platinum gold. When she brushed it, it fell in soft, silken waves down her back. But she never allowed it to be seen like that—she wore it braided and tucked into a hat or kerchief at all times.

Jennifer would take her son, her only child, to church every single day. Tommy's father, Tom Ross, Jr., would not go with them. On occasion, he would try to tell his wife that it was excessive—that her religious fervor was abnormal, and he was afraid that Tommy would grow up with unhealthy attitudes. But she would leave the room. So he stopped bringing it up. He prayed in his own way for his son's mental health, and for his wife's.

Jennifer had disdained sex from the beginning, but she refused entirely after her son was born. She often quoted "Paul" to justify her continued abstinence. Tom waited two years, hoping that his patience and love would eventually win her over and that she would be a wife to him again. But it never happened. Eventually he began staying in town after he closed up the station at night, having a drink or two before going home. It was not long before Tom found that there were many women who were eager enough to spend time with him, in spite of the wedding band he always wore.

It took nearly five years before Jennifer was no longer able to ignore her husband's philandering. He came home hours after the station closed most every night; and frequently not at all. When he did come home, he often stumbled intoxicated to fall asleep on the couch. He had hired Clarence, an otherwise slow-witted young man who was a whiz at auto mechanics, and dependable enough to open the station for him every day. Clarence probably was responsible for keeping the station going altogether, in those last terrible years of Tom and Jennifer's marriage.

The final chapter came one day when Jennifer ran into the most overbearing and gossipy woman in the church. She buttonholed Jennifer in the supermarket, and in a loud, castigating voice, told her that her husband was fornicating with whores every night, and that if Jennifer didn't DO something about it, she and her seven-year-old son would both go to hell for aiding and abetting a sinner "by omission."

Jennifer left her grocery cart in the aisle and took Tommy home. He asked her what "fornicating" meant, and she slapped him so hard that his lip bled. She had never raised a hand to him before. When they got home she made him get on his knees and pray with her for hours and hours. She would not let him get up to eat or drink, and he wet on himself because she would not allow him to stop praying with her. Finally, she took him into the kitchen and made him some vegetable soup which she had laced with rat poison. She watched him until he made it "all gone" and then she put him to bed. Then she went into the bathroom and hanged herself from the shower head.

Tommy started feeling sick, so he got up from the bed and tried to go to the bathroom, but the door was locked. He went around the house calling for his mother, crying from the pain in his stomach and because he was scared. He went outside and a neighbor saw him crying and vomiting. She took him back inside his house and called the police when Jennifer failed to answer from the locked bathroom. Tommy was taken to the hospital and joined by his father once he had been located at the Dog House Bar.

Tommy was released from the hospital after a week, and did not attend his mother's funeral. His father never drank again. He began picking up Tommy after school every day, and would bring him to the station. There Tommy spent his afternoons doing homework, and learning auto mechanics from Clarence. Tommy and his father spent every evening and weekend together, too, and his father never dated again, from the day of his wife's death until his own untimely death a few years ago. That was when Tommy gave up practicing medicine and took over the station.

Tommy didn't remember much about his mother, except for the vision of her on her knees, praying. Constantly praying. *Just like Sydney was right now.* And the tears started flowing down his face, because he didn't want Sydney to be sick like his mother was, and it looked a whole lot like that right now.

He walked around to her on the other side of the bed and knelt down on one knee next to her. "Sydney?" he asked, softly, hoping she would pull out of this state of religious insanity, which he hoped with all his heart was temporary. He touched her shoulders, but she just shook him off and kept up her intense praying, face buried in the bed, hands clasped in front of her. He couldn't make out what she was saying. But just then the door opened. Tommy looked up. Two sentries entered the room.

36/ INTRUSION

"Mr. Ross wants you both to come with us," said the sentry dressed in the Wells Fargo uniform. Sydney did not acknowledge their entry into the room. She continued her silent prayers into the edge of the bed. Tommy reached down and took her by the waist and pulled her, gently but without allowing her any resistance, to her feet.

He was shocked when he saw her face—so were the sentries. Her eyes were red and tear-streaked; and there was a huge red bruise on the side of her face where Tommy had struck her. The edge of her lip was already beginning to swell.

"Oh, my God," Tommy said, as he looked her over, "Oh, Sydney, I ..."

She shushed him with a finger over her lips. She was remembering the moment in the woods on the trail leading up to Billy's Bunion when she stopped to take a drink of water. She had heard Claudette's voice admonishing her, even though she did not see her anywhere. She was sure that had been real! It just couldn't have been her imagination!

"Sh-h-h!" Quiet!" she said in a whisper, when Tommy stopped speaking. "We'll hear her any minute, I just know it! We have to listen for her instructions!"

Tommy didn't even try to stop the tears from streaming down his own face now. He was losing Sydney—he loved her, and he was losing her—just as he had lost his beautiful mother to her own mental disease—and there didn't seem to be anything he could do to stop it. He turned and walked toward the men in the doorway, shoulders shaking as he unashamedly sobbed.

Sydney stayed where she was, but kept looking all around her in the air, as though she expected to see or hear something any minute. But there was nothing. One of the sentries—the one who was dressed in the uniform of a train conductor—went over to Sydney and took her by the elbow.

"Mr. Ross has instructed us to use our powers if necessary, Miss," he said to her, with a slightly sneering look. Sydney took a step toward him, and walked with him out of the room, but she continued scanning the air all around her, ignoring everything else.

When they got to the control center, Ross was frankly surprised at the sight in front of him. Tommy had obviously been crying, and Sydney had obviously been battered in the face. Anger rose up within him, and he glared first at one sentry and then the other, and they saw his skin begin to turn pinkish and both began protesting their innocence loudly and gestured toward Tommy and said in unison, *"HE DID IT!!"*

Ross made a change of plans at that moment. He had been planning to encase both Tommy and Sydney in glass cells of their own—Sydney in particular would have been very useful because of her computer skills—but now things were different. *Tommy had struck Sydney!* He would never have expected that kind of behavior from his grandson! He would dispose of Tommy right now, and keep Sydney down here with him for the time being.

And who knows? Perhaps with Tommy out of the way, Sydney might begin to find him ... somewhat ... attractive ... in a mature sort of way ...

"Franklin!" Ross called the sentry in the army uniform who had been the subject of the levitation experiment when Sydney and Tommy first arrived, and had now taken over Mac McMulligan's place as Ross' first lieutenant. Franklin jogged around the control center until he was directly in front of Ross, and then snapped to attention.

"Yes, Sir!"

"Take this man out," Ross said, finding that he could not look at his grandson as he gave the final order, "and execute him."

Sydney stopped looking around in the air and gaped at Ross, then at Tommy, and then back at Ross again. Surely he could not have his own grandson killed? But as Franklin marched toward the entry doors which led to the parking foyer at the front of the sphereship, Ross never even looked up, and Sydney realized with flooding horror that he *DID* mean to have Tommy murdered!

She started to shout—perhaps she would even have lunged at Ross—but something happened suddenly that stole everyone's attention. Even Franklin stopped marching with Tommy and turned around to see what was happening.

A red light was flashing on the control panel in front of Ross, and a siren began to wail from somewhere overhead. Ross looked at a monitor on the other side of the control center, and said, "It's Unit 968—It's been breached." He looked up and scanned the hundreds of glass honeycomb cells lining the walls, but he could not tell which one was the identified unit.

Ross turned to the computer keyboard he had been sitting at before, and tapped in a few commands. "Nine-sixty-eight ... *Lila Elaine Maxwell* ..."

Sydney heard her niece's name and immediately jumped up and looked at the monitor herself. When she saw Lila's name on the screen, she gasped, and turned around and grabbed Ross by his arms, heedless of any danger, and said, "That's my niece!! Oh, Mr. Ross, please!! I came up here to get her!! *What's happening?*"

Ross forcefully removed Sydney's hands from himself and told her to sit quietly while he had the situation investigated, or he would put her in leg irons. She sat down immediately.

Ross called to Franklin, who had already stopped marching Tommy toward the entry doors, and told him to wait there. He did not want to open the doors until this situation was cleared. Then he motioned to four sentries to go up to Unit 968 and see what the problem was.

Sydney looked at the glass cells and counted up to what she thought might be the ninth level. The hexagonal shapes and honeycombed arrangement made it very difficult to figure out, but Sydney thought it was about halfway up the side of the wall. She carefully eyed each cell at that height, hoping beyond hope that she might be able to spot her dear Lila.

And spot she did. It was easy once she eyed the cell that had two people squeezed into it instead of one.

"There!!" Sydney stood up and pointed to the cell, just over halfway up, with the double occupancy. Ross followed her finger, but his vision would not allow him to see what Sydney had seen.

"What is it?" he asked, curious to know what she had seen there.

"It's my niece! And ... and ..." Sydney could just barely make out the familiar silhouette of the other person in the cell. "... and my *sister? Melva?* Omigod!! Melva's in there, too!!" Melva had just beamed herself into Lila's cell from the Ross mansion attic moments earlier.

Ross looked at Sydney. He would wait and see who was in the cell with the Lila girl, but he was at a loss to figure out how anyone could possibly have gotten in there! The security field extended for fifty yards in all directions surrounding the sphereship. Alarms would have been set off if anyone set foot into the surrounding woods. And no one came through the front draw-ramp, that was certain.

Then he remembered ... The control center in his house in Jiminy Rock! In the attic! Someone could have sat down at the main computer and easily identified the children on screen. Then if they hit

"Enter" they would be molecularly transported at the speed of light into the honeycomb cell listed on the screen!! That was how Ross himself had travelled from the hospital to his home in Jiminy Rock, and to the sphereship!

So Sydney's sister had snooped around looking for her daughter and ended up taking a little jaunt! Well, he would just dispose of her along with Tommy!

None of the glass cells could be entered without a palm-sized laser device which Ross kept himself, to turn off the individual force shields which surrounded each and every cell. This prevented the children from using their telekinetic and pyrogenic powers until he directed them to do so.

Now he handed that control, which looked like an ordinary television remote control device, to the first of the four sentries he was sending up to the unit, and instructed them on its use. Then they headed toward one of two sets of elevator doors at the foot of the glass honeycombs. These were just to the side of the main entry doors.

Ross stared after them ... he didn't trust them. Not really. Really, he didn't trust anyone. And these "sentries" were little more than clowns. Misfits. Failures. Every one of them had been assigned to desk duty, for one embarrassing reason or another, in their former places of employment. That is why they all happened to be familiar with computers, and that is how they were drawn to Ross and the sphereship!

At first he thought it would be a boon, having all these authority figures to give an air of high security to the encased youngsters—not that it was necessary, anyway. But they also provided several right hands for him, like Mac reporting on the number of youngsters landing at the airport, and helping in the transporting of them to the ship.

But these "sentries" were really just goons after all. Otherwise they would have been out in the field in their jobs, or they would have been promoted to higher offices than they were, after being in their positions for so long. Ross was tempted to parboil the whole lot of them on more than one occasion!

It was all they could do to avoid bumping into each other around the control center. They often showed resentment and jealousy toward each other and vied for Ross' attention, like a room full of little schoolkids. He certainly could not trust them with maximum powers—they would burn the whole place down, with as little sense and as much temper as they seemed to have!

So Ross had allowed their powers to fade out, as they would if not re-stimulated electronically by computer every few days. Some of the sentries had asked him about it—one complained that he couldn't tie his shoes without using his hands anymore!—but Ross just told them they would have a "recharging" when everything was in place for spin-off.

That was why Ross had sent Franklin out "to dispose of" Tommy, before they were interrupted. Franklin couldn't do a damn thing to hurt his grandson! He had no powers left at all! And as soon as Tommy realized that, he would have taken off and left Franklin in the dust.

But now this new development—this was really annoying! Ross did not know what to make of it. Someone had gotten inside one of the units! And this Sydney—this red-haired devil-angel—it was *her* sister who breeched his ship! Somehow this Sydney was managing to throw a wrench into things. Everything started to go wrong after *she* showed up. And to think that he was ... he was ... *attracted* to her. What an old fool he was!

Ross looked over at Sydney. The bruise on her face was beginning to darken now. He couldn't help it, no matter how much he wanted to believe that she was against him, his heart pulled in the other direction. Maybe she was not in Dr. Anna's camp after all. It was obvious by her swelling lip that she and Tommy had not been of one mind—maybe the lovemaking had been forced, too! That Tommy was more of a scoundrel than his own son had been! His son had been an alcoholic and a philanderer—until his wife died—but he had never hit a woman!

Ross stood up and reached into his pants pocket, and came out with a long, old-fashioned type of bit key. Sydney thought it looked as anachronistic as the leg irons Tommy was in when she first came into this place! Ross threw the key to Franklin, who dropped it and scrambled over the floor to pick it up.

"Got it, Sir!" he called jubilantly to Ross when he finally straightened up.

"Put the man back in leg irons!" Ross commanded to Franklin, gesturing back to the same bench where Tommy had been held before. "I'm going up to 968," he said—and then he looked at Sydney. "She's coming with me!"

"Yes, Sir, Mr. Ross, *Sir!*" Franklin called back, and saluted crisply. Then he shoved Tommy from the back and said, "You heard the man. March!" Tommy hesitated for only a split second before deciding what to do. For the time being, at least, he would not be taken off the ship nor away from Sydney. He walked toward the bench, a few paces ahead of Franklin.

Ross turned to Sydney. "Come with me now, dear," he said, as gently as he could manage, "and we'll see if that really is your sister up there. Then we'll decide what to do with all of you." Sydney followed.

Phil Maxwell felt a pang of intuitive fear unlike anything he had ever experienced before. He was feeling the same sickening pang of faceless anxiety that Melva was trying to describe when she hastily (he thought) left for Asheville two days earlier, in search of Lila.

He had a vision—the image of his wife and daughter huddled closely together, trembling with mortal fear. The kind of fear that converts people from agnostic to deeply religious. Foxhole fear.

Phil picked up the remote control and snapped off the video he had been watching ("Know Your BMW"). First, he would have to call his mother and see if she could come over and stay with the two younger children for a few days. But really, for how long, he did not know.

Phil's mother would put up a fuss if it were longer than a day or two. And she would never stop tongue-lashing him for letting Lila go visit her "irresponsible Aunt Sydney" in the first place; and again for marrying Melva, "a woman of no social standing whatsoever," in the first place. And if Phil had not insisted on pursuing his "foolish aspirations" in art as an avocation while in dental school, he "would surely have been even *more* successful." And if he had gone on to medical school after dental school and had become a maxillofacial surgeon, he would be able to make "scads of money," and for a mere three years more study he could have added a law degree to his D.D.S. and M.D. degrees, and that would surely have made him the "foremost medico-dento-legal expert in the country, if not the world," and *blah, blah, blah...*

Phil sat back and snapped the video back on. He felt confident that Melva had everything under control.

37/ THE CAGE AND THE BIRD

The four sentries had already disappeared into the elevator. Ross pushed the button beside it, and the elevator next to the first one whooshed open immediately. He stepped in and Sydney followed. He pushed the "nine" button and they lifted so swiftly that Sydney felt as though she weighed four hundred pounds. She definitely left her stomach on the ground floor. It was only a few seconds before the elevator came to a smooth stop, Sydney's stomach now rejoining the rest of her, and the doors slid open in front of them. They could hear the sounds of the sentries arguing somewhere down from them, but they could not see them.

The elevator opened onto a corridor so narrow that there was barely room to swing one's arms. It was short, too. Sydney could feel the top of her hair brushing against the ceiling, and the Gray Man had to stoop over to walk. He walked behind her. The corridor was on a slight incline, and they were walking uphill. Sydney could hear a humming sound below the sentries' arguing voices, which were some distance away, but getting closer as they walked on.

The wall opposite them looked like smooth concrete, but as Sydney's hand brushed it, *it did not seem solid!* She wanted to stop and inspect it, but she was not about to try Ross' patience. The humming may have been coming from within the wall, and it remained constant as they walked along.

Shortly they came upon the sentries. They were arguing about how to use the laser control device, and who would get to use it. Ross lost his temper when he discovered the haggling bunch. "You idiots! I should have known I couldn't depend on you!"

Ross raised his hand and all four men hit the deck and put their arms over their heads. Ross drew back his booted foot and kicked the one nearest him in the side of the head. The man never looked up, just began to tremble and whimper into his arm.

"Who has the laser?" Ross demanded of the four prostrate soldiers. "Give it to me!"

One of the men scrambled to his feet, and with his head still hanging down, handed Ross the laser device. "Now go back down and see if Franklin figured out how to lock the leg irons on properly! See if any of you can figure it out!"

All four men rose and attempted to squeeze down the hallway first, bumping into each other, exiting as quickly as possible.

Downstairs, Tommy had started to move toward the bench after Franklin shoved him in that direction. The elevator had come very quickly and taken Ross and Sydney away, and then Tommy spotted the door next to the bank of elevators. A stairway, perhaps? He looked over at the control center. Five sentries remained there, and they were all milling around and talking about which tubes they might have for lunch. None were watching Franklin and Tommy.

Without giving it nearly enough thought, Tommy turned around and introduced his knee to Franklin's groin. When Franklin bowed over, his breath momentarily gone, Tommy placed his hands on the back of Franklin's head and slammed it into the same knee. It's amazing what you can learn from watching T.V.

Franklin fell to the floor, unconscious. Tommy ran to the stairway door. But was it a stairway? Was it even unlocked? Would the other sentries notice?

Tommy reached the door in a couple of seconds. He grabbed the door handle. The first sentry had just looked up and spotted Franklin in a heap on the floor. Tommy pressed the door handle down. It didn't move. The sentry who spotted Franklin began to yell, and the others looked first at him, and then at Tommy. Tommy threw all of his weight against the door. The sentries began jumping over the control center desk and running toward Tommy.

On the ninth level, Ross stared after the four sentries he had sent back, until they disappeared around the curve of the sphere, going back to the elevators. Then he turned to the wall opposite them and turned a dial on the laser device which he held in his hand. He pressed a button and a blue light beamed out. It was only the thickness of a pencil, but as it hit the wall, the light spread in a little circular pool, and Sydney could see— *she could actually see through the wall* at that point! It was hazy, but she could make out a figure sitting at a little desk, with his back to Sydney and Ross. As Ross moved the pool of light, she could see different areas of the young man and his cubicle.

Then the pool of light ran over something—something which seemed to lie within the thickness of the "wall" itself. Some numbers appeared as the light flowed over them. It looked like fireworks-writing in the sky. Nine ... six ... two. Nine-sixty-two! They must be six cells over from Lila! Ross turned the beam off and paced along the floor another twenty feet or so, and then beamed the blue light onto the wall again. This time Sydney immediately recognized the back of Lila's sweatshirt ("I'm a Dol-Fan from Miami!") and Melva, both squeezed into the little seat and hugging each other and crying.

"Lila! Mel!" Sydney called to them through the blue beam-hole, but they did not respond. Ross put his hand up and told her to step back so that he could release the force field and open the cell. Sydney retreated about six feet back down the passageway. Ross turned another dial on the device and then pressed the center button. This time a bright neon violet light pulsed out in a stream the thickness of a cigar, and when it hit the wall, rapidly spread outward in ripples. The ripples faded out at a radius of about two feet from the central beam.

Now the whole area within the purple light appeared hazy and translucent, and Sydney could see all of Lila and Melva sitting together. Within seconds, the haziness cleared up and the wall had completely disappeared! Sydney reached over and touched her sister on the shoulder, and Melva turned so quickly and screamed so loudly that both she and Lila tipped over the desk in front of them. They stared, each in turn, in disbelief, at the sight behind them. Ross stooped over, his lined and cracked gray face and mega-thick glasses making him look about a thousand years old; and Sydney with her uncombed red hair sproinging out in all directions, and a bruise on the side of her face, and a swollen lip.

"Oh, my God!" squealed Lila and Melva in unison, and with Sydney, they all hugged in a fourth-and-goal huddle. Ross hung back for a few seconds. Now what in hell was he going to do with Sydney and her whole damn family?

He decided. He tapped the young girl on the shoulder. "Lila Maxwell?"

Lila pulled away from the huddle slightly and stared at Ross. "Y-yes?"

"Go sit down!" Ross motioned to her indicating that she should go back into the little cell.

"No! Momma, tell him! *I don't want to!"*

"Listen, Buster," Melva began, pointing one bright red lacquered fingernail at Ross' chest, "You have no right ..."

Sydney held up her hand and stepped in between her sister's forefinger and Ross. Softly, but with great force she said to her sister, *"Mel, do you want to look like this?"* and she touched the side of her face where she had been bruised.

It was a cheap trick, but it worked. Melva stepped back. Then she looked back and forth between Ross and Sydney, and said, "I want some answers! Where are we? Why do you have my daughter in this place? What ..."

Ross started to raise his laser device. As he did so, Melva drew in her breath, and then she pushed Lila back into the little desk chair in the cell. She had no idea what the laser device was, or what it could do, but she knew with absolute clarity that she did not want to find out like this.

Then Ross turned another dial on the laser, pointed it at the cell, and pushed the central button once again. This time a brilliant yellow beam flowed out in waves which broke over the empty space between the three adults and Lila. Melva screamed, but Sydney held her back. Soon Lila's terrified face, streaked with runnels of tears, faded behind a hazy screen, which became a completely opaque wall again in just a few seconds.

When Ross turned off the light beam, the wall looked like smooth, unbroken concrete once again, and there was no clue as to where the cell was behind it. Sydney was still holding Melva, who was speechless. But only for a moment. Then she let loose with a stream of invectives that could have pulverized a real concrete wall.

Ross turned on his heel and walked back in the direction of the elevators.

38/ MAZE-ING

Tommy smashed into the stairwell door with his shoulder and almost fell down as the door swung open. He was two flights up by the time the sentries chasing him reached the door themselves.

Tommy had run up about eight flights before he stopped to catch his breath, and see if he could judge how far below him the others were. He could hear only the faintest sounds of their shuffling progress. They were four flights down, but they were getting winded so quickly that they had already slowed to a crawl. Sitting at desk jobs all day and playing computer games all night had done little for their physical stamina.

After listening for a few seconds, Tommy took off again up the stairs, not having any idea where he was going. He did not know that Ross and Sydney and Melva were walking toward the elevators on the ninth level. He did not know how many levels there were. But he did decide that it might be prudent to get out of the stairwell, as he might have a better chance of losing the sentries on his tail if he got out of there. So, at the next level, he tested the door cautiously to see if it would open.

Deputy Elijah Chester Alston had hiked up to Billy's Bunion, inspected the area long enough to determine the presence of Jeep tracks leading down the other side of the mountain, as well as taking a count of the case of the recently-swilled beer cans crumpled and tossed about, and returned back down the path to where he had left the patrol car parked behind the Volvo. He got into his patrol car and picked up the radio mike:

"Peaches, come in, Peaches. This is Eli." He heard a crackling static which he interpreted as the dispatcher's acknowledgement of his call. "Get ahold of Sheriff Trimble for me, wouldya', Doll?"

"Sorry, Hon'," came back the drawl of Sally Mae "Peaches" Person, "but he's outta the office."

Peaches was an octogenarian who happened to like bragging about the hot times and hell raising she had engaged in as a young woman, when the only pollution in their little mountain town was perpetrated by horses.

"Well, where is he now?" asked Eli, knowing full well that "outta the office" for Sheriff Trimble was a euphemism for "playing poker with his moonshine buddies."

"Durned if ah know, Shugah," answered Peaches, "Didn' give us no I-tinerary." Peaches stopped chewing her gum long enough to blow a large, wet, pink bubble, letting it expand until it burst with a loud snap directly into the mouthpiece of her telephone headset.

"Couldya' try to raise him in the Bird, for me, please, Honey?"

Peaches didn't answer for a moment. She adored Eli, and she knew more about Trimble's snake-like qualities than anyone in Jiminey Rock. But she had no choice.

"Can't, Hon'... He said not to ... Y'know whut ah mean?"

Eli stared at the microphone in his hand and nodded, even though Peaches couldn't see. He hoped Trimble wasn't out still trying to put the make on the undertaker's wife. The mortician let it be known around town that he wouldn't stand in the way of the Lord Almighty if He chose to put a load of buckshot in Trimble's backside if he heard that greasy weasel showed up around their spread again. And he already had a nice box picked out to plant him in.

Eli calmly gave instructions to Peaches to please call another deputy and have him arrange to have the Volvo towed back to town. He signed off and gunned his big Plymouth into gear, screeching off down to the road leading down the other side of the mountain.

He didn't curse Trimble now. He cursed himself. He shouldn't have passed up the opportunity he had last year when the county commissioners wanted him to run for Sheriff against Hollister Trimble with all of their support. He felt that would have been ... disloyal. What a notion! He hit the steering wheel hard with the heel of his hand.

Sydney never thought she would be so happy to see her sister. But she was thrilled. And impressed in a way which also surprised her. How in the heck did Melva get here? She never would have given her sister credit for this much resourcefulness—even if it did land her in Lila's cell! But it was obvious to Sydney that Ross did not know how that happened either.

Sydney took Melva's hand and held it. Melva was between her and Ross, who was leading them back toward the elevators. She squeezed her hand tightly in return, but when she looked back, Sydney just put a finger to her lips.

Sydney thought about what might happen now. *What would I do if I were the Gray Man?* And—something else. Something else was bothering her. Something was nibbling at the back of her mind that she couldn't quite put her finger on. A clue. But what?

Tommy had gone only about ten steps out of the stairwell door on the ninth level when he heard the footsteps coming toward him down the passageway—it was Ross, Sydney and Melva. He thought about running back to the stairwell, but he did not know how far the sentries had ascended by now. Then he thought of getting into one of the elevators, but he decided that he did not have enough time to wait, if the doors didn't open up right away. So he padded back in the other direction as quickly as he could, on the declining passageway. He walked quietly but swiftly. Nothing but concrete all around, it seemed. He walked for what seemed like a long time, before he came back around to the stairway door and the elevators. There was an "Eight" painted on the wall, where "Nine" had been when he first stepped out of the stairwell. He had walked in a slightly descending spiral around the entire outer shell of the sphereship and descended one floor!

Suddenly he heard loud and clear the sounds of the sentries in the stairwell. "I can't go anymore," one was saying, "my legs feel like rubber!"

"You need to go on a diet and get rid of that pot belly, then you could go another four, five flights without breathing hard!"

"Yeah, well you're breathing like a buffalo yourself!" he answered, "and I don't see you catchin' up with nobody!"

"Let's get off here and take the elevator."

"Mr. Ross will kill us!"

"Well, he'll kill us if we don't get up there and catch that dude, and we'll kill ourselves if we don't take the elevator. Ya' comin' or not?"

"Yeah, okay."

Tommy didn't think he could lose these guys forever if he took off running down the ramp the same way he came. It was hard enough walking stooped over. He decided to hit the elevator button. If it opened right up, he would get in. If it didn't, he would take off through the passageway again. It opened right up.

Ross had changed his mind. At first he thought he would lock both of these women downstairs in the master quarters, where he had kept Sydney before. But then he decided that it would be better to keep this Melva woman separate from Sydney. Together they were bound to be more trouble! And he couldn't just dispose of her. He was still, in the back of his mind, hoping that something ... just might ... work out ... between himself and Sydney. Something. Oh, she seemed infatuated with his grandson ... but if he were patient ... in time, surely she could be won over by the superior qualities of experience, knowledge and maturity that he had ... surely ... maybe ...

And it would be better if he spared her sister. So when they got back into the elevator—just after Tommy heard them approaching and took off down to the eighth level—Ross pressed the very top button. Level twenty-nine. The doors whooshed closed and Sydney's stomach was parked on the ninth level for a few seconds again, until it caught up with the rest of her.

When they stepped out onto the twenty-ninth level, Sydney was surprised at the sunlight flooding the passageway. And there was no low ceiling! The concrete "wall" ended just above Sydney's head, and there was empty space between it and the giant window above, which was at the very top of the sphere. This window-cap could be seen from the ground floor of the sphereship, but it was so far up that it did not give much "feel" of sunshine streaming in, as it did now that they were right next to it.

Sydney stared up through the huge window, awestruck in the sunshine, in spite of the pain in her eyes, as a man on the desert would be if he saw an oasis. Then she saw the helicopter in the distance and nearly cried out with joy at the prospect of being discovered ... saved!

But Ross, anticipating her thoughts, said, "It's not actual sky you're seeing." Sydney and Melva both turned to him. "It's just the reflection of the sky. We are totally hidden by mirrors here, and that is one you are looking into right now, which is reflecting the surrounding skylight."

Sydney felt sick at this—as though she had leaped for the brass ring, but fell on her face. Melva's lower lip was quivering and Sydney knew that she felt the same sinking disappointment, especially in light of the helicopter, the sight of which had given them such a surge of hope.

Ross stopped and took the laser device out once again and pointed it at the wall. The blue pencil-thin light pooled to show an empty cell behind it, with just a desk and chair.

"Good," he said, almost inaudibly, more to himself than to his company.

Suddenly Sydney was filled with terror once again. She realized that Melva—and perhaps herself, too—would be encased in one of these glass cells, to sit, for ... ten years?! A hundred?? Or whatever time it would take for the Gray Man to pull off his huge stunt. Or blow them all to kingdom-come! She couldn't let him encase Melva here! But what could she do? He was turning the dial on the laser to the next mark. Now the violet light was washing over the concrete wall and making it translucent. Her thoughts raced wildly.

Tommy stepped into the elevator on the eighth level. He gathered from the bits and pieces of the sentries' conversation he overheard that they were headed for the very top floor. Perhaps they would travel down the ramp from there, checking the stairwell on each level, looking for him. He also learned that if the sentries notified the Gray Man that Tommy had escaped somewhere in the sphereship, his location could be pinpointed immediately from the control center, with video monitors located everywhere—but they were too afraid to tell him they had lost him!

Tommy decided to go halfway up—and wait—and think. He punched "seventeen" and the elevator pulled up quickly.

The five sentries did indeed go directly to the twenty-ninth level. However, in the meantime, the four sentries that Ross had dismissed from the ninth level, because they had been arguing and diddling around with the laser, got to the ground floor and were met by the sight of Franklin struggling to get up, a grunting, pained expression on his face. Immediately they knew something was wrong, geniuses that they were.

"Franklin! Are you okay? What the heck happened?"

Franklin could hardly get his breath, but he finally managed to say, "He got away!"

"Who?"

"Tommy! Tommy! Ross' grandson, you idiots! Who do you think?!!"

The four looked over at the bench where Tommy was to have been re-shackled and saw that it was vacant. Then they helped Franklin to his feet.

"The others went after him. He went up the stairwell," he finished saying, and then nearly passed out again from the pain in his groin. The four sentries half-carried, half-dragged him over to the bench and laid him down. Then they decided that at least two of them had better stay down here and guard the control center in case the grandson got back here. The other two went up the stairwell. If only Ross had re-charged their mental powers, they could have notified him of these problems by telepathy! Damn him! He deserved for things to go wrong!

Tommy got off the elevator on level seventeen. He crouched down between the elevator and the stairwell doors, and looked at his watch. He would wait fifteen minutes, and then go up to the top. That should give them time to have searched the top level, left it, and be one or two levels down. He waited—and reviewed the layout of the sphereship in his mind. The entry way doors ... the control button which opened them ... a plan for exit.

The two sentries who had just left Franklin and entered the stairwell to join the chase lasted only five floors until they were too winded to do anything but gasp and wheeze. One thought for a minute that he might throw up. That was when they, too, decided that they would not make it unless they took the elevator. They decided to go to the top level, and work their way down.

Sheriff Hollister Trimble ran his fingers through his greasy black hair, which fell back over his eyes as soon as he finished the sweep. He and the pilot of the "Bird" had combed over every inch of the mountainside without spotting any movement whatsoever. Trimble went over and over in his mind the sparse information he had: A speeding blue Volvo with a red-headed driver, female, caused a patrol car to flip over due to her razzle-dazzle driving. She then took off up to Jiminy Rock and abandoned the Volvo just beyond the Ross mansion. No one lived there since Mrs. Ross died a couple of months ago—although there had been some strange reports of haunting voices in the area at night.

Peaches had passed that information to Hollister. She had known Mrs. Claudette Ross since they were both very young. Peaches even sort of hinted that Mrs. Ross may have had something of a wild nature, herself—but her eyes darted around and her voice dropped when she got onto that subject, as though she were afraid the recently-departed woman might be listening in. So she stopped short of proffering any further details of such "wildness," and let the listener's imagination do the job.

Trimble scratched at his pockmarked face as he rolled over the sparse facts in his mind. Suddenly he jerked upright from his usual slumping position. The pilot of the Bird looked over at him.

"Sheriff? What is it?"

Trimble had just remembered that Mrs. Claudette Ross herself had owned a blue Volvo! She hardly drove it, though—and what did that stupid vanity-license plate say? Chaingang? Gangplank? Gangbang? Something like that. She got that car a few years ago, and only drove it on those rare occasions when she went to visit her husband. He was locked up in the state nut house after going on a shooting spree when he went completely crackers.

Ross. Hadn't thought about him in years. Wonder whatever became of him? He picked up the radio microphone.

"Peaches, Honey," he drawled into the mike. Even his own mountain drawl got exaggerated when he spoke to her. "See if you can raise Broughton Hospital for me, okay?"

"Roger, Sugar ... Roger and out." Peaches knew exactly whom he was checking on.

39 / THE CLUE

The wall of the cell on the twenty-ninth level had just disappeared completely under the wash of violet radiance when the elevator arrived. As soon as the doors opened, the five sentries all blinked their eyes at the radiant sunlight, and also at the three others standing there. Ross, Sydney and Melva turned around and stared back at them.

"What in the hell are you doing up here?" Ross demanded to know, turning deep red around the neck. The five sentries all drew back together, and the elevator doors bopped open and closed, open and closed, as they stood astride the doorway, trembling with fear at having angered Ross.

Finally, one of the sentries found the courage to speak (Douglas "Stop Sign" Ludwig, formerly a high school crossing guard). "He ... He got away ... SIR!"

Rage swept across Ross like a shadow over the land when a cloud overtakes the sun on a bright day. "Tommy? My grandson?" he sputtered, *"He got away?!!!"*

All five sentries nodded largely in unison. Ross stepped forward so that his nose was less than its own length from Ludwig's. "You find him and bring him to me," he all but whispered, between clenched teeth.

They were all still now, no one nodding his head anymore. Someone had reached in and pressed the "Open" button so that the elevator doors would hold still.

"DO YOU UNDERSTAND??!!!" the Gray Man shouted, spittle flying into Stop Sign's face.

"Yes, Sir, SIR!!" he said, and they could barely squeeze past each other fast enough to get back into the elevator and get away from there.

On the seventeenth level, Tommy looked at his watch again. Only twelve minutes had passed. His heart was pounding with anticipation. Should he continue to wait? What would he do once he got to the top level? He forced himself to stop wracking his brain and just continue with his present plan. Once he got to the top, he could plan further.

When Ludwig and the others were safely out of range of the Gray Man's presence, they all turned to each other.

"What now?"

"I don't know. That Ross is a madman!"

"We'll have to find the grandson or else we'll all go like ..." he trailed off without finishing the sentence.

He couldn't say it. None of them could. None of them wanted to call up the image of what Mac McMulligan had looked like after Ross had telepathically microwaved him.

"Maybe we should ..." Krep Hamner, formerly a night watchman at a sausage factory, started to speak, but couldn't finish. He did not want to be the first to utter words of mutiny.

"Maybe we should *jump ship*," Chucky Zablocki finished for Hamner. The others just stared at him. No one could say anything. Just at that moment, the doors of the elevator swept open again. Someone had accidentally hit the open-doors button.

Ross and the two women had taken only a few steps back toward the open cell where he had intended to encase Melva, when the elevator doors whooshed open. There were the five cowering, and now mutinous, sentries. All of them, including Sydney and Melva, swallowed hard and held their collective breaths in anticipation of a murderous explosion of rage by the Gray Man.

But he just looked at them in the elevator. He smiled. Then he walked over to them and said, "You have to push a floor button to go anywhere." He pointed at the panel of buttons inside the door. Then, like a kindergarten teacher addressing a class of five-year-olds, "Split up. Some of you go to twenty-eight, some to twenty-seven. Search each floor, but don't go alone." He smiled.

Ross had detected their fear and instinctively worried about the possibility of a mutiny if he did not restrain his anger—even though he attributed to these gentlemen not a shred of competence to carry off such an endeavor. But he needed what little he could get out of them right now. He had to have Tommy contained.

"Go on now," he smiled again, and the sentries smiled back, greatly relieved and eager to do Ross' bidding. They hit the button for level twenty-eight.

No one mentioned jumping ship again. Ross seemed to them like the kindly father they had originally felt he was. And even kindly fathers sometimes lose their tempers, don't they?

After the doors closed again, Ross' smile fell from his lips and he muttered something to himself. He again turned his attention to Melva & Sydney and the open cell.

"Get in," he said in a stern, but calm voice.

Melva stood her ground.

Fifteen minutes had elapsed, Tommy noted, as he looked at his watch. Time to go. There were five elevators along the wall next to the stairwell door. He started to hit the button for one, when he wondered if there were other stairwells around the building. In case of power failure, would there be only one stairwell to evacuate so many hundreds of people? Of course, his grandfather was completely mad, insane. He may not have given any consideration to these youngsters whom he held captive, in the event of a catastrophe of any kind. He thought with a sickening feeling that felt like a punch in the gut that his grandfather may not care what happened to these kids if his glorious plan were not successful.

Tommy decided just then to look for other stairwells, rather than go right up to the top. He took off around the seventeenth level. He had not remembered seeing any other doorways as he had travelled around below from the ninth to the eighth level. But at that time he had been running from the sound of the sentries' voices, and was not looking for any other doorways. It was worth a more thorough search.

Peaches dialed up the Broughton State Hospital, while Sheriff Trimble waited on hold, hovering above the mountains of Jiminy Rock in The Bird.

Thomson Alva Ross, Senior. Even in her golden years, Peaches could still feel a thrilling rumble of long-forgotten excitement at the mention of his name. The feeling rent the cobwebs which had curtained the memories of so many decades past...

It was in the Old West. Thoughts of that hot, dry, wide open landscape that seemed to go on forever were like scenes from another planet. During the Great Depression, there were hundreds, thousands of people traipsing westward in search of jobs, farmland, food, opportunity. Peaches' family was among them. So was Claudette's. Ross had emigrated from across the ocean. Peaches and Claudette met in the same town, earning a living in one of the only ways unmarried women could in those days. At the local saloon. That's where Peaches got her name. Claudette was known as Sugarbee.

It was a hot and dusty night. The kind of night that packed the saloon with thirsty ranch hands, field hands, cowboys, and others who supported themselves in less savory ways.

Peaches was sitting on top of the piano, waiting for Ivory, who played the piano like Scott Joplin himself. Peaches had a sweet, sultry voice, and when she and Ivory began to sing and play, a quiet descended through the smoke and chatter of the saloon.

Sugarbee stood at the top of the stairs, leaning casually on her elbows over the rich wooden bannister. She was generously built, with wide, soft hips, and a tiny waist that needed no corseting. She always wore scarlet. Sequined camisole, feather boa, satin slip, spike-heeled slippers. Scarlet all.

That was the night Peaches and Sugarbee first met Thomson Alva Ross, Senior. He swung open the saloon doors, and both women noticed him at once—partly because he was new in town, and partly because of his striking handsomeness. He wore a round bowler hat, a brown suit, faded brocade vest with a gold watch chain; and his spectacles were not nearly so thick as they were now.

Peaches and Sugarbee cast a glance at each other. As soon as they looked back at Ross, they realized that he had tuned in on them. Both women felt the strength of his will instantly—and it was both frightening and immensely seductive. The rest of the saloon fell away from their vision—the rinky-tink piano, the clinking glasses, the laughter and raucous conversation all dimmed for them. Peaches and Sugarbee were caught in the steel grip of Ross' stare, and they neither could escape nor did they want to. Ross' will was almost like a physical force. And it was irresistible.

He walked past Peaches at the piano, and she slid off, ignoring Ivory's raised eyebrows, but he didn't miss a note. She followed Ross up the wide, winding staircase, and as they passed Sugarbee, she fell in step next to Peaches, behind Ross. He led them into one of the rooms at the top, and they followed obediently.

The staircase in the Ross mansion in Jiminy Rock was an exact replica of the one in that long-ago saloon.

The other two sentries who were on their way up after discovering Franklin on the floor, arrived at the twenty-ninth level just as the door closed on the five sentries on their way to the twenty-eighth and twenty-seventh levels.

Ross cursed under his breath, as he was once again interrupted in his effort to get Melva into the cell. The two sentries stepped off the elevator, not noticing the exasperation in Ross' face and voice. They had not been there when Tommy clobbered Franklin and took off into the stairwell, so they did not feel fearful of telling Ross what happened.

"I know, I know!" Ross cut them off. He was glad they at least had the good sense to leave two sentries down at the control center, in case Tommy should return there. Along with Franklin, if and when he recuperated, they could probably hold Tommy there.

"Okay, very good," he told them. "Ludwig and the others have split up and are searching the next two floors down. You men stay together and start on twenty-six."

They liked it when he called them "men."

"Yes, Sir, Mr. Ross!" they both snapped to attention and saluted. Then they turned and went down the elevator.

Ross turned his attention back to Sydney and Melva.

"Now," he said, seeming to try and decide how he would approach this without having to resort to force. He gazed at Melva and said nothing. As he continued to gaze at her, Sydney noticed that Melva's body was beginning to relax. Her hands, which had been balled up into fists at her side, slackened open. Her shoulders drooped slightly. Her eyes, which had been wide with anger and defiance, now began to close.

When Sydney realized what was happening, she was stunned: He was hypnotizing Melva with his gaze! At that very instant, the "clue" that had been eluding Sydney dawned on her.

"NO!!! STOP!!!" she screamed at the top of her lungs.

Melva seemed to snap out of her hypnotic descent and balled her fists up once again. Sydney lunged at Ross, now hoping and praying that she was right in what she had just figured out—that he could not harm them with any "powers" where they were!

She hit Ross with a flying tackle and knocked him to the floor, as he was caught completely off guard for such an event. His glasses flew off his face and hung on one ear, and the laser control device fell about four feet from him.

"Grab it and run!!" she shouted to Melva, who did just that.

Ross easily pushed Sydney off of him, but she grabbed his spectacles, which put him off balance for just the seconds she needed to scramble to her feet and run in the opposite direction from Melva.

Ross tore at his hair with rage and fury at being bested by these two females. They had both his laser and his glasses! But that did not worry him nearly as much as the fact that he had no powers at all while he walked through these passageways! That was the "clue" that Sydney had figured out! When Ross was describing his plan to Tommy and

Sydney after they had arrived—bragging about how he had accomplished such a feat—he mentioned that all of these youngsters had been imbued with powers of telekinesis and pyrokinesis, through his computer programming wizardry. But he also mentioned that while they were encased in these glass cells, the force shield behind them, which kept them imprisoned inside, also interfered with their powers, so they were powerless to do anything to help themselves.

Once the force shield was reduced, they could, under Ross' natural ability of hypnotic mental domination, and through the computers in their cells, regain power and help him direct it through the window cap at the top of the ship, to destroy all life on earth. But until then, they were just powerless captives.

But *Ross' powers were also* obstructed when he went into the back passageways! Only the laser device could counteract that! And now it was in the hands of Sydney's sister! He had to catch up with her before she gave it to Sydney, who might be able to figure out how to use it.

Ross groped his way back to the elevators. He was virtually blind without his glasses. But he was still a big man, and stronger than some men half his age (like those couch potato sentries), and if the two women came back around to the elevator bank he felt sure he could take both of them. He listened keenly, with the super hearing of those who cannot see. He listened for the sound of footsteps.

40 / THE CHASE

Deputy Eli drove his patrol car slowly over the craggy rocks and leaves of the back of the mountainside. He felt a little anxious knowing that Hollister was whirling around overhead somewhere in The Bird, playing incommunicado games. He was sure that Hollister had picked up on the trail of the blue Volvo, and was hoping to break the case before he did.

He also felt anxious about the terrain over which he was driving. He needed a four-by, and, although his Plymouth was pretty rugged and reliable, he could easily get stuck out here. The mountain road which he was following down from Billy's Bunion became less and less negotiable as it went on.

And where the heck was he going, anyway? What would he find?

Suddenly he heard the beating of chopper blades. He was under a canopy of hardwoods and pine trees, but just a few feet further would take him into an open clearing where he could be seen by the helicopter overhead. He stepped on the brake, stopping the car just short of becoming visible to the chopper.

He watched as the Bird flew over the trees and on into the distance. When it flew beyond his visibility range, he slowly stepped on the accelerator. The big Plymouth with the big deputy inside lurched, but made no forward progress. Eli could feel the car sinking as the wheels spun freely on no traction. Along with the car he could feel his heart sinking.

By the time Tommy had completed his circle of the eighteenth level, moving upward along the inclined passageway, he realized why he had not run into any other stairway doors. This passageway ran in a spiral up the entire surface of the sphere. If they needed to be evacuated, the prisoners would only have to run down the incline, and it would eventually take them all the way to the ground.

Prisoners. He wondered how they would get out of their cells, anyway. He saw nothing but smooth concrete. No break of any kind to indicate any doorway into the cells. Perhaps, he wondered, with a sickening sadness, perhaps his grandfather never intended for them to get out. He would keep the youngsters encased within their glass cells until they died!

Now he found himself back at the bank of elevators. He hit the button, and within three seconds, the doors parted. He stepped in and then punched the top button—level twenty-nine.

Ross listened and listened, but he heard nothing but the cables of the elevator moving behind the closed doors now and then, and assumed it was the sentries searching for Tommy. He expected that Sydney and Melva would try at some time to come around and try to get to the elevator doors. Then, suddenly, he heard the mammoth grinding of machinery, and looked up. He knew, even though he could see nothing without his glasses but the brightness of the sunshine above him, that the women had found the switch along the wall on the other side of this passageway, which opened the huge window cap! As it slid back, grinding slowly, he knew where to find the women. He ran along the passageway to the opposite side of the sphere.

Melva handed the laser control device to Sydney, and started up the ladder which had automatically come down when the window was opened. Sydney held the ladder, and started up behind Melva as soon as the lower rungs were free. They both heard Ross' footsteps as he ran around the corridor toward them, feeling the wall as he went along, which slowed him only slightly.

Melva stepped up the last rung, swung her legs over the side one at a time, and turned around to begin making her way down the narrow foot-hold steps which appeared to extend down the outside of the sphere as she stepped. Sydney was halfway up the ladder inside, the laser device in one of her jeans' pockets, and Ross' glasses in the other. She swung one leg over the edge of the open window cap, when the laser fell from her pocket and clattered to the floor. She could hear Ross coming around the bend.

Instinctively, she felt that his powers would be increased if he had the laser in his possession. She jumped back down from the top of the ladder and grabbed for the laser. Ross could make out the shadows of her movement in front of him, and raced to grab her. Sydney's hand closed around the laser and she hopped up to the third rung of the ladder in one smooth movement, and climbed as fast as she could, with the laser in one hand. Ross lunged at the ladder and caught Sydney by one ankle. She tugged hard and kicked at him with her free foot, but she just slipped off the ladder and fell down into his waiting grasp.

Ross held her in a vice-like bear hug, and her squirming and kicking were useless. He found her wrist and squeezed hard so that she had to drop the laser. He did not let her go.

"You could have ruled the new world with me, Sydney," he whispered into her hair, and she tried to pull away from him with all of her strength, but he held her fast. "I could have made you happy ..."

They both froze as they heard the elevator doors whoosh open and Tommy stepped out. Ross twisted around and held Sydney tightly with one arm, pulling her down with him as he bent to swoop up the laser and pointed it at Tommy. He stopped in his tracks.

Sydney shouted, *"He has no power without ..."* but Ross' hand came up to her throat, and cut off her words. He spoke in a deadly monotone.

"I'll snap her neck if you come one more step." Sydney realized that he must turn some dials on the laser before he could use it against Tommy. She had stopped squirming, but now she began again. Ross' hand tightened on her neck, and she realized that he did not need a laser to kill her if he wanted to. But first he intended to use her as a hostage to get around Tommy until he could reset the laser, or get them down to the ground control center where his massive telekinetic powers would be restored.

Tommy stood still. "What do you want me to do, Grampa?"

Ross recoiled only slightly at the endearing term that defined his bond to this young man—but he stiffened with resolve to do what he had to do to keep his grand plan from being sabotaged.

"Walk toward the elevators and push the call button."

Melva had climbed down about twenty feet outside of the sphereship, new rungs seeming to extrude below her, somehow triggered by a sensory mechanism which responded to her own position and progress. Suddenly she realized that Sydney was not behind her! She was riveted by indecision. Should she go back and see what happened? Or should she climb on down and get back to civilization and get help? What if there were sentries down at the bottom who would just take her right back inside? She decided to creep back up as stealthily as she could, and try to take a peek through the window cap.

When she got back to the top, she slowly looked over the edge of the window cap. There she saw Sydney in Ross' grip, and Tommy several feet away. Ross was pointing the laser device in Tommy's direction, and Melva thought he could probably kill him just by pressing a button. She decided to back away a little and collect her thoughts. Then her foot slipped—she should have worn better walking shoes, darn it, she didn't always have to worry about looking nice or running into someone she needed to impress—and she let out a scream as she tumbled from the ladder.

Ross whipped around at the sound of the scream, letting Sydney pull away slightly. At that moment, Tommy rushed at him with his shoulder and head down, connecting with his grandfather squarely in the midsection. The breath went out of him and Sydney tore herself away. Tommy grabbed her hand and ran swiftly around the bend of the passageway, back to the stairwell door.

Ross lay gasping for his breath, and finally managed to get back up. He squeezed the laser to confirm that it was still in his hand. He was only slightly relieved that he no longer had to worry about the Melva woman, who fell off the outside of the sphereship. He raced around the passageway and ran through the stairwell door after Tommy and Sydney.

Ludwig, Hamner and Zablocki stopped by the stairwell door at the twenty-fourth level. "Let's go in here for a few minutes to stretch, Zablocki suggested. It was difficult searching the passageways which were so low that they had to walk bent over. They opened the door into the stairwell, and heard the sound of Tommy and Sydney flying down from above, taking the stairs three at a time.

Melva sat trembling where she had landed, in the curve of one of the dimple-like indentations on the outer surface of the sphere. She was only twelve feet or so from the area where the ladder rungs extruded, but she was fearful of making another wrong move and falling to her death on the ground below.

Slowly she moved, first one hand, to test her grip on the surface, then she tried sliding her torso just a fraction of an inch in the direction she needed to move. She held fast, and slowly, very slowly, pulled her feet along after the rest of her. Then she moved her hands another fraction of an inch.

Deputy Hollister Trimble spoke with Dr. Anna over his helicopter radio. Peaches had raised her on the telephone. And was listening in on the whole conversation. She heard Dr. Anna review the details of the disappearance of Thomson Alva Ross, Sr., from the hospital just a few days ago. She reviewed how his grandson had come to investigate the old homestead. All the while, Peaches had visions of that fantastic night that she and Claudette had, the first time they set eyes on Ross.

And now ... she realized ... he was free again!

"We gotta head back, Hollister," the pilot of the Bird was saying, for the third time in ten minutes.

"Okay, okay," answered the sheriff, sweeping at his greasy forelock and then scratching his craggy face as he did when he was angry or frustrated. Not that the two ever occurred separately in Sheriff Hollister Trimble. No, frustration was not something that he handled well and it invariably made him angry. He did not want to turn back and take a chance that Deputy Eli might wrap up this case before he did.

Then he spotted it. It was just a glare at first—a glint in his eye coming from somewhere within the forest.

"Swing around to the east one more time!" he commanded.

"But Hollister, we're gonna ..."

"Swing around, I said!!" And with the sheriff's eyes turning to red coals, the pilot leaned on the throttle and the Bird slid into an eastern arc.

As they came around, he saw the glint shoot out again. If Hollister was seeing what he thought he saw, it looked like another sun shining through the trees! The sun was clearly up in the sky where it belonged, though—how in thunder could it be in another place, shining through the trees? Something weird is happening down there!

"What is that, Chief?" Hollister asked the pilot—a direct descendent of the Chief of the Cherokee Nation before they were herded west on the deadly "Trail of Tears."

"It looks like a reflection of the sun to me, Sheriff."

Hollister looked at the Chief. A reflection, of course! These injuns always did know what was what!

"Let's take her down for a look-see!"

"No can do, Sheriff," the Chief replied, about to deliver a strong warning regarding the dangerously low fuel level in the Bird. But he didn't get a chance to finish. The Bird began lurching and sputtering. Then it started to drop.

When Ross regained his breath and was able to stand up again, he started to go down the stairwell where Tommy and Sydney had escaped from him, but quickly realized that he would be in a much better position if he got back to the control center. From there he could monitor every passageway, and his powers would quickly return. He could seal all doors and quickly have the renegade pair apprehended. He stepped onto the elevator and pushed the button for the ground level.

When Tommy and Sydney got to the twenty-fourth landing, and were met by Ludwig and the others, they recognized the look of surprise and incompetence on the men's faces—not to mention the labored breathing of couch potatoes undertaking unaccustomed exertion—so they didn't stop to chat, but kept right on racing past them, down the steps, three at a time. Ludwig and Zablocki stared after them for only a few seconds before they shouted down the stairwell to the other searchers that Tommy and Sydney had just passed them on twenty-four.

Van Bumpass and Claybourne were ready. They were probably the two most competent of all of the sentries. They were only two landings below, on twenty-two.

When Ross got to the ground floor, he immediately ran to the control center, ignoring the questions by Franklin and the other two sentries who had remained there. He threw all five switches of the elevators, shutting them all down at once.

Tommy and Sydney heard Bumpass and Claybourne below them on the next landing. They did not know if they could pass them without the element of surprise as they had the three above them, so they decided to rush out the stairwell door at the twenty-third level. Tommy opened the door and yanked Sydney after him. He pushed the elevator button, knowing that the elevators came within seconds, and they could get several floors away before the sentries in the stairwell would know where they were.

Only no elevator came this time. And as the sentries converged on the twenty-third landing, ready to come through and pounce on Tommy and Sydney, they discovered that the door was sealed. Ross had done so in order that there would be no access to the inner passageways from the stairs or the elevators. But the last two sentries, Fuller and Weatherby, who had originally come up with Ludwig, Hamner and Zablocki, were still in the passageways. They were on twenty-five, and descending via the spiral passageway.

Tommy and Sydney realized that the elevators had been shut off, and now the doors to the stairwells had been locked. Ross had to be back at the control center, and it was likely that the window cap had been closed and sealed as well. They had no idea who else might be in the passageways with them.

Melva inched closer to the rungs, now closer still. She was eight feet away and moving painstakingly slowly, but surely.

Deputy Eli Chester Alston got out of his patrol car to survey the situation. Both of his rear wheels had sunk into the muck and mud, and would have to be pulled out. He opened up the trunk of his car and pulled out a track and shovel, and started to dig diligently for about five minutes—then he heard the sound of the helicopter blades whirring back in his direction. He looked up and saw the Bird swinging back in an arc to the east. Then he heard the blades slow down and sputter. He watched as the Bird began to lose altitude. He dropped his shovel and began running in the direction of the Bird.

Tommy and Sydney decided to bide their time. They sat down in the passageway, and caught their breath for a minute. The five sentries were banging their fists on the stairwell door, seemingly oblivious to the fact that it would not open. Then Tommy looked at Sydney, her disheveled red hair still gleaming like burnished copper from the little available artificial light. He touched her lightly on the cheek and felt an overwhelming desire to tell her something, but she interrupted before he began.

"Tommy, it's not necessary, I know, believe me." Then she hesitated and started to say something else. "I just want you to know that ... well ... if we don't get out of here ..."

Tommy finished for her. "I love you, Sydney—more than I ever thought I could love someone in my life." They embraced and kissed, and ... and ... and they heard the approaching footsteps.

Fuller and Weatherby came around the last bend, and Tommy immediately got to his feet. Sydney was right behind him. There was no longer anywhere to run.

Fuller grabbed Sydney roughly and that made Tommy angry. He threw a fist into Fuller's belly and followed it with an uppercut that not only cracked his jaw, but caused his head to bang against the low ceiling, giving him a concussion. He dropped like a puppet whose strings had been cut. Then Tommy bent low and rushed at Weatherby, who caught him on the chin with his knee. Tommy saw stars momentarily, and he started to stagger backward. But he held on and came up with his foot directly into Weatherby's diaphragm, causing him to lose his breath. Tommy followed with a crashing fist into Weatherby's mouth, sending him flailing back onto Fuller. Then he grabbed Sydney's hand and they were off once again. They ran down and down, around and around the spiral passageways.

Ross was tracking their progress on his video monitors. He instructed Franklin and the other two to wait by the exit door. When Tommy and Sydney arrived there, he would unseal it and let them through.

41 / THE GREAT DESTRUCTION

Melva did not know how much time had passed since she tumbled from the window cap to this position. She was too afraid to make the slightest wrong move, such as looking at her watch, for fear of slipping again, and falling to her death several hundred feet below. But she was nearing the foothold now, still inching along, fighting the impulse to make a lunge for it. She kept her mind off Lila. If she thought of her baby she would surely start crying, and that might break her concentration and steady progress. So she thought of nothing but a little saying that kept running over and over in her mind:

> *Life is hard,*
>> *By the yard,*
>>> *But by the inch,*
>>>> *It's a cinch!*

Tommy and Sydney felt as though their legs were clad in lead boots. Their backs were aching, even though they stopped to rest every few minutes or so. Finally they were approaching the last level. The number on the elevator banks was "one" so this would invariably take them to the ground level. They had no idea what would be waiting for them down there, but they knew that it was useless to try to go anywhere else.

And if they just had a chance to talk to Ross—they had been able to sway him in the past. He had felt great affection for both of them. Perhaps they could get through to him. Maybe they...

They reached the end of the final passageway, and the door which led out was directly in front of them. They stopped for only a second, hoping to embrace one last time, when Franklin burst through, followed by four others. All of the sentries who had been trapped in the stairwell when Ross sealed it off had come back down. Now only Fuller and Weatherby were still up there, probably still unconscious from Tommy's blows; possibly making their own way down the passageway by now.

The sentries surrounded the two fugitives, and they all walked in a group toward Ross at the control center. As Tommy and Sydney stood in front of Ross, with the sentries at parade rest behind them, they knew how the victims of the Inquisition must have felt.

"You have betrayed me for the last time," Ross said, slowly, deliberately.

"Tommy broke in, "Grampa! Why are you doing this? You're my grandfather! We only have each other left ..."

Ross stood up and slammed his hands down on the table in front of him. "*QUIET!!* You are no kin to me!! You're in league with the Conspirators!! You two and Dr. Anna, and all of her coven ..."

His speech was interrupted suddenly. The console showed the flashing red warning light once again, and sirens wailed from the speakers surrounding them. Ross looked down at the monitor and tapped a few codes into the computer.

"Outside ... Someone's outside."

"You stupid redskin!" Sheriff Hollister screamed at the Chief as The Bird seemed almost to stop in mid-air, and then began to fall in an accelerating plunge. "We shoulda' killed all ya' stupid savages when we had the chance!!"

The Chief did not look over at Hollister during this outburst. Nor did he look the least bit ruffled. He kept his eyes on the control panel. He turned some dials and flipped some switches. Suddenly the helicopter's plunge began to slow. Then it stopped again in mid-air, and then began to rise.

Hollister stopped his vitriolic barrage in mid-sentence. "What th'... How'd ya' do that?"

"Spare tank," the Chief stated in his eloquent Native American manner of using the minimum number of words to convey maximum information.

Before Hollister could form a reply, and before the smile maxed out on his face, the Chief drew out a silver-handled hunting knife, which had been handed down to him through generations from his great-great-great-grandfather, the Chief of the Cherokee Nation.

But the smile faded from Trimble's face as he saw the glint of the knife blade.

"Why you dumb redskin fool, whataya' think yer doin'?"

The Chief tilted the knife deftly in his hand, and the silver gleamed from the many years of care and hand rubbing it had received.

"No blood on this blade," the Chief pointed out while still looking straight ahead and the Bird hovered lazily over the forest several hundred yards below. "Don't want any now."

He pushed the tip of the knife toward Hollister's seat belt. Trimble waved his hands in front of the Chief as the reality of the situation set in.

"H-hey, there, Buddy! You're my man, you know that! I've got a nice bonus for ya', too—I'll show ya' where I stash my cash! Got some real good fire-water, too! Fresh brewed, real good! Let's go back now, okay?"

The Chief deftly sliced through the seat belt, while at the same time turned the Bird in a sharp leftward swoop.

Deputy Eli did not hear Sheriff Trimble pealing off one scream after another as the sliced seatbelt flapped in the wind over his flailing form, tumbling to the forest below. He did not hear the Sheriff's final pathetic moans as he hung impaled on the sharp stump left by a tree that had been struck by lightning and severed into a jagged spear. He did not hear Hollister's last words before his vessels emptied in sanguine rivulets, forming a widening red lake around the tree's venerable old roots: *"Should'a never let that injun l'arn to fly..."*

Deputy Eli did not hear these things because the sound of the chopper blades coming back full force drowned them out. By the time he reached a clearing where he had a view of the helicopter again, it was flying off back toward Jiminy Rock. Thank God they're all right, he thought.

Melva had reached the footholds and had climbed all the way down to the ground outside the sphere. As soon as she did so, she set off the alarm system which Ross had designed so that he would not have to rely on outside sentries. Now Ross moved the control on his panel of instruments, and the video monitor zoomed in on Melva. She was racing barefoot through the underbrush, having thrown her shoes away after they had caused her to lose her footing on the side of the ship.

"Franklin!!"Ross commanded so sharply that all the sentries jumped. "Take Bumpass and Claybourne and go get that woman!"

"Yes, *Sir*!" Franklin replied. Then, "Uh ... What should we do with her when we get her?" he asked.

"Bring her back in here!" Ross snapped. He himself was the only one he trusted to dispose of this woman, and the others, too. Then he turned to the other sentries. "Hold these two now, all of you! Don't let them move an inch or you'll all disintegrate together! I promise!"

When Franklin and the others got to the entry way doors, Ross hit a switch on the control panel, and the doors slowly slid open. Beyond them Sydney could see the foyer where the Jeep was parked. When the doors fully opened, the sentries walked through, and Ross hit another switch. This time the huge ramp, which was cut from the side of the sphereship, began to lower. The sentries would walk down that ramp to the surrounding woods, and go right to where Melva was, since the video had pinpointed her precise position.

As the ramp lowered, rosy late afternoon sunshine flowed in, and Sydney was filled with a sadness that shocked her. The sun was there, just as it was every afternoon back in Atlanta, when she would look out of her window, wrap up her work for the day, and plan what she would do that evening. Now, in the middle of the nightmare which could be the end of her life, the sun still shone. She started to sob, and she wasn't even sure when she heard the trumpet blast, whether it was real or imagined.

The trumpet sounded again, and Sydney realized, with some curiosity, that she was listening to the opening fanfare of the *William Tell Overture* by Rossini—which used to introduce the old television show, "The Lone Ranger." And as she recognized the sounds, she realized that they were coming from a quadraphonic sound system ...

The sentries had just started down the ramp when they spotted the blue Volvo, half hidden among the pine and hardwood trees, revving its engine, then letting it slow, revving again more powerfully, again and again, until finally it slipped into gear and peeled out with a screech that left rocks and leaves and dirt flying out from under its wheels, as all the while the Berlin Philharmonic Orchestra beat out the hoofbeats of *William Tell*.

Franklin reached for his shoulder-holstered nine-millimeter Luger semi-automatic pistol, to aim at the windshield of the Volvo which sped faster and faster toward him, headlights glaring like demon eyes—when he realized that he wasn't wearing his shoulder holster. The Gray Man had taken all of the sentries' "mundane weapons" away, which they had gladly relinquished when they sampled the powers he was able to substitute for them ... at least until he took those away, too.

Oh, well, thought Franklin, when he noticed that no one was behind the wheel anyway. A shot through the windshield would have done no good—*No one behind the wheel*???!!!

Franklin felt the warm liquid spreading down his crotch just as his vision clouded over and all conscious thought ceased in his brain. Franklin fainted just as Wolfgang barreled up the ramp and ran over him and the other two sentries.

When Ross spotted the Volvo, he did not immediately recognize it as Wolfgang—the car his wife, Claudette, had purchased shortly before her death, to replace their old car, which she used to drive to Broughton Hospital and visit him so faithfully over the years. Wolfgang came when she finally traded in Ingrid, her previous Volvo, which had three-hundred-ten thousand and some odd miles on the odometer at the time. When Claudette died, Wolfgang had exactly seven hundred point-zero miles on the odometer. It still did.

Ross kept cool. He looked down at the control panel and found the button which would close the huge entryway doors. They were made of an alloy of metals which he himself had invented, and were virtually indestructible, as was the entire outer frame of the sphereship. If he could prevent the car from passing through those doors, he could blow it up in the entryway foyer.

The massive doors began to grind closed after Ross pushed the button. Wolfgang sped up the ramp and his front wheels came over the edge. Ross was rapidly computing in his mind how fast the doors would need to close to prevent the car from entering the ship. Even as he was computing, he began to focus his destructive pyrokinetic force as a backup, in the case the car DID get through.

Wolfgang's rear wheels began to spin as his front wheels came off the ramp at the edge of the foyer and were momentarily airborne. Ross watched as the entryway doors moved closer together, slowly ... one-fourth of the way closed ... one-third ...

He leveled his gaze and focused squarely on the car's front grill as he felt his pyrokinetic power—and his body temperature—building rapidly.

Wolfgang's front end slammed down into the foyer, but his rear wheels remained behind the front edge, spinning freely several inches above the ramp underneath. The doors to the control center were already half-shut and the entryway was rapidly reaching the point which would not allow enough room for Wolfgang to get through. He had only seconds left to make it, if he were to succeed.

Ross narrowed his eyes into slits and clenched his teeth. The entryway doors continued to close off. Wolfgang's rear wheels then tipped back onto the ramp, and with the traction suddenly available against his wheels spinning at ninety miles per hour, he shot forward and flew through the entryway doors, even as they closed on him and scraped both sides of his fenders with a teeth-gritting screech.

Ross took a deep breath and prepared to propel a cannonball of flame as the car careened straight towards the control center where he stood. Sentries were diving out of the way, and Tommy had picked up Sydney and swept her away to the farthest wall.

Suddenly Ross was jolted by a shock that he could not have anticipated with all his brilliance and self-possession. It robbed him of his breath and he lost his focus. His temperature dropped rapidly as his pyrokinetic potential receded, and he stood helplessly watching, in total disbelief of what he had just seen, as the car barreled toward him at the helm of the control center.

Behind the wheel suddenly appeared his dear departed wife, his sweetheart, his darling, his Claudette! Bigger and more beautiful than he had remembered her! Long, shimmering silken hair flowing behind her! A vision in luminescence! And young again with roses still in her cheeks! Whitish cheeks, but nevertheless, a rosy glow on them.

Ross blinked—and the vision disappeared. The headlights of the Volvo glared so brightly as they raced toward him, he felt certain that his imagination had just played a trick on him. Perhaps he should try to get more sleep.

At that moment, Ross tried to get out of the way, but he had barely gotten the desk entryway lifted when Wolfgang smashed into the control center. Sparks flew everywhere, and then there was a small explosion in the instrument panel, and then another and another. The last one sent a chunk of metal flying and it hit Ross squarely in the back of the head just as he was about to get away.

"Tommy, this whole place is going to blow!" Sydney shouted, as she watched one explosion after another. She wondered if Wolfgang's gas tank would be ignited by the explosions. Then she thought of Lila and looked up at the walls of glass honeycombs.

The force shields had all disintegrated when Wolfgang smashed into the control center. All of the young people were leaving their cells as the "walls" behind them vaporized and left them free to enter the spiral passageway.

"Tommy, Lila must be free! Let's go find her! Please!" Sydney said, tugging at his arm.

"Don't stay here, Sydney! Go outside! I have to see if my grandfather is all right! Go!"

"No!" she said, "I'm staying with you!" Tommy didn't waste time arguing. They walked swiftly over to Ross, prostrate on the floor of the control center. Tommy turned him over carefully and smoothed the hair back from his face.

"Grampa?" he asked, feeling for a carotid pulse in Ross' neck. "Grampa!"

Ross didn't answer, and Sydney watched as Tommy's eyes began to well up with tears. He whispered, "Grampa" one last time. He laid his head on Ross' chest and squeezed his eyes shut.

Sydney watched him as he sagged with grief, and then she reached over and touched his shoulder and squeezed it gently. She said, "C'mon, Tommy, we've got to get out of here! Please! Help me find Lila! We've got to go!"

Tommy straightened up and wiped his eyes with the back of his arm. "Okay, Sydney," he said as he rose up on one knee, and took her hand.

"Don't let them do it to me, Tommy." They both heard the nearly inaudible whisper coming from Ross.

"Grampa?!"

Ross' glasses had flown off when he fell, and now his big, charcoal gray eyes opened wide and looked up at both of them. "Don't let them do it to me, Tommy. Promise?"

Tommy didn't know what his grandfather was talking about, but he didn't stop to ask. "Grampa, we've got to get you out of here!"

"NO, Tommy, please!" Ross responded, and Tommy was amazed at the strength left in his grip as his grandfather squeezed his hand. "Please leave me here! I'd rather die here than go back to that hospital and let them do what they want to me!!"

"What, Grampa? What do they want to do?" Tommy tried to reason with Ross in the hope that he would not resist so strongly, and they could get him to leave with them. "What do you think?"

"They want to give me a lobotomy, Tommy! That's what!"

Tommy would have burst out laughing if the situation were not so grave. "Grampa! They don't do that any more! That's ridiculous! They haven't done those in fifty years!"

"Yes, they do, Tommy." Tommy was astonished to hear this, calmly coming from Sydney. He just stared at her, not knowing what to say.

"Really, it's true!" she went on, and Tommy had visions of her appearing to lose her mind again as he had thought when she was frantically praying in the sleeping quarters, what seemed like an eternity ago.

But she just went on, seemingly oblivious to his incredulity: "I do word processing for a psychiatrist at the medical center, and he wrote a paper recently with all the details. Lobotomies have been greatly refined from the crude prefrontal cleaving that they once were ..."

Tommy just gaped at her, speechless, as she continued her discourse. Ross had lifted his head, listening thoughtfully to her dissertation.

"... and they're conducted in operating theaters now, just like other neurosurgical procedures, with much less trauma to outlying brain tissue." When she finished, she fell silent, and they seemed to have forgotten the turmoil and screaming and explosions going on all around them.

Finally, Ross spoke: "Help me up, will you, Tommy? I think we need to leave now."

42 / WHEN AN IRRESISTIBLE FORCE MEETS ...

Peaches leaned back in her swivel chair in front of the quiet switchboard. Ross is free! She had overheard the conversation between Sheriff Trimble and Dr. Anna at Broughton Hospital. Her mind slipped back to replay the events of that night in a dusty old saloon out West, so many decades ago ...

She in yellow, Claudette in red, they fell irresistibly into step and ascended that magnificent stairwell, to follow Ross into the bedroom at the head of the stairs. It was the finest room in the house. The walls were covered in rich European satin; silk drapes imported from China graced the tall windows; and wood molding of the finest oak was hand-carved to depict in vivid detail the revelry and decadence of a Roman bacchanal.

The room had a magnificently ornate crystal chandelier in the center of its arched cathedral ceiling. Items of clothing from the two women would rest overnight on its burnished branches.

Peaches had only a faint recollection of the remainder of that night. She could only remember that, although she knew she was totally under the physical and mental control of this strange man, she was so utterly intoxicated with pleasure that she never felt a single moment of fearfulness.

In the morning, she awoke to find herself alone in the huge pink satin bed, fully clothed, and the room appearing completely untouched. She walked downstairs and was told that Claudette and the stranger had left the night before.

Now, finally, fifty years later, it was Peaches' turn! Claudette had passed away and Ross had escaped from the hospital! Peaches never really believed he was mad. Love is madness anyway. All she knew was, she had loved Ross for more than fifty years, and now it was *her* chance to have him!

"Oh, no, you won't, honey!" A sharp voice pierced her reverie and she whirled around to see who was there. *No one* was there!

Great, she thought, now I'm hearing voices! Maybe I need a rest ...

"No, you don't, Sweetcakes," the voice rang out again, so loud and clear that Peaches nearly fell out of her chair as she whirled around to see who had spoken. There was a shocking vision.

Sitting across the credenza on the opposite side of the room—much like Peaches herself sat across the top of the piano and sang as Ivory played his saloon music decades ago—was Claudette! She was dressed in a red sequined camisole slip with a red feather boa around her neck. A red satin headband hugged her forehead, and a huge red ostrich feather was held in it next to her right ear. Long diamond and ruby earrings swayed from her ears, and every long, white finger of her hands had a different gemstone ring on it. Black fishnet stockings outlined her shapely legs. She was as curvaceous and buxom and radiantly youthful as she was the very last time Peaches laid eyes on her.

Peaches closed her eyes and shook her head from side to side. But when she opened her eyes again, the image remained. Peaches tried to speak, but her throat suddenly went as dry and parched as that old West landscape outside the silk-draped window of her memory.

"Lost yer voice, eh, honey? said Claudette, sliding off the credenza and walking slowly toward Peaches. When she reached her, she swept the feather boa across Peaches' throat. "Pity! A fine singer like yerself!"

She moved her face to within an inch of Peaches' own. The odor of corned beef was strong, and Peaches felt a sense of revulsion and sheer terror. She wished this were not really happening, and that she were just losing her mind.

Claudette spoke again, and her voice pierced Peaches like a scalpel, so sharp that it didn't hurt until after she stopped: "You didn't *really* have plans of going after my man, didya', Honey?"

Peaches shook her head violently from side to side, and tried to form the word "no", but nothing came out.

"I take it that's a 'no,' since your mouth looks something like a fish right now." Her eyes flashed with sparks of anger. "And that's good! Very good! Because, you see, it would be so awful for someone to be found, for example, with a feather boa wrapped around her chubby neck and hanging from a chandelier somewhere, don't you agree, Honey, hm-m-m-m-m-m?"

Peaches stopped shaking her head from side to side abruptly and immediately began nodding it up and down. Claudette's image faded slowly along with her gleefully screeching, echoing laughter. Peaches fainted.

When Tommy and Sydney had gotten far enough away from the ship for safety, half carrying, half dragging Ross with them, they gently helped him lie down in the grass. His eyes fluttered closed.

Tommy checked his pulse again. This time he could not find one.

"Grampa?" he said, shaking him lightly at the shoulder, and then more urgently. "_Grampa!_" Tommy's voice cracked, and he felt a hot coal in his throat. "Grampa, please ..."

Ross lifted his head and looked at Tommy, then at Sydney, then back at Tommy. "She admitted it!" he said triumphantly, lifting an index finger in Sydney's direction. "They DO want to do a lobotomy on me! I knew it!"

"No, no," Sydney said, "_not on you!_ They still do lobotomies these days, but only for severe depression and obsessive compulsive disorders," she said, remembering what the paper had described. "I don't think you would qualify."

"That's right," Tommy added, trying to hide his own astonishment at Sydney's knowledge of a subject unfamiliar even to most medical doctors. "You have mood swings, Grampa—manic-depressive illness, remember? You're not a candidate for psychosurgery. You just need to take your lithium, okay?"

Ross looked from one to the other with a look which they could only describe as something akin to beatification. And then, slowly, like icicles melting from tree branches in the spring, slowly, and then increasingly faster, the madness which had gripped Ross' mind began to vaporize and was carried off by the spring breeze. His eyes began to clear and lighten. His iron gray hair began to darken, and shimmer with a youthful brown shine again. The multitude of lines in his face began slowly to fill in, as a raisin would if it could turn back into a grape.

When he finally stood up, he looked as though twenty years had dropped from him and blown away. He looked youthful and vibrant. And sane.

Tommy and Sydney only gaped at the transformation before their eyes. When Sydney found her voice she said, "Mr. Ross—_how did you do that?_"

Ross smiled, and took a deep breath. "Well, my dear, you know how I explained the effects possible when you restimulated the thymus gland in a certain ..."

His words were cut off by an enormous explosion. Tommy and Sydney felt a lancing pain as the sound of it hit their ears. It was followed by a bright flash of light which filled the sky and made it fluorescent for a few seconds; and then a searing wave of heat followed, as the entire sphereship blew up and was enveloped in flames. The explosion was heard on the other side of the mountains, as far as Gatlinburg, Tennessee.

All the youngsters from inside the ship had gotten safely away. When the smoke cleared, and their ears had stopped ringing, Ross asked Tommy and Sydney if they would take him back to Broughton Hospital. It wasn't long before the helicopters arrived with first aid. Ross was flown by Life-Flight helicopter back to Broughton, where Dr. Anna met him and took him back to his ward. Tommy and Sydney drove back to Atlanta in Tommy's truck, which had been left in his grandmother's driveway. The sphereship was nothing but a pile of charred remains, having blown up with a force equivalent to a nuclear bomb. No trace of Wolfgang could be found.

EPILOGUE

Tommy and Sydney were married in her parents' home in Miami, and bought a three-bedroom ranch style house in the suburbs of Atlanta. Sydney kept her condo, and continues to work there in her computer business, and has a staff of three employees. They have two children, Claudette, Jr. and Tommy the Fourth. Tommy was born exactly nine months to the day after his parents made love in the sphereship. Both children have candy apple red hair.

*

Lila graduated from high school and was offered a scholarship to the University of Florida at Gainesville. She visits her Aunt and Uncle and two cousins in Atlanta every chance she gets. Her Aunt Sydney and her mom, Melva, have been much closer since their adventure in the Smoky Mountains. As a matter of fact, to see them now, one would never guess an ill word had ever passed between them.

*

Tommy turned the gas station over to Clarence, who kept up the good reputation of the place. Kareem used his savings along with a partial scholarship to attend Columbia University to study market economics, and is now a consultant with a prestigious New York brokerage firm. Tommy himself applied for an was accepted into a residency to complete his training in internal medicine at Emory University Medical Center.

*

After Sheriff Hollister Trimble's funeral, the Alston County Commissioners installed Deputy Elijah Chester Alston as acting sheriff; and that fall he was elected unopposed.

*

The sentries who did not get their old jobs back joined up with a paramilitary survivalist clan in Palestine, Texas, and are planning a strategy for taking back the South.

Thomson Alva Ross, Sr., is alive and well, and living in the old homestead in Jiminy Rock. Twice a month he drives down to Broughton State Hospital for a check-up with Dr. Anna, and a refill of his medication. From time to time, late at night in the old Victorian mansion, in a bedroom on the second floor, bits and pieces of conversation can be heard; sometimes with boisterous laughter, sometimes with the softer sounds of lovemaking; always with the pungent smell of corned beef.

Sydney never could bring herself to trade in her trusty old Toyota. She still drives it to and from work, and Clarence keeps it in tip-top shape. On weekends, she drives a late model blue Volvo, which has never had a thing wrong with it, except that the odometer sticks at seven hundred miles. One of these days, she's going to have to get that looked at.

Dear Reader,

Leslie, my sixteen-year-old-daughter's sixteen-year-old friend told me how much she loved to read.

I told her that she should read some Saul Bellow. She told me that I should read some Stephen King.

Well, I didn't want to tell her that his books are just a bunch of dungola, because ... well ... I'd never read any of them. So I told her to recommend one.

She gave me SKELETON CREW. I was hooked.

Then I read THE STAND, CHRISTINE, THE DEAD ZONE, and PET SEMATARY. By the time I finished reading TOMMYKNOCKERS, I couldn't thank Leslie enough for introducing me to this genius of classic horror. I just thought he needs to lighten up a little.

VIRUS 2.0 is the result.

I originally published this as TOMMY'S CRACKERS —a play on the title TOMMYKNOCKERS —but my daughter suggested VIRUS 2.0.

We should listen to our kids more often.

Yours truly,
Norah